unCONventional
Isaac Sher

Cover Art Design by: Kelly Moran/Rowan Prose Publishing
Photo Credit: Adobe Images/Deposit Photos
First Edition

ISBN: 978-1-961967-47-2
Rowan Prose Publishing, LLC
www.RowanProsePublishing.com
Published in the United States of America

PRAISE FOR ISAAC SHER:

"A fast-paced ride."
-Author Eve Forward
"Diverse, inclusive, and compelling."
-Author D.N. Frost

*Dedicated to the very real man who inspired "Prowl,"
taken from us far too soon.
We miss you terribly, J.J., and always will.*

CHAPTER ONE

FELIX

Felix Jackson stood outside the massive Grand Royalty Hotel & Convention Center complex, taking in the afternoon scene. Another year, another Anime Horde convention, and another long weekend of shared wonder, joy, new discovery, reunions with old friends, Japanese pop culture, and giddy sleep deprivation.

At least it isn't raining this year, he thought to himself. *Yet*.

"Man, can you believe this beautiful weather? They might actually get to do some outdoor cosplay shoots this time, yah." Felix turned around to find Prowl walking towards him, towing a massive suitcase. Prowl was a huge blond Viking of a man, whose booming voice was still thick with a Minnesota accent despite living further south for over a decade. "I parked in the lot up ahead, but I saw you standing here as I pulled in. I even honked, dont'cha know!"

"Sorry, I guess I was lost in thought. Good to see you, Prowl." Felix laughed, and adjusted the collar on his green polo.

Prowl raised an eyebrow. "Lost in thought for, what, ten minutes? Took me a bit to walk back here after I parked, man. Thinking about the show on Saturday?"

Shaking his head, he grabbed the handle of his rolling suitcase. "Nah. All the crap from last year. C'mon, let's get our room keys from Staff HQ."

"Last year was a shitbag of a time, no kiddin'." Prowl fell into step beside him, the pair heading towards the hotel's main entrance, already chock-full with arriving attendees and other staff members. "I'm sure this year will be better, but you gotta stop dwelling on it and let it go. We all make mistakes. Lord knows, I did, oof."

Felix turned to look closer at his friend's expression. "Considering how badly Natalie stabbed you in the back last year, you're handling it a lot better than I would've. And what's with the 'let it go' talk? Are you going to break into song on an ice-covered mountaintop now?"

"Ha!" Prowl's huge laugh echoed off the hotel's glass walls, startling a few other convention goers nearby. "Good one, Felix. But I'm serious. Natalie was bad news, everyone said so when we started dating, and last year just proved 'em all right. I may have lost months of my life to her bullshit, but I'm not gonna let her take any more by allowing her to sit in my head."

The laughing Viking turned around to look at all the other people milling around in the hotel courtyard. "Besides, there's plenty of other women around here who are just as big a bunch of nerds as we are. I'm sure we'll both meet someone nice this year."

Felix shook his head, adjusting the strap on his shoulder bag. "Oh, no. You go 'on the prowl' all you want, bud. That's what got me in trouble last year. This time, I'm just going to relax, concentrate on my responsibilities as con staff, and not worry about being single. Still."

Prowl held open the hotel door for his friend as they passed into the gloriously air-conditioned lobby, the lush purple carpets obscured by the press of the already substantial crowd of incoming congoers. "It is possible to ask girls out without giving off *Eau de* Desperate, Felix. Just relax, don't worry about it, and just...be yourself. It's not rocket science, man."

Felix chuckled, and switched his voice to a thick German accent. "Vunce the rockets go up, who knows vere they come down? That's not my department..."

Prowl joined him in a sing-song voice on the last line, "Said Wernher Von Braun!"

They shared a chuckle, and gave each other a familiar fist-bump.

"Tom Lehrer! Good one, Felix."

"Gotta love the classics. Anyway, let's get to Ops and report in. We're going to need all hands on deck to get everything set up tonight, so let's get to it."

CHAPTER TWO

IRIS

Clicking on the "Receive Call" button on her laptop screen, Iris sat down at her bedroom desk, an ice cold bottle of her favorite soda in hand. "Isaiah! How've things been since last week?" As she spoke, the video image came into view, the face and broad shoulders of an incredibly handsome dark-skinned man in his mid-twenties.

"Hey, Iris! Things are quiet here, but I wanted to ask you—are you going out to the convention tomorrow?" Isaiah spoke with a rich, deep, bass pitch, and Iris always felt a little thrill of excitement at the sound of his voice.

"Yup. That 'Anime Horde' thing I told you about, out near the airport. Uncle Marcus has the week off, so the whole family is going. Him, Aunt Abby, my two adorable little cousins, and me: one mid-twenties layabout." She watched her friend's face as she sat there in her favorite white t-shirt, so ridiculously over-sized that she used it as a nightgown. "What about you? Got a hot date planned in the wild steel canyons of Manhattan?"

Isaiah held up a thick textbook. "Oh yeah, a sexy hook-up with more med school reading. No rest for the wicked."

She sat forward, her eyes flashing with annoyance. "Isaiah West! We talked about this. You're far too good a human being to not have someone dragging you out into the city for some romance. I know for a fact that there are several women we both knew from college who would snap you up in a heartbeat." She unscrewed the cap of her cola and took a swig. "Probably more. When you and I broke up, half the girls in my dorm were asking me permission to swoop down on you like a hawk."

"No offense to your old friends, Iris, but I am not interested in being some white girl's 'I dated a *Black guy*, oh my gosh' fantasy object." He ran a hand across his close trimmed beard. "Besides, look who's talking."

She stuck out her tongue. "Hey, I'm not like that. I asked you out because, unlike most guys in our school, you didn't freak at the idea of a mere girl knowing more about Marvel superhero movies than you do. Come on, Isaiah, you know me better than that."

"I do know better, and that's not what I meant." He pointed directly at her through his screen. "I mean, you're getting on my case about not going out this weekend? You haven't hardly left your aunt and uncle's house since you moved in with them. It's been, what, seven months now? If anyone needs a night out, it's you."

"I do not need a boyfriend, Isaiah. Last thing on my mind, and I am going out! To the con!"

"And that's a good start." He gestured with his coffee mug. "But you really need to be doing something that doesn't involve you hiding behind your family like they're a phalanx of Spartans."

"I do no such thing!" She brushed a long lock of her thick hair out of her face, the curls a very dark shade of auburn. She wished her hair was a true red like her cousins had, rather than just taking on red highlights in the sun. She frowned at her hair as if it had personally betrayed her, and brushed it out of her eyes again. "I'm social! You're talking as if I'm one of those '*hikikomori*' shut-ins or something."

"You're social online, sure. You'll go out if your aunt is with you. Since you moved there, when was the last time you talked to someone face-to-face, without anyone from your family nearby to back you up?" Isaiah took a loud, slurping sip from his mug.

"Uh…"

"Can't remember, can you?" He nodded. "Look, Iris. You know I want you to be happy, right? Unlike everyone else, I'm not trying to say you need to move back to New York…"

Her eyes narrowed angrily. "That is *not* going to happen! *I am not*…" She paused, and held up a hand. She clenched her eyes shut for a minute, and took a deep breath. "Shit." She rubbed her temples, her eyes still shut. "You still there, Isaiah?"

"Not going anywhere, Iris. It's okay."

She opened her eyes, and he was still sitting there on the other side of his screen, an understanding smile on his face. She groaned, incredibly annoyed with herself. "You even made a point of saying you weren't asking me to come back, and I flipped out on you anyway. No wonder we broke up years back, I'm obviously some sort of psycho."

"Stop it, Iris—and don't use that word." He sighed, and seemed to think for a moment before speaking again. "We've been friends instead of lovers for five years, and I honestly think we get along better this way. You've said so yourself. Since you're still my friend, as much as I miss seeing you around town, I really do think you getting out of New York was the best thing you could've done for your mental health."

She sniffed. "Thanks. I'm glad someone from back east understands." She grinned suddenly, tugging downwards on the overlarge collar on her shirt, displaying more than a hint of her generous cleavage. "But let's be honest, you know you miss these, at least."

"Oh, don't you start!" He held up both hands in front of him, looking away with a laugh. "Put the 'weapons of mass destruction' away, Iris. Save 'em for someone in a better position to appreciate you."

She released the collar, letting the shirt conceal her chest again. "Spoilsport."

"But to be serious, I do have one request, Iris." He tapped a finger against his lips, seemingly pondering how to phrase things. "When you're at the con tomorrow, I think you should go off by yourself for a bit. Let your family do their things, you just go and take some time to do some Iris things. Pose for some photos in the great costume you made. Chat up strangers who might like the same shows you do. Watch a movie you haven't seen yet. Just...do your own thing for a few hours. Get some fresh air, and on your own terms. Take charge of your life again, like the Iris I used to know."

She looked down, her lips pursed. "I'm trying to be better than the 'Iris you used to know', Isaiah, but I get what you mean. I'll think about it."

He nodded. "That's all I ask. Have fun with your fellow geeks, funny-voice-lady." He held up one hand to his heart. "May the Force be with you, Iris."

Rolling her eyes, she put on her best Yoda voice. "Adventure. Excitement. An Iris craves not these things." She cleared her throat. "You don't need to try and fly the geek flag, Isaiah. On a 'mundane' like you, it just sounds weird."

"Just showing my support for you glorious weirdos, Iris. G'night." With a last wave, Isaiah disconnected the call.

Standing and stretching, she walked over to the mannequin in the corner that was currently wearing most of her planned costume. The paint had dried, the glue had held, and everything looked perfect. The replica armor had taken months of careful work, and tomorrow would be its public premiere. She idly wondered if any reporters would be there—it seemed like even major news magazines made time for "check out these amazing cosplayers" articles these days. *Wouldn't it be something if a picture of me went viral...*

On a whim, she turned towards her full-length mirror, and pulled her t-shirt over her head, leaving her completely naked. "Weapons of mass destruction, huh." She cupped her heavy breasts in her hands and shook her head. "More trouble than anything. Thank God for professionally-fitted bras."

She struck a pose, her arms over her head as she cocked her hip to one side. Her first college roommate had called her a "pin-up girl brought to life," joking that if she'd been around during World War II, her likeness would've been painted across the entire fleet of Allied bomber planes.

"That's a good thing," she mused aloud. "Right?" She didn't have the slender hips of a modern fashion model, but she thought one could use the term "hourglass" when describing her without too much snickering.

She looked lower and frowned. She hadn't bothered to shave her legs or do any sort of trimming in months, and now that she really looked, she disliked what she saw. She kicked the discarded shirt up into her grasp again, and then threw it at the mirror.

"Goddamnit, Iris. You're just going to a con, not a beauty contest."

She looked in the mirror for a moment longer—and then stomped into the bathroom to look for her razor. "I should at least get the legs done," she muttered angrily.

CHAPTER THREE

PROWL

As Thursday afternoon waned into early evening, the Grand Royalty Hotel's grand ballroom slowly transformed into Anime Horde's "Main Programming" hall. Prowl was sitting at a table set up near the stage, typing away at his laptop and making last-minute edits to the Costume Contest's entry forms.

"Serves me right for not proofreading more closely," he muttered under his breath.

Felix stood on the empty stage, talking with two of their staffers. "When we set up for the Costume Contest on Saturday, the podium needs to be right here, downstage left, almost in the corner, so let's mark that spot now—no, use the yellow tape. Blue is for the Game Show on Saturday morning. After you're done, head to Panel Room Two, Enrique's going to need some more help in there soon. Thanks, guys."

As the assistants bent down to apply spike tape to the stage, Felix jumped down and walked over to his friend's makeshift desk. "Prowl, who is Main's room manager this year? I need to get a chair count."

Prowl took a brief pause in his typing. "Lorenzo's still in the hospital, so Amanda stepped up."

Felix grimaced. "Amanda Diamond or Amanda Zeller?"

"Diamond." He pointed towards the tech station in the back of the room, facing directly opposite the stage. "She's right over there."

"Crap. God is cruel." Felix looked upwards in silent prayer. "Zeller at least shot me down nicely. Diamond probably wants to feed me to a piranha tank."

The two of them turned to look towards the back of the room, and Prowl allowed himself a moment to enjoy the view. Standing by the main console and making adjustments to it, Amanda was a short, but rather curvy college student, with one side of her head shaved nearly bald, and the other side a shimmering wall of purple and blue hair reaching just above her shoulders.

Felix spoke up again. "Prowl, can you..."

"Nope." Prowl looked back down at his laptop, pointedly resuming his typing.

Felix's voice grew plaintive. "Come on, dude. She hates my guts. You ask her for me. Please?"

Prowl shook his head, still staring at his computer. "Even though this room's all but done, I really need to finish the last bit on this paperwork, you know that, and she doesn't hate you, I don't know where you got that from. Just ease up a bit on the hormones, and you'll be fine." He looked up, and gave his best Harrison Ford impression. "'I don't know, fly casual.'"

Felix gave an aggrieved Wookie-style growl, and turned toward his fate.

Prowl watched his best friend approach Amanda as if he was convinced there was a ticking bomb under one of the tech station's tables. *Jumping Jesus on a pogo stick, Felix,* Prowl thought to himself. *It's not like she swore unholy vengeance on you or anything. Yes, she's got a damn lovely body, and the fishnet stockings are always a winner, so just don't stare, calm down, and you'll be fine.*

After another moment's hesitation, Prowl closed the lid on his laptop, and surreptitiously made his way forward, moving from chair to chair on the central aisle until he got close enough to keep tabs on this situation. Felix had been doing pretty well over the last few months, but convention nerves had a way of ungluing even the most level-headed. If things went pear-shaped, he would be there to make the save. How exactly he'd do that, he had no idea, but it was the thought that counted, right?

As Felix reached her location, Amanda stepped forward from around her table, hands on her hips. "Felix."

"Amanda, hey."

"Can I help you with something?"

He nodded, and turned to look off to one side. "I wanted to get an idea of how many we can seat in here this year, on account of the new stage setup. That way I can mention it to the audience during the show."

Amanda paused before answering, giving an amused look at the back of Felix's head. "Okay, then. Well, we've been cleared for just over three thousand seats in here, and I'm sure we'll fill every one of 'em on Saturday night. Does that answer your question?"

Felix nodded, still looking out over the room. "Sure does, thanks, and I wanted to say thanks for taking over for Lorenzo on short notice."

"Felix." She scratched around the ring in her left eyebrow. "C'mon, I don't bite. Is there a reason you won't look at me? Do I have something on my face?"

Prowl winced, and almost stood to pull Felix back, but then hesitated. *It's early yet, Prowl. Give your bud a chance.*

Felix turned back to face Amanda, albeit slowly, and from Prowl's vantage point, it looked like Felix was fixing his gaze on a point in the middle of Amanda's forehead, as if there was something on her face that demanded his utmost concentration. *Well, it's better than staring at her tits, I suppose. Calm down, Felix, you can do this.*

"Sorry, Amanda. I just didn't want to make things weird again."

She leaned forward against the console, a twisted smirk on her lips. "You're kinda making it weird now, oh high and mighty Department Head." She curled a bit of her hair around one finger. "It's cool, I get it. I mean, I did turn you down last year, but does that really make me so scary?"

Stuffing his hands in his pockets, Felix gave a nervous shrug. "I was more worried I might be making you uncomfortable. I really got into your space last year, and I still feel bad about that." He took a deep breath. "And since we haven't really talked since then, I haven't apologized properly yet. So, I'm really sorry about being a creep last year."

"Huh." She let her hair fall from her fingers, and rubbed her chin. "Well, I appreciate the thought, but dude, you're not a creep, and you weren't 'in my space'. You were definitely giving off the desperate and gloomy vibe last year, but all I did was turn you down. No harm, no foul."

"If you say so, but every time I thought about it, I was sure I had really messed up." He rubbed his eyes. "Last year was a wake-up call, and I've been trying to do better ever since."

Amanda glanced upwards. "And that explains why you didn't look at me at first, and why you're staring a hole through my forehead now instead. You're trying not to stare at my chest."

Felix kept his eyes firmly on her face. "After the third time, you very pointedly said, 'my eyes are up here', I did eventually get the hint. I still feel like an ass about all that."

She gave a kind laugh. "Felix, I said it once, and I was laughing when I said it. You're a straight male, and I've got E cups. You're going to look, I get it—that's just how most guys are wired. Did I notice you looking for half a second? Yes, and that's normal. Did I think you were doing the extended creep stare? No." She put her hands on her hips, and squared her shoulders. "If anything, you're kinda missing out by being so careful this year, I'm not even wearing a bra tonight."

Felix's eyes went wide, and he immediately lifted his chin to stare at the ceiling, apparently to stop his eyes instinctively flicking downward.

Prowl's eyes, on the other hand, agreeably moved due south, and he allowed himself a quick glance. *Damn. I mean, DAMN, that's a hot body. I wonder if Amanda's single?*

Amanda burst out laughing, and Prowl pulled his eyes back upwards.

"Oh, my God! Don't give yourself whiplash, bud!" She laughed again, one hand over her mouth. "I'm sorry, Felix, that was mean of me. But I appreciate your gallant effort to not drool on my knockers, seriously." She reached out, touching the tip of his nose with her fingertip, guiding his gaze downward to meet her eyes. "Take a deep breath, and relax. Look at me. I wasn't mad at you last year, and I'm not going to tear your head off now. You asked me out a year ago, and I said no. That's all."

Felix took the requested breath, and let his shoulders relax. "So, we're cool?"

"We're cool, yes." As he exhaled in relief, Amanda held up her hand. "However, I would like your opinion." She gestured to herself. "Be honest. How do I look tonight? Seriously."

Prowl cocked his head to one side, like a curious dog staring at a record player. *Is she...? No, couldn't be.*

"Since you asked...um, okay." Felix's gaze flickered briefly up and down her person.

Prowl followed suit, again enjoying the view. Black leather high end boots, black fishnet stockings, skin-tight jean shorts, a wide leather belt that brought out the sway of her hips, and a very formfitting black *"Dethklok"* t-shirt. Prowl snickered as Felix's eyes bugged out for a split second when he realized she hadn't been kidding about going braless—the points of Amanda's large nipples were firmly outlined underneath the taut cotton that hugged her ample bosom.

Felix quickly dragged his gaze upwards again, and Prowl nodded approval.

Amanda cocked her head to one side. "Well?"

"You look good, Amanda. Real good." Felix cleared his throat. "You wear that outfit really well, and the blue in your hair nicely matches your eyes. If you're trying to get someone's attention, it'll work."

Amen to that, hell yes, Prowl thought with a grin.

"See, that wasn't so hard." She clapped her hands. "Congratulations, you have passed the test."

"Wait, that was a test?"

She nodded. "You looked without staring too long, and you gave me a nice compliment without sounding like a skeezy stalker." She held out an open hand. "We're now super-officially cool and totally leaving behind last year's non-drama. Let's shake on it."

Felix shook her hand happily. "'So, it shall be written, so it shall be done.' Glad to get the weekend off to a good start, Amanda." He briefly checked the screen of his phone. "I need to head out in a second, but I have one more question."

"Con stuff or more you-and-me stuff?" She gave him a warm smile.

"You stuff. You asked me how you looked—is there actually someone whose eye you're trying to catch? Anything I can do to help there?"

Amanda just shook her head. "Ah, Felix. A lady's got to have her secrets, after all." She gave him a shoo-ing gesture. "You go on and do your thing. Maybe I'll tell you later." Her hand shot out, grabbing Felix by the wrist. "Actually, wait. I wanted to ask someone, and you've probably seen it—is *Kabaneri of the Iron Fortress* any good?"

Felix blinked, already half turned away before she'd grabbed him. "Oh! Well, the art is absolutely amazing, I can tell you that."

Nodding, Prowl made his way back to his laptop. No need to listen to general anime chatter, and he did have work to do still. *Not too bad, Felix. Pity that you're about as dense as a yak when it comes to girls flirting with you, though.*

A few minutes later, Felix returned, and Prowl looked up from his computer. "Well, how'd it go?"

"Pretty good, I think." Felix glanced back to where he'd come from—Amanda was now chatting amiably with Kalli and a couple of other staffers from Security, who been helping out with odd jobs here and there. "She went braless tonight, and then made a point of mentioning it to me, just to see if I'd stare at 'em again. Which I managed *not* to do, and I've apparently proven that she and I can be friends again. I think."

Prowl grinned. "Yeah, I spotted that earlier. If she leaves the con without a new boy toy, I'll be very, very surprised." He laughed. "You were never not-friends to begin with, ya know. That's all in your head, but in the meantime, if you have no objections, I may audition for the role of 'boy toy number one' myself."

"Why should I object?" Felix raised an eyebrow. "She's hot, you're both single, what do I have to do with it?"

Prowl shrugged, typing in another line of text. "I figured you might want first shot, since you two are getting along so well now." He looked back up. "You've been single for over four years, with just one kiss from that Raye girl two Hordes ago to show for it in all that time. I've only been on my own for one year, so I don't mind being patient. The weekend's just getting started, don'tcha know."

"While I would very much like to see what she looks like without that t-shirt on—I'll pass. I doubt she'd be interested." Felix gave a resigned sigh. "You should go for it, though."

Prowl rolled his eyes. "Oh, ye of little faith," he whispered to himself.

"Faith in what?"

"I keep forgetting how sharp your ears are." Prowl snickered. "Don't mind me, I'm just being a goof." He typed in another bit of text, hit the Save command, and looked back up to his friend. "We're just about done in here—you off to have your 'Balcony Moment'?"

"Yup. Want to come along?"

Prowl shook his head. "That's your con tradition, y'know, not mine. You go relax for a bit, and then text me when you want to grab dinner."

As Felix walked towards the ballroom doors to head towards the hotel lobby, Prowl took a look around. Amanda was still chatting with Kalli, the other security staff having moved on to other tasks. They both looked over in Felix's direction, and their conversation became even more animated. Prowl chuckled as he watched, unable to make out their words, imagining instead a calliope soundtrack playing over the scene, like an old silent movie.

Amanda grinned widely, at one point gesturing to her own chest and then mimicking Felix's rushed look to the ceiling from before. Kalli seemed a little more subdued at that, but when Amanda gestured in the direction Felix had left with a two-handed "no, please, after *you*" motion, Kalli nodded, and then walked in that direction herself.

Prowl looked at his laptop and shut it down, gathering everything into his computer bag. Felix's encounter with Kalli last year had been a little awkward from what he'd heard. *Maybe I should...no. Felix has to learn how to handle these things himself, and he's doing fine so far.* He looked up back towards Amanda, who was busily working with her equipment, whistling a happy tune to herself. *Nah. I'll talk to her later. Chatting her up right now would just be weird.*

CHAPTER FOUR

FELIX

Standing on a balcony on the mezzanine level of the hotel, Felix looked out over the lobby, watching the staff and congoers come and go. The floor was thick with teens and twenty-somethings, some already in costume. There were an assortment of middle-aged suit-wearing men and women heading towards the door—they'd no doubt been here for a trade show that just ended. From the baffled looks on their faces, they had no idea what this swarm of strange youngsters pouring in was all about.

Felix's gaze flickered back and forth, picking the cosplayers out of the crowd. *Looks like Attack on Titan* is *still in vogue*, he thought. The *Homestuck* fad looked to have passed, but still plenty of *Sword Art Online* guys in black coats, no shock there. A smile grew on his lips when he noticed one young woman dressed as a gender-swapped version of Kaito Kumon from *Kamen Rider Gaim*, a character not often seen at American conventions. He made a note to walk by later to compliment her work, and ask if she would enter the Costume Contest. It certainly looked well-made from his vantage point.

Leaning against the balcony railing, he took a swig from a bottle of water. His gaze returned to a group of teenagers that had taken over some tables in the lobby's corner, watching their body language, listening for words through the murmur of the crowd.

His ears perked, and he looked back over his shoulder at the sound of approaching footsteps. "Evening, Miss Calderon. Or would you prefer 'Kallista'? What can I do for you?"

The well-tanned Puerto Rican woman walked up, and leaned into the same railing about five feet away. She was several inches shorter than Felix's six feet, and her sleeveless t-shirt revealed an impressively chiseled physique. A tattoo on her right shoulder showed a pair of crossed flintlock pistols in gold on a green shield, with a gold banner below that read "Assist—Protect—Defend" in green letters.

She crossed her arms over the railing, and rested her chin on her forearm. "Don't be so formal, Felix. My friends call me Kalli, you know that."

"I wasn't sure I had the right anymore." He watched one teenager in particular stand up and walk a short way away from the rest of his group.

He narrowed his eyes, trying to get a closer look.

Kalli scratched her arm. "Trust me—if I didn't consider you a friend anymore, you would know beyond a shadow of a doubt." She turned to look at him, and then tried to follow his gaze. "What are you looking at?"

"That guy, looking at himself in the fountain pond." Felix pointed. "Every con I go to, I like to stand on the balcony on the Thursday night before, soak in the atmosphere, and do some people-watching. This guy's got an interesting story going on."

"Is he wearing a pocket protector?" Kalli leaned forward as well, an amused smile on her lips. "I haven't seen one of those in years. Between the button-down tucked-in shirt, the big glasses, and the hiked-up pants, the poor white boy's a nine-point-five on the Nerd Richter Scale." She gave a soft chuckle. "Not like we're ones to judge, being massive nerds ourselves."

"Yeah, but that's not the whole story." Felix took another swig of his water. "His mom dropped him off fifteen minutes ago, and he's been desperately trying to fit in with that group there ever since. They clearly know him, I think they're class-mates or something, but they don't really know what to make of him, and he has no idea how to talk to them."

"So, what's so interesting about him? Just another awkward teenager, right?"

Felix shook his head. "We're watching a real-life transfor-mation happen. When he walked in, his hair was slicked back. Just as you walked up, he walked around that column to get by himself, and shook his hair up a bit. He's trying to make it look a little more stylish, and watch his shirt, he's been fiddling with it."

Kalli turned back to the pale student just as he untucked his shirt from the waist of his pants and unbuttoned it entirely, revealing a t-shirt beneath bearing a *Power Rangers* logo across the chest.

Felix continued. "He was also slouching a lot more a few minutes ago, but after looking at himself in the fountain, he's been trying to stand up straighter. I swear, it's like watching a montage from an 80's teen romance movie."

As Felix and Kalli watched, the lanky young man pulled the waistline of his pants down a couple of inches from where they'd been hiked up around his bellybutton, and unrolled the cuffs around his ankles.

"Will you look at that." Kalli pointed. "He's shaking."

"He's terrified." Felix rested his chin on his crossed arms. "He's realized that somewhere along the way, he's made a huge mistake, and he's trying to fix it before it's too late."

Kalli turned back toward him, eying him closely. After a moment, she looked back to the young man below, who'd just put his glasses in his pocket. "I hope he doesn't walk into any walls without those on," she remarked. "The glasses didn't look too bad."

Felix shrugged. "Maybe they're more for close reading than anything else. Cross your fingers...and there we go."

The youth looked down at his reflection one more time, and then looked hard at the pocket protector in his chest pocket.

"I bet someone important gave him that," Felix murmured. "It's hard for him to imagine himself without it."

Finally, the boy removed the pocket protector and carefully put it in the backpack sitting at his feet. He took another look at himself in the fountain water, took a deep breath, and turned around to head back towards his classmates. However, this time, he circled around to a different part of the student group.

"Oh, my gosh, he's going for it." Kalli broke out into a huge grin. "Look, look!" She pointed towards someone on the edge of the crowd.

Felix followed Kalli's gesture, their young man was walking right towards a pretty young Black girl dressed in a blue *Power Rangers: Ninja Storm* suit, who hadn't noticed him approaching yet. The boy paused, clearly nervous as hell, and suddenly turned around, retreating.

"No, no, no!" Felix gripped his water bottle. "Come on, guy. You can do this. Just walk up to her. Say hello. Don't panic."

Kalli had clasped her hands in literal prayer. "Be brave, be brave, come on. Stand tall. Come on."

Just as suddenly, the young man turned back around, crossed the distance between himself and the blue ranger of his dreams, and nervously reached out to tap her on the shoulder. The girl turned, and was clearly quite surprised. The words "Morty, is that you?" echoed across the lobby. She pointed to his t-shirt with a huge smile, and then a moment later, she pulled out a chair so that he could sit down next to her.

Kalli pumped a clenched fist. "Yes, that's how it's done! Good job, Morty."

Felix nodded agreement, and then after a moment's thought, he pulled his phone from his pocket, typing in commands at a rapid pace.

"Uh, Felix? What are you doing?"

Felix flipped through some images on his screen, his eyes flickering quickly over a list of names. "Morty... Mort... Mortimer... Ha! Got you." He held up his phone, showing a profile page from Anime Horde's online message board. "Mortimer Tuck Jr., age seventeen. Pre-registered for the con three months ago." The picture showed Morty in all his ultimate nerd garb glory, posing nervously in front of a *Power Rangers* movie poster.

Putting the phone away, Felix reached into his other pocket, and pulled out a business card holder and a pen. "Kalli, you're working the doors for the Costume Contest on Saturday night, right?"

"Yeah, why?"

"Follow my lead." He took a moment to write something on one of his cards, and then headed towards the escalator.

Kalli hurried to follow. "Felix, what are you doing?"

At the top of the escalators, Felix turned to face her. "I know I was a serious idiot last year, but I'm asking you to give me the benefit of the doubt. We're going to help Morty out. I know what I'm doing."

As they descended, Kalli responded. "I am giving you the benefit of the doubt, Felix. You're a good man. I just don't follow what you're planning, that's all."

"Coming from someone who was well within their rights and ability to break off my arm last year, that means a lot, Kalli. Seriously."

As they got off the escalator and navigated through the crowds toward where Morty was sitting, Felix lowered his voice to a whisper. "You don't need to do anything fancy, just be the security staffer you are. Okay, here goes."

Carefully weaving through the congoer crowd, Felix approached where Morty was sitting, deep in conversation with his fellow *Power Rangers* fan.

"W-well, I have to admit that *Dino Thunder* is my favorite season so far, with Tommy coming back, and the *Lost & Found in Translation* episode—but *Ninja Storm* is really cool, too!"

The young woman twirled one of her microbraids around one finger, giving Morty a warm smile. "You're just saying that because I'm cosplaying that show."

Morty waved his hands in front of him. "No, honest! Cam's Green Ranger is one of my favorite characters ever!"

Felix cleared his throat and stepped forward. "Excuse me, are you Mortimer Tuck? MisterMorty on the Anime Horde website forums?"

Morty looked up in surprise, pushing his hair out of his eyes. "What? Uh, yeah, that's me."

Felix gave a friendly wave. "Sorry to interrupt, I'll just be a second. I'm Felix Jackson, the Master of Ceremonies for the con..."

Morty's face lit up. "Oh, yeah! I was at the Costume Contest last year. You were great!" He turned back to the young woman next to him. "Karen, did you get to see the show last year?"

She frowned. "Actually, no. The room filled up before they got to us in line. I heard it was fun, though."

"Well, I have good news." Felix held out the card he'd written on to Morty. "We selected a person at random from the site forums, and you're our lucky winner. I was going to announce it at Opening Ceremonies, but since I spotted you here, I figured now was as good a time as any."

"W-winner?"

Felix grinned. "This card will get you, and one friend, front row seats for the costume contest this year. All you have to do is show this card to Kalli here—she's working security for the event—and she'll let you in." Next to him, Kalli gave a friendly wave.

Morty was stunned. "Front row? Seriously?"

"Absolutely." Kalli stepped forward. "If you don't see me, ask any security staffer for me, ask for Kalli, show them the card, and they'll find me for you. You won't even need to wait in line."

"And one friend." Morty looked at the girl next to him. "Karen, do you...do you want to go to the contest with me?"

The words spilled out of him, as if he wanted to finish asking her as quickly as possible before fear kicked in.

Karen clasped Morty's hand with a genuine smile. "You want to share that with me? Not one of your friends?"

Morty's face stiffened.

He doesn't have any other friends, does he? Well, hopefully that's about to change.

Morty broke into a nervous smile. "I'd... I'd really like you to be one of my friends, Karen. Front row, then?"

Squeezing his hand again, Karen's eyes lit up. "Morty, you are *awesome*." She looked at Felix and Kalli, and beamed a beautiful smile. "Thank you so much!"

Placing the card in Morty's open hand, Felix flipped it so that only Morty could see the additional message written on the back:

FORTUNE FAVORS THE BOLD. NEVER FORGET THAT. —FELIX JACKSON

Morty leaned back slightly to better read the message without his glasses, and then turned to look at Felix with wide eyes.

Felix gave him a smile and a nod, and patted him on the shoulder. "Have a great con, Mr. Tuck."

Mortimer stood up suddenly, and grabbed Felix's hand for a grateful handshake. "You, too, Mr. Jackson. Thank you so much."

A minute later, Felix had returned to his original balcony perch with Kalli still keeping him company.

She gave him a friendly mock-punch on the shoulder. "That was really sweet of you. And I'll make sure the rest of the door squad knows to let them in."

"Thanks. He reminded me a lot of myself ten years ago." He pointed towards where Morty and Karen were still sitting, still conversing as eagerly as before. "I didn't do the pocket protector look or anything like that, but I was branded the 'weird kid' for years, and only had a couple of friends in high school. I know I could've used a little help back then, so I figured, why not?"

She gave him a beaming smile. "You might have just changed his life for the better with that 'little help'. I have to tell you, Felix, that was really something else. You should be proud of this."

He ran one hand through his thick hair and shook his head. "The hard part was all Morty's doing. He worked up the nerve to talk to her, I had nothing to do with that."

She looked like she wanted to say more about that, but instead, she gestured in his direction with an open hand. "And now that your deed is complete, you're back at your perch, watching over the lobby again."

Kalli pulled her dark hair out of its ponytail, shook it, and then tied it back anew.

Closing his eyes, Felix took a deep breath and focused on the sounds echoing around him, taking in the background murmur of the lobby. "There's just something about the night before a con. People trickling in from all over, the hotel filled with this slowly building whisper that, by tomorrow morning, will be like the roar of the ocean. You see a lot of reunions on Thursday night, people who only see each other at these cons. Or those who don't fit in well in the outside world, but in here, they manage to find a tribe." He smiled, and opened his eyes again. "There's a lot of good feeling in the air on a Thursday night. The quiet before the storm."

They watched the lobby in silence for a few minutes, taking in that quiet together.

After a time, Kalli suddenly blurted out a question. "Do you know why I said no to you last year, Felix?"

He looked over at her. She was watching him, an odd expression on her face he couldn't decipher. "Because I was a frantic idiot, getting way too far into your personal space."

She shrugged, tilting her head to one side. "You weren't that bad, but 'frantic' describes it well. You were this whirlwind of desperation last year, but that's not what I was getting at."

Standing up straight, he pursed his lips. "I'm listening."

"And I appreciate that." She paused. "When you started hitting on me that Sunday morning, I was pissed off because I thought you were taking pity on me."

He blinked in surprise. "Pity? Kalli, that wasn't it at all."

"And I know that now, but back then, I was seeing red." She gestured to herself. "I had this broken record going in my head that no one would ever want me anymore."

"Why wouldn't they? You're awesome."

She gave a soft smile, looking down. "Thanks, Felix. But last year, all I could think about were three things. One, that most of the guys I knew were scared of the fact that I could easily break them in half. Two, that I'm all ugly muscle with no pretty curves. And three, I couldn't stop thinking that missing a couple of fingers was grossing people out."

"Anyone shallow enough to give you crap about any of those things wouldn't be worth your time anyway, Kalli." He gestured to her left hand. "I'm not a trained combat veteran like you, but if I saw someone being cruel to you, I'd find a way to kick them in the head on general principle."

She looked at the hand, touching the stumps of her shortened ring and pinky fingers. "I know you would, and thank you, but last year, I was starting to think I was a hideous freak-creature who was never going to have a date again as long as I lived. Then, all of a sudden, you were flirting with me, and I panicked."

"I can never apologize enough for that. I was flailing, and couldn't even pause for a second to think about what I was doing." He scratched his neck. "I'm still amazed you're willing to talk to me at all now."

"You're not a bad person, Felix. You were just really lonely, and you were trying to reach out—if a little awkwardly." She took him by the shoulder and turned him to face her. She then touched her left palm to his sternum. "I very nearly did hurt you last year. When you were leaning towards me, reaching out for my bad hand? I was about to one-inch-punch you, right here, but I caught myself, and just pushed you away instead. The next morning, I got on the horn to the VA office and got an appointment with a counselor. You shouldn't be apologizing to me for a harmless flirtation, Felix. I should be apologizing to you for what I almost did."

Kalli's hand lingered on his chest as she continued. "I talked about you and that morning with the doctor a lot, and I realized you weren't pitying me, you were just so damn lonely that you'd gone a little bad in the head. I was so damn lonely I'd gone a little crazy myself, just in a different way. All I could believe was that you didn't actually like me, because I was convinced that no one could actually like me anymore, that I was damaged goods."

"I like you a lot, Kalli—I'd even go so far as to say that you're one of my favorite people at this con, seriously." He gestured in her direction with two open hands. "I mean, look at you. You're a bona fide badass who's saved people's lives. You're the most moral person I know, and I'm not just saying that because you refrained from putting my idiot ass in the hospital, even though I deserved it. You're a hell of a lot smarter than I am, that's for sure."

She let her hand fall from his chest, a half-smile on her face. "What, no 'beautiful' or 'pretty'? I'd settle for 'striking', that'd be nice."

Felix put a hand over his heart. "I'm trying to be good this year, and not be a flirty creep again. But I will say this: I did notice you've let your hair grow long since last year, and I think it looks really nice."

Her mouth parted in a slow smile, her cheeks showing hints of a blush. "You like it?" She looked away. "You know, it doesn't hurt to flirt a little bit. I mean, Amanda was flirting with you pretty hard back there. I saw that whole thing."

"Nah, no way she meant it like that." Felix laughed, and turned back to leaning on the balcony railing. "A bit of friendly teasing with the whole 'have I mentioned I'm not wearing a bra' thing, sure. I deserve a lot worse. If I can just keep it mellow this weekend, and manage to salvage some of the friendships I damaged last year, like with you, I'll be happy with that."

"Trust me on this. You and I? There's nothing you need to fix." She put a hand on his shoulder, and gave it a warm squeeze. "You know, just because things went bad last year doesn't mean that you have to—"

The radio on Kalli's hip squawked to life. "Dispatch to Kalli, come in."

Muttering a curse under her breath, Kalli released Felix's shoulder and pulled her radio from her back right pocket. "Go for Kalli."

"Kalli, what's your twenty, over?"

Kalli sighed. "Megan, I'm on the mezzanine balcony. With Felix. Why?"

There was a pause on the other side of the radio. "Oh. Shit, sorry about that. But we need you down in Video Three, there's a drunk down there giving folks crap, and no one knows where hotel security is. You're closest. Sorry."

Kalli let out a long breath. "You owe me big, Megan. I'm enroute, over and out."

Felix winced sympathetically. "Looks like the storm is starting early. Sorry about that. Can I help?"

"No, I've got this. It's my job, after all, but I want to continue this conversation later, okay?" She pointed right at him as she backed away. "You're a good man, Felix Jackson, don't let anyone, yourself included, tell you otherwise."

As he watched Kalli turn and jog away, he wrenched his gaze away from staring at her pretty backside, perfectly framed in the tight jeans she was wearing.

He spoke quietly to himself as he rested his chin on his crossed arms. "A good man? Yeah, right." His attention glancing to and fro across the hotel lobby, he settled in to watch the growing crowds.

CHAPTER FIVE

FELIX

It was early the next morning as Felix stood naked in front of the hotel room mirror. He looked into his own eyes. "Be yourself," he said. "Be yourself." He took another deep breath, trying to calm his nerves. "Easy for you to say, Prowl. I don't even know what I really want yet."

Prowl's voice echoed from inside the bathroom. "What?"

"Just talking to myself, dude. Take your time in there."

"Oh, I plan to! Shouldn't have had those garlic fries last night. Oh, man."

Felix laughed and rolled his eyes, and then looked back at himself again. A little taller than average, a little larger than average. He pinched the fat at his waist with a frown. If he didn't get back into his old walking routines and other exercise, that 'little larger' was going to get worse. Dark brown hair that was thick and wavy, green eyes, and a face his mom had always said was handsome—but that's what moms say regardless, right?

I am not going to worry about that for right now, Felix thought. *This weekend is about making sure Anime Horde is the best convention it can be, and not about trying to find some woman to bed. That was last year, and last year was, let's be honest, a total disaster. This year, I'm not going to worry about this four-year dry spell, I'm just going to enjoy being a fan, and being here with my fellow fans. Seriously.*

As he adjusted how he fit into the boxers, he tried very hard not to think about how long it had been since someone else's hands had touched him there.

"Looking good, Prowl." Felix and Prowl had paused at a large mirror, right at the edge of the convention center lobby, which was next door to the hotel. Despite the early hour, the sun was already quite bright, illuminating the huge crowds through the many skylights in the convention center roof.

"And yourself, as well, sir! Our illustrious Con Chair might be an ass sometimes, but I think the dress policy is one of Brian's better ideas."

Brian had been adamant about this at a staff meeting two months ago. "It is imperative that all department heads and con officers be dressed formally for Friday," Brian paced the meeting room. "We only get one chance to make a good first impression, and I want our leadership to be that good first impression." So, both Felix and Prowl were in their black job-interview suits, adjusting their ties in the convention's official colors of red and blue. They both wore their staff badges on lanyards hanging around their necks, and Prowl had added an additional flourish on one lapel—a diecast pin bearing the likeness of his namesake, one of the original "G1" *Transformers.*

"Strictly speaking, Prowl, you didn't have to dress up. It's department heads only."

"Bah. A lowly *assistant* department head of the Costume Contest I may be, but I still like to put my best foot forward. Besides, the ladies love a man in a good suit."

Felix shrugged as they turned and walked towards the open lobby area. "I'll take your word for it."

As they approached the convention center, Prowl gave him a sidelong look. "I heard Kalli was looking for you last night. Did she find you?"

"Yup, found me at my balcony spot." Felix took a deep breath, glancing around at the attendees they were passing. "We had a good talk, actually. She looks really pretty with the longer hair, but I didn't want to make a thing out of it." He turned to look back at Prowl, a sly grin on his face. "What about you? Any luck with Amanda?"

Prowl shook his head. "She got really busy after you left, so it didn't seem the right time. I'll talk to her later."

The convention center lobby was a huge open area with a thirty-foot high ceiling. Sunlight poured in through numerous skylights, and the cleaning crew had polished the faux-marble tile floors to a beautiful shine. Various convention sponsors had set up displays or hung wall banners depicting famous anime characters, and the convention staff had placed numerous signs about, directing attendees to various notable locations.

To one side, a hallway led to a series of smaller meeting rooms, home to panel discussions and anime screening theaters. A large open gate led to another area that was home to the massive registration desks, and then the largest gate of them all led to the convention's dealers' room and artist alley, where hundreds of thousands of dollars of anime-related swag would be on sale.

Easily two thousand people were milling around with room to spare, ranging from small children to senior citizens, although most of the crowd looked to be in their late teens or early twenties. This was the tip of the iceberg. The early arrivals—before the end of the weekend, well over ten times that many people would be circulating through this massive complex. Most people were dressed casually, but a significant number of the crowd were decked out in incredible costumes, from student uniforms from fictional high schools, to the occasional giant robot suit made out of cardboard, fiberglass, and a serious time investment. Some of those cosplayers were posing for photos being taken by other attendees, while others just sat or stood around, talking to their friends like most of the rest of the crowd was doing.

Felix smiled, enjoying the feeling of being among his fellow fans, remembering many conventions ago when he'd been an attendee rather than staff, hanging out just like these people were.

He turned to Prowl. "So, you remember the drill, right?"

The bearded Viking nodded, adjusting his glasses. "You betcha. We're looking for families with little kids, especially kids who came in costume, we offer to take them to the front of the registration line, and tell the reg desk to knock ten bucks off each person's badge fee."

Felix nodded. "Bingo. Make sure to talk up how Anime Horde is a 'family friendly' con to the parents."

Prowl adjusted the lanyard holding his staff badge, already heavy with several extra ribbons with various anime in-jokes written on them. "That might be a little difficult, Felix. The amount of weaponized sex appeal in this hall is already pretty intense—not that I'm complaining, no sir. I mean, look at everyone! I know you're trying to play it mellow this year, but as for me? This is what heaven looks like. Oh, yeah."

Felix could only sigh in agreement. The amount of people who'd shown up last night and were still pouring in this morning meant that Anime Horde was certainly going to break its own attendance record again, and the amount of artfully bare or tightly-clothed flesh on display was enough to make even a devout monk or nun think twice. Young men cosplaying the latest bare-chested pretty boy characters, with washboard abs right out of fitness magazines, and young women with mouth-watering figures posed in elaborate costumes that did everything to flatter every possible body part.

"Ah, we're too old for most of these folks anyway, Prowl." *I am not thinking about the fantastic ass on that leather-clad vampire woman to the right, or the dream-inducing cleavage on that ninja beauty to the left. Eyes front, Felix. Focus on the job.*

Prowl snorted. "We're only four years out of college, man. That's not so old."

"Just make sure you're checking their ID, dude." Felix made a *tsk-tsk* sound in mock reproach. "Don't want a repeat of 'The Nausicaa Incident' from two years ago.'"

"Hey, now. I wasn't the only one hanging around with jail-bait cosplayers that year, Mister 'Raye just needed a shoulder to cry on.'" Prowl snorted. "And it's not my fault that the Nausicaa girl lied about being eighteen! Besides, I never even touched her."

Felix held up one finger. "First, Raye was actually eighteen, she made a point of showing ID to one of the onsite cops to show she wasn't violating curfew." He lifted a second finger. "Second, I was trying to talk her down from a nervous break-down after her 'friends' basically stabbed her in the back."

"Yah, I remember. A cadre of little shitheads, that bunch."

Felix frowned, and lifted a third finger. "Lastly, she kissed *me*, not the other way around."

Prowl patted Felix on the shoulder. "Gee, if only you didn't have, y'know, morals. You could've ended your dry spell right then and there with some hot cosplayer nookie. She wanted you something fierce."

With a deep sigh, Felix looked upward in resignation. "Don't remind me. She was in a bad way, seriously vulnerable. I was not going to take advantage of that."

"No matter how nice it would've been to have a hot Califor-nia blonde wrapped around you all night." Prowl snickered and made little kissy-face noises.

Felix turned and glared. "But anyway. In your case, you were laying the flirts on Nausicaa pretty thick, and the only thing that saved you was her friends showing up and yanking her away before you could get that first kiss. You dodged a bullet that year, Prowl."

"Yeah, and ended up with Natalie at the end of the con instead. Out of the frying pan and into the fire."

Felix winced. "Sorry about that. I didn't mean to bring She Who Shall Not Be Named up again."

Prowl waved it off. "Pssh. It's history, man. I'm just focused on the now. Hey, I think I've found our first family, down there by the drinking fountain. Let's go."

CHAPTER SIX

IRIS

Iris was already nervous as hell, and all they were doing was standing around a bench on the edge of the lobby, waiting for her uncle to show up.

The armor fit perfectly, like she knew it would. She'd gotten every detail exactly right, and the interlocking tabs and locks held it together snugly and comfortably over her body. She was the spitting image of her favorite character in all of anime, and no one cared.

As she leaned on her character's signature war staff, Iris berated herself. She knew that this anime was obscure, so it was to be expected that no one recognized it. Besides, wasn't the point of cosplay to be doing it for your own enjoyment, not for what other people thought?

"That's the theory, anyway," she grumbled to herself. A few people passing by had complimented the costume and asked if they could take her photo, which was nice, but when every single one of them followed it up by asking her, "So, who are you cosplaying as, anyway?" It had ripped a little more wind out of her sails each time.

One thing she was happy about, though—the signs placed all around the convention center that read "Cosplay Is Not Consent" seemed to be working. She hadn't spotted any other cosplayers having to swat away creepers. When one guy taking her picture then moved around behind her and was about to take a photo of her ass without permission, his friend had immediately reprimanded him with an elbow to the gut and a stern, "Dude! Not cool," apologizing to Iris as he pulled the offender away. Iris had been ready to smack the jerk over the head with her war staff, but it was just as well that she didn't have to.

Like usual, her Aunt Abby was a rock, sitting calm and composed on their bench despite all the noise and chaos around them. How Abby managed to keep her cool while riding herd on two hyper daughters was something Iris had always admired, and her aunt was in top form today.

"Angelica, don't go wandering too far, stay where we can see each other. Tracy, do you want another juice box? Iris, how about you?"

Iris blinked, not realizing at first that she'd been addressed. "Oh! No, thanks, Aunt Abby, I'm good. I don't want to have to take the costume off in the bathroom again just yet."

Abby smiled, smoothing out her own flawless Mon Mothma cosplay gown. "I can certainly understand that. You did such an amazing job on that armor—but that's to be expected for a character so near and dear to your heart."

Iris gripped her war-staff tightly. "I needed a project after everything went to pieces, and this... Well, it helped."

Little Tracy looked up where she sat next to her mother, a precocious ten-year-old dressed as Kujo Jotaro from *JoJo's Bizarre Adventures: Starlight Crusaders*, black duster jacket and all. "When are you going to let me watch that character's show with you, Iris? It's not like there's naked stuff in it."

Iris smiled awkwardly. "No, but it does get pretty violent. Maybe when you're a little older."

Tracy rolled her eyes. "If I can handle *Jojo*, I can handle *Yoroi Senshi: Damashii Knights Daitai*," speaking the Japanese words flawlessly. "If it helps you feel any better, we can watch the subtitled version instead of the dub."

Angelica wandered back, fifteen-years-old and decked out in her natural blazing red hair, a domino mask, and a disturbingly form-fitting yellow bodysuit. "Give it a rest, Tracy. We can watch DKD later when Iris is feeling better."

Iris still boggled at how quickly her young niece was growing up. Had she been that developed at fifteen? *Must be something in the water around here.*

Tracy looked up and bolted for the crowd, accidentally kicking over Iris's shoulder bag in the process, sending its contents scattering across the floor. "Daddy!"

Iris knelt to gather her things, but turned to watch where Tracy had run off to. The crowd had parted like the fabled Red Sea, making way for the giant that was her Uncle Marcus, who had finally returned from parking the family van. Nearly seven feet tall, muscled like a superhero, and dressed in a bright purple bodysuit with ornate shoulder pads, facial appliances, an oversized wig, and many other accessories, Marcus was an awe-inspiring presence, drawing impressed stares. The instant Tracy reached him and jumped into his arms, the other con-goers took even greater notice.

"Oh, my God! Jotaro and Star Platinum together! I have *got* to get a picture of you two!"

"Jotaro and his Stand! *So Cute!*"

"Do the pose! Can you do the pose?"

Camera flashes went off like firecrackers, and father and daughter obligingly posed and soaked up the attention with huge grins.

Abby smiled, and zipped her shoulder bag. "Now that we're all here, we should get in line for registration. That's going to take forever, but such is life."

Iris was still kneeling to gather her things when an unfamiliar but warm voice addressed her aunt.

"Actually, I can help out with that."

CHAPTER SEVEN

FELIX

Felix was impressed. It was fun to see families that went all-out for conventions like this. They had just helped a single father and his three kids (dressed as Ozzy, Slash, and Flea from *Chrono Trigger*) and it was time to find the next family. As he scanned the room, he noticed the crowd surrounding a father/daughter duo doing a series of dynamic and exaggerated poses, and decided they would be a good next choice.

"Prowl, check it out, a little Jojo and Star Platinum!"

Prowl turned, his face breaking into a huge grin at the sight. "I'll bet you good money that those two are going to go viral on YouTube in *minutes*. That's just awesome."

"No bet." Felix pointed with his thumb towards the benches along the nearby wall. "I saw Jojo sitting by that Mon Mothma at the bench beforehand, so let's do our thing, and put a good foot forward for the con."

As they approached, Felix caught the apparent mother say something about having to wait in line, and he smiled at how perfect the timing was.

"Actually, I can help out with that." He approached, holding up his staff badge. "My name's Felix Jackson, and I'm the Department Head and Master of Ceremonies for the Costume Contest."

Prowl stepped up and nodded a greeting, his hands behind his back. "First name Jackson, last name also Jackson, but everyone calls me Prowl. I'm the Assistant D.H. for the Costume Contest."

The Mon Mothma cosplayer raised an eyebrow, and beckoned her husband and daughter back from their admirers. "Felix Jackson and Jackson Jackson?"

Prowl and Felix smiled and said, "No relation," in unison.

Felix cleared his throat. "So, as part of Anime Horde's welcome wagon, if you will, we like to show that we're a family-friendly convention. If we see families who are coming to the con together, especially if some, or all in this case, are cosplaying, then we like to give them a bit of a hand and speed up their registration process. If you'd care to follow me, we'll take you all to the head of the registration line."

The mother nodded in appreciation, returning their smile. "Very, very kind of you. I'm Abby Weinberg, this is my husband Marcus."

"Yo." Marcus gave the two young men a friendly wave.

Felix reached out to shake the giant's hand. "That is the best Star Platinum cosplay I've ever even heard of, and your girl's a perfect Jotaro Cujo. Great stuff, man."

Marcus shook the hand eagerly, clearly proud of his work.

Abby continued, "The little girl in the Jojo costume is my daughter, Tracy, and my eldest daughter Angelica is doing a classic this year."

Prowl gave a thumbs up. "Firestar! I have every episode of *Spider-Man and his Amazing Friends* on VHS, that is seriously great work." The teenager beamed in response.

Abby smiled. "I thought I'd do a little bit of *Star Wars* this year, and this is my niece, Iris."

The woman Abby pointed to stood from where she'd been kneeling behind her aunt, apparently picking up some fallen belongings. She looked up, and Felix's world abruptly changed.

He was almost struck speechless. "Oh, wow." While he did register that she had done an impeccable job recreating one of his favorite characters, that wasn't what had really gotten his attention. Rather, it was because of her raw physical beauty, in no way diminished by the bulky costume armor she wore. Her hips were wide and enticing atop long and graceful legs, narrowing to a curvy waistline that fit her proportions perfectly. While the armor's breastplate did conceal the full impact of her figure, it was still quite clear that she was very generously endowed.

But it was her eyes that had the tightest grip on him. Large and alight with life, they were such a pale and striking shade of blue as to be almost white. Combined with a full and very kissable mouth, and a cute nose that further hinted at the Jewish ancestry implied by her family's name, her face's immediate allure hit Felix like a speeding bullet train. It was impossible for him not to stare into her eyes, and all conscious thought went completely forgotten.

CHAPTER EIGHT

IRIS

Iris shivered as she sensed his gaze upon her. The brown-haired man watching her was easy on the eyes, that was for certain, with broad shoulders, and handsome green eyes that made him look thoughtful and intelligent, but it was that deep voice that really sent a tingle all the way down to her toes. He looked to be about her age and height, and he wore his suit well, although the tie of red and blue made him look a little flushed.

Or was he blushing because of her? It had been far too long since the last time someone looked at her like that—as if she was the only woman in the world worthy of adoration. It was a big improvement over someone undressing her with their eyes, with leering faces of predatory intent. Blushing fiercely herself, a warmth traveled from her flushed cheeks and down through her neck and breasts. Her gaze drifted down his body. As her gaze reached his badge hanging at his chest, her mouth moved before she had time to consciously think about it.

"Oh, my God! You watch *Shurato*!"

Felix blinked in obvious surprise. "Uh, yeah!"

He held up his staff badge, custom-made to include an image of his choice, which Iris had heard was the practice for high-ranking staff at Anime Horde. He'd used a picture of a sinister looking albino swordsman in black and red armor that she knew very well, and his next words confirmed he hadn't picked the image at random.

"Yasha-Oh Gai is my favorite anime villain of all time. I'm convinced that *Final Fantasy VII* ripped him off when they designed Sephiroth."

Her smile broadened. "*Totally*, although I still wish they'd given Nara-Oh Renge a bigger part."

He leaned forward in apparent agreement. "I know, right? I mean, they cast Megumi Hayashibara and then barely gave her anything to do! She's such a great character."

Putting one hand over her heart, Iris was almost swooning. "Hayashibara-san is my inspiration, she's just the most amazing voice actress..."

Abby coughed. "Iris, I think we're getting off topic."

They both blushed again, and Felix spoke first. "Sorry, didn't mean to geek out there."

As she fidgeted with the straps of her armor, Iris nodded, but had a hard time looking away from him. "Likewise. Sorry, Aunt Abby." She self-consciously stepped back to stand next to her two young cousins.

Tracy tugged at her big sister's elbow, and Iris overheard her whispering in confusion. "What was that all about? It reminded me of that one chapter of *Lone Wolf & Cub* where the two samurai imagined a sword fight in their heads while they stared at each other."

Nodding sagely, Angelica whispered back, "It was *exactly* like that, but with kissing instead of katanas. You'll get it when you're older." She looked at Iris, a gleeful smirk over her lips.

Tracy rolled her eyes in exasperation, muttering in Japanese under her breath. "*Yare yare...*"

Prowl put his arm around Felix's shoulder as if shaking his friend out of a trance, and was grinning like someone who'd just been hit with Joker Venom. "So, if you'll all step this way, we'll be glad to get you all registered."

Hoisting her bag onto her shoulder and stepping away from her giggling cousins, Iris gave Felix a sheepish smile. "Waiting in a long line is never fun, so thanks for this."

She turned and shot Angelica a murderous look, but the teenager just rolled her eyes.

CHAPTER NINE

FELIX

Felix adjusted his collar and tie, smiling while his mind raced furiously.

Dear Lord, what a voice! A husky alto, sensual and rich.

I want to hear this woman whisper my name…

Gah. Down, boy. Chill. Focus.

He took a breath. "We, ah, like to think of it as a recognition of all the hard work a family has to put in for an outing like thi…"

His voice trailed off as something of concern caught his attention, his eyes narrowing, but no longer looking at Iris.

Iris looked at him with a concerned expression. "Felix? Everything okay?"

He raised a finger to his lips, his eyes scanning the crowd, and his head suddenly shot to the left, his eyes intent. "Excuse me for a moment, Iris. Mrs. Weinberg, if you and your family could wait here, please?" He pulled a radio out of his back pocket and spoke into it. "Felix to Security, priority response please."

A woman's voice crackled from the radio a moment later. "Go for Megan at Security Dispatch, Felix. What's going on?"

He started walking with purpose towards the direction he'd been staring, realizing as he moved both Prowl and Iris were following him. "Megan, please send a team to the convention center lobby immediately. We have a lost child. Have them meet me by the *Pokemon* banner on the east wall."

"Affirmative, Felix. I've got River and Kalli nearby. I'll get them to you, stat. Dispatch out."

Prowl looked around. "What child?"

Felix pocketed the radio and pointed to the large banner he'd referred to, now twenty feet away. "Behind that." As they looked at the large image of *Pokémon*'s favorite electric rodent mascot hanging from the wall, a tiny pair of sandaled feet were just barely visible at the banner's bottom edge.

He stopped a couple of feet away from the banner. "Hey, are you okay back there?"

A small Asian girl of perhaps four years pushed aside the fabric she'd been hiding behind. "I'm sorry, I'm sorry!" Her face was streaked with tears, her ponytail covered in lint from the back of the banner. She wore a t-shirt with the same image of Pikachu as the banner held.

Felix sat cross-legged in front of the girl so that his face was about level with hers. "It's okay, you don't need to apologize. Did you lose your mommy? I heard you calling for her."

As the child nodded, Iris whispered to Prowl. "He heard her in this crowd?"

"*I* sure didn't," Prowl responded, "but he's always had better ears than me."

Felix turned his attention back to the girl. "Where did you see your mommy last?"

She rubbed at her runny nose, sniffling. "It was dark. I wanted a drink of water, but I can't find her now. Where's Mommy?" The tears started flowing again.

He cleared his throat, and pitched his voice several octaves higher to a voice that was almost a squeak. "Pika pika!"

The girl blinked and looked up. "You sound like Pikachu!"

Iris had stepped around to Felix's right, and had an impressed look on her face. "That was really good, Felix. Good sound there."

Felix nodded, but didn't turn away from the girl. "I like doing impressions, it's fun." He switched back to the Pikachu voice. "Pika pi? Pika? Chu! Chuu!"

The girl was giggling now, her terror forgotten.

Iris stepped forward and dropped to one knee. "What other Pokémon do you like, honey?"

Wiping away the last of her tears, the girl looked at Iris. "You're pretty."

Felix bit his lip, restraining himself from loudly agreeing with that assessment.

Iris beamed. "Aw, thank you! And so are you! Do you like...Squirtle?"

"I like Snugglypuff." The girl looked confused. "Why?"

Iris thought for a moment, and then opened her mouth to sing, doing a flawless imitation of the little pink puffball monster. "Snugg-a-ly puff, Snug-a-ly-y-y-puuuff."

The girl clapped her hands, but then put them over her ears while grinning. "Oh no, I'm gonna fall asleep!" Her sniffles had turned to giggles.

Felix put his own hands over his ears, playing along. "It's the perfect Snugglypuff lullaby! She's gonna put us to sleep! *Oh, no!*" He fell over onto his side, closed his eyes, and made loud snoring noises, getting another giggle from the girl.

At this point, two staffers wearing red and blue baseball caps with "Security" written on them walked up. One was a slender Caucasian fellow with androgynous features and short blond hair, and the other was Kalli, who had changed into a US Army t-shirt this morning.

"Felix, everything okay here?"

He stood up slowly, brushing the dirt off his side and back as he spoke. "Hey, Kalli. You're exactly who I wanted to see." He gestured to the young girl. "So, our little friend here is lost. From what she said, I think her mom's in one of the film rooms nearby. She snuck out to find a drinking fountain and no one noticed, and then she couldn't find her way back."

"Gotcha." Kalli waved to the little girl. "Hey, sweetie, my name is Kalli. What's yours?"

"Annette."

"Okay, Annette. I work for the convention show, and my friend River and I are going to help you find your mommy, okay?"

"Okay!" Annette suddenly ran up and hugged Felix around the legs, and then ran back over to hug the still-kneeling Iris as well. "Thank you, Pikachu! Thank you, Snugglypuff!"

Felix smiled. "You're welcome, Annette. Everything's going to be fine." He turned back to his friend. "Kalli, can you radio me when the mom is found?"

Kalli nodded. "Of course, Felix." She leaned in, lowering her voice. "So, are you Pikachu or Snugglypuff?"

"Pika pika!" Felix chuckled.

Shaking her head with a laugh, Kalli paused, and then looked over at Iris, who was still making faces and voices for Annette. She frowned. "I'll let you get back to your date with Snugglypuff, then."

Felix blinked in confusion. "Date? Oh! No, no. She and I just met, we're getting her family registered."

Toying with a lock of her hair, Kalli gave a warm smile at this news. "Oh! That's, ah, good to know, good to know. Well, um, we should get to stepping. We'll talk soon, okay Felix? I still want to finish our conversation from last night." She walked up, and gently took the lost girl by the hand. "Annette, let's try these rooms over here first."

As the security guards walked away, Iris stood. "So, you know those two?"

Prowl gestured to the departing guards with a pointing thumb. "River's new to staff this year, but came highly recommended by some trusted friends, and we've known Kalli for a long, long time. She's ex-Army military police, and she's also the closest thing I've ever seen to a real-life Lawful Good Paladin. Annette is in good hands, oh yeah."

Iris turned to Felix. "You seriously heard that girl from over thirty feet away?"

"Barely." Felix brushed his hands over the backs of his thighs, hopefully removing any dust and dirt from sitting down on the lobby floor. "The crowd noise had dimmed a bit while we were talking, and suddenly there was a tiny little 'mommy?' on the edge of my hearing." He frowned. "I got really badly lost in a department store when I was that age once, and I remembered making exactly that sound when it happened. Sorry about shushing you back then, I was trying to pinpoint her."

Iris shook her head, smiling. "You have absolutely nothing to apologize for. Quite the opposite, in fact."

Felix smiled. "Kind of you to say so. Thanks for coming along. You were a big help there, but let's get back to your family. They're probably wondering what happened."

CHAPTER TEN

IRIS

As she followed Felix back to her family, Iris looked him over with interest. *He's handsome, he has empathy, he's good with kids, he looks at me like a goddess, and I could listen to him talk all day with that sexy voice. What's the catch? Did I really just meet someone this amazing at a con, of all places?*

As the reunited family walked across the convention floor towards the distant reservation desk, Felix turned to speak to her. "I didn't get a chance to say before, but it is so cool to see someone cosplaying Bronwyn Davies from *Damashii Knights Daitai*."

She was stunned. "You actually know about DKD? Everyone else either has to ask what I'm cosplaying as, or even worse, they assume I'm doing Kain from *Final Fantasy IV*, and then mansplain how Kain uses a spear instead of a staff."

Felix shook his head. "Ugh, sorry you had to deal with that crap. I love all the detail you included, though! You got the perfect shade of green for the armor's main color, the design of the dragon-helmet couldn't have been easy to make, and you even included the little trim on Bronwyn's war staff. It was so good, it just took my breath away."

She bit her lip, and looked at her feet. "My *costume* took your breath away. Ah, I see. Well, it was a nice feeling while it lasted." *And the other shoe drops. Damnit. If he turns out to be gay, I'm going to cry.*

"I'm sorry?"

"Never mind, it's nothing." *Hold on, Iris, this isn't a total loss.* She looked back up and managed a smile. "But I'm really glad to meet a fellow fan!"

He shrugged. "Well, I'm a huge fan of that genre. Super-powered martial arts heroes in magic armor, banding together against evil, and all that. *Saint Seiya, Samurai Troopers, Shurato,* and so forth. So, when I heard that someone was making a new show in that style, I had to check it out." He pitched his voice to a deep bass rumble. "'Let the hunt begin'," he quoted Lord Orion, one of DKD's villains. "Such a shame it only lasted thirteen episodes, though. I would've thought they could get a whole year out of that story, at least."

He flicked away a bit of lint from his sleeve as he continued. "I guess when your show gets released at the same time as a mega-hit like *Attack on Titan*, it's easy to get lost in the shuffle." He turned back to look at her. "Have you seen the dub of DKD yet?"

Iris froze mid-step, and forgot how to breathe. "Um."

Prowl was handing all the members of the Weinberg family some paperwork. "And we've arrived! Okay, we'll need each of you to fill out one of these forms, should only take a few seconds, and then we'll get you into the computers."

Felix blinked. "Huh. I didn't realize we'd reached the desk already." He handed Iris a pen. "Sorry, I'll stop blathering at you about DKD stuff."

She just nodded, and as Felix walked a few steps away, she bent her head to fill out her form at the counter, her strained smile falling away into a twisted frown.

CHAPTER ELEVEN

PROWL

"And here you go. Pen, form, and clipboard." Prowl smiled at the young woman before him. "Angelica, right? Any questions?"

Angelica made a show of assessing Prowl as she took the clipboard, a smile forming on her bright red lips. "Why do we have to fill these out, anyway?"

"Well, for one thing, we like to get an idea of what age groups we get at the con." He gave her an apologetic shrug. "If you'd really rather not answer, we're not going to force you to, but it does help us out."

She put one hand on her hip and struck a flirtatious pose, giving Prowl a very warm smile. "Oh, I'll help you out, alright. I can be as old as you want me to be, big man. *Ow!*" She wheeled on her cousin. "Iris, you hit me!"

Iris frowned, gesturing with the staff she'd just poked her cousin with. "And you thoroughly deserved it. Stop teasing him, Angie." She turned to look at Prowl. "Just so you know, my little cousin here is only fifteen, but I don't blame you for thinking she's older. It weirds me out, too."

Prowl's eyes went as wide as dinner plates, and he made a point of taking a large step backwards and away from the curvaceous minor. "I'll just be over here, then."

As Abby turned to gently admonish her oldest daughter, Prowl looked back and forth between Iris and Felix, the latter talking with a staffer behind the registration counter.

He grabbed his friend by the shoulder. "Felix, can I talk to you over here for a second?"

After getting dragged a few feet away, Felix regained his balance. "Dude, what the hell?"

Prowl leaned in and lowered his voice. "Answer me one question, friend, 'kay?"

"Uh, okay."

"When that Iris girl stood up and you got all tongue-tied, why was that?"

Felix scratched the back of his neck, suddenly not able to meet his friend's gaze. "Why are you asking me this?"

"Indulge me. Answer the question."

Felix gave a small cough, clearing his throat. "Okay, fine. She's got these really pretty eyes, okay? I've never seen eyes that pale blue before, and her face is just gorgeous. Not to mention everything else about her."

"And yet you told her it was because of her costume."

Felix rolled his eyes. "Well, I didn't want to be a creep about it! 'Hi, nice to meet you, my name's Felix, and I'm suddenly lost in your beautiful eyes.' I'm trying not to be some massive horndog on the hunt this year, remember? And besides, it really is an amazing costume, so it's not like I was lying."

Prowl looked past Felix's shoulder, where Iris was filling out her form, a frown visible on her face. He looked back to Felix, and whispered intently, "I'll say this as clear as I can, so there is no chance you'll not get this. *Tell her you think she's pretty.*"

"But—"

"No! No buts." He pointed at Felix's chest. "She's upset right now because she thought you were staring rapturously at her because she was a beautiful woman, only to find out that it wasn't her, it was only her cosplay." Prowl hung his head for a moment in frustration, and then looked back at his old friend. "And furthermore, you need to get it in your head that flirting with a woman does not automatically make you a creep. Do you know why you got shot down by everyone last year?"

"Because...?"

"Because you didn't actually care who you were hitting on. You were so lonely and horny that you just wanted to bang someone, anyone, so long as they were halfway attractive, and every single woman last year could tell that, and that's why you struck out. You didn't care about who they actually were."

"Prowl, I—"

"I'm almost done. This woman behind you likes the same obscure anime you do, is so damn gorgeous that she leaves you speechless, and then when you and her *did* get to talking, it was as if you'd known each other for years already." Prowl pulled off his glasses and rubbed the bridge of his nose. "I swear, if you don't at least offer to buy her a drink before the day is over, then I will step in and ask her out myself, because she is, indeed, hella hot."

Felix grit his teeth. "Please don't."

Prowl held up a finger. "You have twenty-four hours. Ask her out, or I will. If you don't, you will always regret it, never mind what she says to me. You really, really need to do this." Prowl paused for a moment, and then added, "If it helps any, if you do ask her out and she says no, then I'll leave her alone. You understand why I'm doing this, right?"

"Um, excuse me, Felix and...Prowl, you said?" Mrs. Weinberg stood only a couple of feet away.

The blood drained from Prowl's face. "Oh, God."

Felix turned to face Mrs. Weinberg, his face frozen in a terrified rictus grin. "Yes, ma'am?"

She gestured back to the registration counter. "There seems to be a mistake. They're charging us less than they're supposed to."

Prowl smiled. "Oh! Actually, that's no mistake at all, ma'am. When we do family programs like this, we give a ten dollar discount off each person in the family as a courtesy. We just hope you'll give our convention some positive word-of-mouth in return."

Mrs. Weinberg nodded, looking down at the form thoughtfully. "Very kind of you, Prowl, and I think we can certainly do that for you. Oh, but one other thing. Felix?"

Felix adjusted his tie. "Yes?"

She stepped a little closer and lowered her voice. "I did happen to overhear what you and Prowl were saying just now."

Felix winced. "Ma'am, I am *so* sorry."

She smiled, waving away the apology. "Please, you two need to stop calling me 'ma'am', I'm only forty-five. Just Abby is fine, or Mrs. Weinberg, if you must, but what I mean to say is, I think it would be wonderful if you asked out my niece."

Prowl and Felix just blinked, and said, "What?" in perfect unison.

"She just moved here a few months ago, and had a very rough year leading up to that move. She hasn't had a chance to make any friends in town yet, much less go on any dates. Do you think she's pretty?"

Felix visibly and audibly swallowed. "Incredibly."

"She really needs to hear that more often, especially since it's true. If you can be honest with her about that, it will be exactly what she needs to hear right now. So, don't you worry about me, I'm rooting for you."

Felix glanced over to where Marcus was standing, looming over everyone else present, eyeing daggers at a teenaged boy nearby who was staring at Angelica. "I just don't want her uncle breaking me in half for being too forward."

"Oh, don't you worry about him, either. I'll let him know what's going on, and he'll feel the same way, trust me." With that, she turned back and returned to the registration counter.

Felix turned to Prowl, shaking his head in disbelief. "I don't think my blood pressure can handle this."

Prowl clapped him on the shoulder. "Now you really have no excuse, man. Twenty-four hours. Ask her out."

They turned to where Iris was standing just in time for her to pull off her elaborate helmet, and shake loose a gorgeous cascade of dark auburn curls.

Prowl smiled appreciatively, but when he looked over at Felix, it was clear that his best friend was completely captivated by the sight.

Felix rubbed his forehead. "I won't need that long. Thanks, Prowl."

The radio at Felix's hip beeped. "Kalli to Felix?"

Felix picked up the radio, but kept his eyes on Iris. "Go for Felix. How's our lost girl doing?"

"You called it, Mister Pikachu. I found the mom wandering outside Video Room Five, about to have a panic attack. She never noticed Annette sneaking off in the dark while the show was playing, but they're okay now."

Felix breathed a heavy sigh of relief. "I appreciate the good news, Kalli. Great work."

"You, too, Felix, seriously! I want to meet up for a meal today, alright? If you'll buy this soldier girl a stiff drink afterwards, you're going to hear some crazy stories. This con is off to one hell of a start. Kalli out."

Felix looked back at Prowl, a confused look on his face. "Um, truer words were never said, Kalli. Felix out." Pocketing the radio again, he scratched his collar. "Kalli drinks? That's new."

Prowl looked at Felix's radio, then to Iris, and then back to Felix. He shook his head incredulously. "I think I might need a drink myself. You have no idea, do you."

"No idea about what?"

"Exactly." Prowl rubbed his eyes again. "Look, aside from Iris, is there anyone else at the con this year that you were thinking of asking out?"

"No, nobody." Felix looked utterly lost. "What are you getting at?"

"And you really do like Iris? You're not just going to ask her out because I badgered you about it?"

Felix held up both hands. "I really do. The more I think about it, the more I realize you're right. If I don't at least say *something* to Iris, I'll regret it for the rest of my life. I just hope I manage to say something halfway interesting."

Prowl nodded. "There you go, then." *Sorry, Kalli*, he thought to himself.

CHAPTER TWELVE

ANGELICA

Watching her mother walk off to talk to the two convention staffers, Angelica took off her Firestar domino mask, and tapped Iris on the forearm with it. "You're awfully pissed for no reason."

"What? I'm not pissed, I just..." Iris pushed hair out of her eyes. "I just don't want to get my hopes up when I'm clearly misreading everything. Like always."

"It wasn't your cosplay he was checking out, cousin. Trust me."

Iris rolled her eyes. "Oh, like you'd know."

The teenager smiled. "There are five guys within fifty feet checking me out right now, so I'll have you know, I know exactly what I'm talking about."

"Oh, really?" Iris turned to face her spandex-clad cousin. "And how many people are checking me out right now, oh great and wise mistress of the heart?"

Angelica tossed back a wave of fiery red hair with a practiced gesture. "Two guys in line were staring at your butt when you were bending over and filling out your form. The girl in the

Sailor Mercury cosplay thirty feet to your left has clearly been working up the nerve to talk to you ever since we walked over here, but the one that really matters here is a certain deep-voiced staffer in a suit, who has done everything but kneel in your presence and declare you his muse since he met you a few minutes ago."

Shrugging dramatically, Angelica heaved a heavy sigh. "But you'd know that if you trusted your eyes and didn't immediately assume the worst about yourself." She looked at Iris. "Seriously, you should be schooling me on this, not the other way around."

Iris just stared, and her cousin continued. "In fact, I'll bet you a week's worth of chores that Mom and that big yummy Prowl are plotting right now to get you two together. And when they fire off that plan, you should at least give the guy a chance to admit what he was really staring at back there, because it sure as hell wasn't your armor. Time to woman up and take charge of your life, cousin."

With that, Angelica gestured to her mother, who was walking back from where she'd clearly been talking to Prowl and Felix, an enigmatic smile on her face. "Admit it. I'm right."

Iris pulled off her helmet and shook out her thick mane of curls. She opened her mouth, paused, closed it, and then finally managed to find her voice again. "You're growing up entirely too fast, Angie."

Angelica put her mask back on, and gave her cousin her best smile, one that her dad had once described as "like a cat set free in a fish market." "I'm telling you, Iris, life is a ride, and you just have to grab the steering wheel and never let go."

CHAPTER THIRTEEN

IRIS

Iris looked over her freshly printed badge, and she had to admit, she was impressed. In no time at all, the entire Weinberg family had all been officially registered and badged, and were ready to hit the convention in style.

Aunt Abby gathered her daughters for a quick review. "Alright, you two. We've all got our phones with batteries charged. You don't need to stay right with us, but you do need to be in line of sight of at least one of the adults so no one gets lost. If you do get lost, you should go to the *Crunchyroll* booth, and then you call Dad or me. Stay there until we come for you. Don't go with anyone else, no matter what they say, unless they have the code word."

Felix leaned slightly to whisper to Iris, the two of them standing off to one side. "Dare I ask what the code word is?"

Iris chuckled. "Technically, I shouldn't say, but I suppose I can trust you." She flashed him another dazzling smile. "The code word is Superfly Swanton Bomb."

Felix smiled, looking rather amused. "Your aunt and uncle are awesome."

Her smile grew broader. *Another mark in your favor, handsome.* "You have no idea how true that really is."

"Iris, dear?" Aunt Abby glided over, a suspiciously serene smile on her face. "I know that the dealer's room bores you. If you want to meet us later so you can go to some panels, that'd be fine."

Iris raised an eyebrow. *Since when did I say anything about the dealer's room being boring?* "Uh..."

Abby continued, still smiling like a Buddha. "And you know what? You did say you'd like to meet some of the local anime clubs. Felix, do you think you could introduce her around to people? If you're not too busy?"

Prowl immediately chimed in. "His schedule is *totally free* for the next few hours until Opening Ceremonies, and even after that, I've got first shift at the Costume Contest office after our lunch meeting. Dude, you should bring her around to meet some of the other staffers. Maybe she'll want to join staff next year, and then bring her to Opening Ceremonies and the staff lunch, too! That'd be great! Bye!"

Felix and Iris were suddenly left standing alone as Prowl and the Weinberg family faded into the convention crowd like legendary ninjas.

She broke the silence first. "Well, I did actually want to do some shopping at some point, but maybe meeting some of the staff would be nice?"

He scratched the back of his neck. "And I could've sworn I had first shift of the Contest office this afternoon, but I suppose I could be wrong."

Her shoulders shook in a silent laugh. "Subtle, Aunt Abby. *Real* subtle."

He looked to where Prowl had gone, and if Iris was any judge, Felix was weighing options of either thanking or murdering his friend. "If it's any consolation, Friday morning isn't the best time to hit the dealer's room, anyway. Everyone rushes it first and clogs the aisles, thinking there might be rare collectibles that'll be gone after the first five minutes."

"Are there actually any collectibles like that?"

"Rarely." He pointed in the direction of the hotel next door. "But seriously, I could go for a cold drink. Care to join me?"

"Absolutely."

"So, it turned out there was already a con a couple states over called Anime Allies. Someone at the meeting jokingly suggested Anime Horde instead, and it stuck."

As they leaned against the counter of the hotel bar, Iris sipped her juice thoughtfully, enjoying the sound of Felix's bass voice. They'd been chatting for the better part of an hour, and she was having the time of her life. "That's a *World of Warcraft* reference, right? I never played, but I remember Hardison making jokes about it in some episodes of *Leverage. For the Horde,* and all that."

Felix's jaw dropped. "My God, you watch *Leverage* as well. You have impeccable taste." Felix's jacket was hanging over a nearby barstool, next to Iris's war staff and helmet, and he signaled the bartender for another round of cranberry juice.

"I will watch or read anything with John Rogers involved in it," Iris confirmed, idly stirring the ice in her near-empty glass. "The man's a brilliant writer. I'm still hoping they make a *Blue Beetle* TV show based on his comics one day. A girl can dream, can't she?"

Felix made a show of pinching himself. "I'm practically dreaming right now." Which pulled another blushing smile from Iris. "I mean, you know what I'm talking about when I mention *Shurato*, you don't assume I'm an idiot for enjoying professional wrestling, and we both think Jackie Chan's best movie was *Drunken Master II*, which is just awesome. I can only hope my fandom confessions have been half as interesting as yours."

Iris took a deep breath. She loved the close clean scent of him, and it made her smile. "You like the Moy Brothers run on the *Legion* comics, you love *Discworld*—although I will say *Night Watch* is a far superior Vimes novel to *Thud!*, in my humble opinion. You knew what I was talking about when I mentioned *Daigo of Fire Company M*, and I should let you know right now that my heart skipped a beat when you said that *Bridge of Birds* was your all-time favorite novel, because it's in my top five, seriously. This all speaks very well of you."

As she smiled at him, he took a deep breath and met her gaze directly, his green eyes intent, but nervous. "Well, then I have another confession to make, oh fellow DKD fan."

She took a comically loud slurp from her straw. "Your name is actually Ford Prefect, and you're from a small planet somewhere in the vicinity of Betelgeuse?"

Felix shook his head. "Actually, it's from when we first met this morning."

Standing a little straighter, Iris braced herself. "Okay."

"When I first got all tongue-tied, before you spotted my Yasha-Oh Gai badge, I wasn't speechless because of your costume. Although, it is a seriously awesome cosplay."

She blinked, holding her breath. *Oh, my God, Angelica was right. I am such an idiot.*

He broke eye contact for a moment, rubbing grit from the corner of one eye. "Man, I'm bad at this." He looked back up. "I was dumbstruck because you literally, and I do mean literally, this is not hyperbole, have the most beautiful eyes I have ever seen."

Iris's jaw dropped. "I do?"

"When you look at me with those amazing blue eyes, Iris, I forget my own name for a minute." His gaze met hers, and she reached up to brush away another errant curl. "But I was so damn terrified of coming across like some sort of creep, that I was afraid to say it."

She ran her gloved fingers through her hair as she cleared her throat. "You're definitely not a creep, and I really appreciate what you said. Thank you, Felix." She stepped a little closer. "So, what got you to speak your mind?"

He picked up the fresh juice that had just been left by the bartender. "Prowl knocked some sense into my head, and threatened to ask you out himself in twenty-four hours if I didn't muster up some courage."

She picked up her own refilled juice. "You'll have to break the bad news to Prowl. I'm not really into burly blond guys with beards. Besides, Angelica would kill me if I poached her new prey of choice."

He laughed, and raised his glass as if making a toast. "And what do your tastes run to instead?" He leaned in just a tiny bit.

She broke into a wide smile. "I'm starting to find some real appreciation for men with deep green eyes and even deeper voi—"

Something heavy had hit Iris in the back like a battering ram, and sent both her and her drink flying right at Felix. As if in slow motion, her cranberry juice splashed across the front of Felix's shirt and face, and as she collided with him, his own drink spilled, drenching the side of her head and a good chunk of her hair.

Suddenly, she was nose-to-nose with him, her gloved hands clinging to his shoulders for balance.

That moment seemed to last for years. No sound but their breathing, and his face filled her entire world. Her lips parted, and she found herself wanting to lean in even closer.

"Oh, my God, I am so sorry, I didn't realize the springs were wound that tight!"

Iris and Felix blinked in unison, and turned to look beside them.

A young woman stood there, short black hair touched with red highlights, wearing a black and red ruffled dress with matching black stockings, and holding two pieces of what looked to be a giant scythe made out of wood and plastic.

"I made it to unfold automatically with a spring, and I guess I made it too powerful. I am so sorry that it flew off and hit you like that." The cosplayer's soft brown eyes widened as she looked closer at Felix's drenched face. "Oh no. Felix Jackson. Oh no. Not like... Please don't kick me out of the con. I swear I didn't mean it!"

Iris grabbed some napkins and dabbed at the juice all over Felix's face and chest. "Looks like you're famous. You okay?"

"Well, I have been the con's Master of Ceremonies for a few years now. People know me here." Felix suddenly noticed the state of his shirt and tie. "Aw, dammit. Look, it's cool, I'll live."

The young woman in black looked ready to die of shame. "Totally my fault. The top of my prop scythe flew off and nailed your friend in the back, and I am so, so sorry."

As the young woman said this, her eyes fell on Iris again, and widened further—as if in recognition.

Iris straightened and was about to ask when something poked her hard in the shoulder. Probably a piece of her costume, but it was hard to tell. She yelped in pain and surprise.

"I am so, so, so, *so* sorry!"

Felix shook his head. "Look, miss, uh..."

"Rachel."

"Rachel, right. Accidents happen, it's totally cool, just make sure it doesn't happen again, okay? I'm sure this will all come out in the wash." He looked down at his shirt and grabbed another napkin to wipe his eyes. He gestured to the bartender. "Hey, D'andre? I'm going to have to bail here. How much do I owe you?"

Whatever piece had come loose from her costume was really digging into Iris's shoulder and back. She needed to fix it.

The bartender just shook his head and handed Felix a clean towel. "You've got enough to worry about, man. Go clean up, it's taken care of."

"Thanks, man. I appreciate that." He wiped his face with the towel. "Iris, I'm so sorry, but I really need to get cleaned up. Meet me at Opening Ceremonies?"

She frowned. "Actually, can I come with you? Something in my costume is trying to stab me in the back here. I need to get somewhere private to peel myself out of this armor, and my folks don't have a hotel room here. Is that okay?"

Felix nodded. "Yeah, that's fine. You'll have privacy in the bedroom while I'm showering this out of my hair." He ran a hand through his thick mane, grimacing at the mess. "*Oy gevalt.* Rachel, it's a pleasure to meet you, and hopefully we can have a normal drink sometime rather than dump them on my head."

Rachel nodded, nervously looking back and forth between Felix and Iris. "I will absolutely make it up to you. I promise. You're still the Costume Contest MC this year, right?"

He swiped the towel across his neck. "Yep. If you want to compete, don't forget to sign up with us at the contest registration office ahead of time."

Rachel nodded again. "I will totally be there, but you two go ahead and get cleaned up. I'm really sorry about everything."

Iris nodded her thanks, and she and Felix made their way toward the elevator.

Looking back, she noticed Rachel watching her. The young woman's lovely face was still agog in surprise and recognition. Iris held the woman's gaze for a moment, wracking her memory for a hint, but to no avail.

A gaggle of the woman's fellow cosplayers approached to console her, and Iris turned away to follow Felix.

CHAPTER FOURTEEN

FELIX

"Be it ever so humble, there's no place like temporary home." Felix held open the hotel room door for Iris, and she walked in, still hunched over on account of the damage to her armor.

As she set down her shoulder bag in front of one of the beds, she pulled off her gauntlets and started fiddling with the straps on her armor. At the same time, he kicked off his shoes, hung up his jacket, peeled off the cranberry-soaked button-down shirt and the t-shirt underneath, and tossed the soggy garments into a plastic hotel laundry bag.

"At least the jacket and the pants didn't get hit." He looked down at himself, and it suddenly hit him that he'd just pulled off half his clothes in front of this woman without even thinking about it. *Oh, nice one, Felix. That's not creepy at all.*

"Small favors, I guess." Iris winced, and hadn't looked at him yet. "If I don't get out of this in five seconds, I think something's going to break the skin. Damn, this hurts."

Felix eyed the bathroom door, debating if he should immediately dash inside. "Um. Do you need a hand with it?"

"No, I'm good, you go on ahead and shower."

Felix nodded gratefully, and quickly closed the bathroom door behind him. As he slid off his pants, boxers, and socks, he looked at himself in the mirror, muttering under his breath. "Talk about your crazy mornings." He met his own gaze, naked in a mirror for the second time that day. "Don't panic, Felix. She needs a place to change in private. You can just wait in here until she says she's done. No harm, no foul. You're not doing anything wrong."

He took another breath, and wiped another errant drop of juice from under one eye. Turning to the bathtub, he twisted the knobs to start the shower, when a sudden loud noise and a cry of pain rang out.

"Iris? Iris!?" Without thinking, he flung open the door and ran back inside the room.

CHAPTER FIFTEEN

IRIS

Iris cursed herself as a damned fool. The last catch she needed to release to get the breastplate off was in the small of her back, and when she twisted to try and reach it, she tripped and fell on her side. "Shit! Ow! God dammit."

Moments later, she looked up to discover Felix was standing over her, naked as the day he was born, a concerned look on his face.

"Are you okay?"

"Oh, wow." She couldn't help but stare. This man was real, he was right in front of her, and the sight of his nakedness sent a warm shudder down her neck, all the way to her toes. He may not have been as sculpted as some men she'd known, but he had strong-looking hands and arms to go with those shoulders. Her gaze fell upon his revealed length, and her throat tightened. "Um, I need help. I tripped."

He reached out and helped her to a standing position. "I hope nothing's broken?"

"Just my dignity." She grimaced in pain as the broken costume continued digging into her back. "Can you get that catch back there? I twisted too far trying to…"

As the breastplate and backplate loosened, the pain in her shoulder immediately stopped. Gingerly lifting the last of the costume off her, she lowered it onto the bed.

"Yeah, there's the culprit. That piece right there got bent when I got hit, and was digging into my back. I can fix it, though."

He brushed the spot on her shoulder where a small bruise was forming. "Doesn't look too bad. I'm glad you're okay."

Shivering a little at his gentle touch, she turned to look at him, and then glanced down at herself. From the waist up, she was wearing nothing but a sports bra, and she was in a hotel room with a naked man whom she'd only met a couple hours beforehand. A thousand fantasies rampaged through her mind in that moment.

"I'm…glad you came to check on me."

He suddenly seemed to realize his lack of clothing. "Well, it was, um, yeah. I wanted to make sure you weren't hurt." He glanced around nervously. "I…I should finish cleaning up. I'm still all, uh, sticky."

As he turned and walked back to the bathroom, she watched his backside move with each step, and she realized she was licking her lips.

She stood motionless for a moment, and then as the thump of Felix stepping into the shower resonated, she took a deep breath. She started undoing the remaining armor around her legs, and then peeled off the tight black yoga pants she wore under the leg plates.

"*Carpe diem*, Iris."

CHAPTER SIXTEEN

FELIX

Felix stood under the hot spray, the juice washing off his body, and a stir began between his legs. The sight of her curves in that sports bra had sent his hormones into overdrive, and he had barely been able to avoid staring right at her beautiful breasts.

"Down, boy," he muttered to himself. "Don't read too much into this. Just get clean, and you'll figure it out when you get out of the shower."

There was a knock at the door. "Felix, can I come in?"

Don't read too much into this. Don't, don't, don't. Just relax, Felix. Be yourself.

"Yeah, okay."

The door creaked, and footsteps padded. "Are you almost done? I want to talk for a second."

He pulled his head out of the spray and rubbed the water from his eyes. "You know I'm naked, right?"

"Nothing I haven't seen already."

He gave a nervous chuckle. "Well, ah, you have a point. One sec." He pulled back the curtain, stepped onto the towel he'd laid on the floor, and stood there nude in front of her.

"What can I do for...*oh.*"

She was leaning against the sink counter, dressed in nothing but that black sports bra, and a pair of lacy pink underwear with a high and narrow waistband. With her voluptuous figure on full display, he took a moment to drink in the sight of her. She was real. She was right there in front of him. And she was looking right at him with those mesmerizing eyes.

His pulse tripped and his heart thundered.

"It didn't, um, seem fair I got to see you naked, but not the other way around. So..."

Her gaze locked onto his, and she pulled her sports bra up over her head, revealing breasts Felix would see in his dreams for decades to come. Full and beautifully round, with pretty pink nipples that were already stiff and eager.

She set the bra aside, then reached down to slide her panties off of her delicious hips.

He held his breath, painfully trapping it in his lungs.

Her thick curls were the same dark auburn as her hair. For a moment, she instinctively covered that revealed area with her hands, but then moved to instead grip the edge of the counter on each side of her.

There was a long moment of no movement, no sound but the white noise of the shower.

"You're so beautiful." He didn't even want to blink, afraid she'd suddenly disappear.

She grinned bashfully. "Can you say that again?"

He swallowed. "Absolutely, breathtakingly, beautiful. Your eyes, your body, your voice..."

She straightened and stepped right up to him. "I could say the same for you and that rich voice of yours, mister."

He smiled, and wrapped one arm around her waist. "If I'm dreaming, don't wake me up yet. Please."

She cupped his face. "Thank you for being real. Thank you so, so much. Now kiss m—"

He practically lunged, his lips dancing with hers, his tongue teasing as he held her close, his fingers gliding across her ears, and down through her soft hair. His respirations increased the more tangled they became, his heartbeat a frenzied drum solo inside his chest.

The kiss seemed to last forever.

When it ended, she bit her lip as she ran her hands along his arms, breathing heavily. "I actually do need to use the shower. Got some of that damned juice in my hair. May I join you?"

He left a line of kisses along her neck, pulling soft gasps from her lips. "Absolutely."

Later that morning, Felix led Iris by the hand, jogging their way down the staff passages of the hotel and into one of the backstage entrances to the hotel's Main Programming ballroom. They'd had to splash cold water on their interlude because of his duties.

"Iris, I'm so sorry things got cut short. I have to do this bit during Opening Ceremonies. All I do is introduce the chair and some other folks, but I have to say a few words onstage at the start and at the end, so I can't leave until it's done. The whole thing should only take an hour."

He'd changed back into his black suit pants and jacket, and had replaced his soaked button-down with a plain black t-shirt instead.

"Maybe you could grab a seat in the audience, and I'll meet you at the back of the room afterwards?" He lifted her hand he'd been holding, and tenderly kissed the inside of her wrist. "Like I said before, you're breathtaking. I want to spend as much time with you as I can."

She'd changed into a set of jean shorts and a form-fitting tie-dyed blue tank top from her bag, and her nipples hardened visibly as he gently placed a kiss. "And you're...I can't even describe how you make me feel, Felix, but trust me, it's all good. So, so, good." She pulled him close for a quick peck on the lips. "I'm already thinking about picking up where we got interrupted, so don't keep me waiting too long. Now, get going, handsome."

He grinned, but as he turned toward the door, it opened to reveal the Convention Chairman, a hard frown on his thin lips.

"I thought I heard your voice, Mr. Jackson. Where have you been? You're tardy, and this is not conduct becoming of a Department Head."

Brian McHenry was tall, slender, and pale, with a long face and longer legs. He'd developed a slight bald patch on the top of his light brown hair during his year as Chair (Felix and Prowl had wondered if it was stress-induced), and had a ponytail that reached the small of his back.

Felix held up his hands, palms outward. "First off, I am not tardy, the show doesn't start for a few minutes yet. Second, an attendee accidentally dumped cranberry juice all over me at the bar, Brian. I have witnesses." He gestured to Iris, and then down at his outfit. "Luckily, only my shirt and tie were ruined, so I cleaned up as best I could, and improvised. I'm here, aren't I?"

Brian's eyes narrowed. "I would request you stop grinning about it. We're starting very soon." He turned to glare at Iris. "Miss, I will thank you to not distract my senior staff from their responsibilities. His presence is required."

Felix hadn't even realized he was smiling, but Brian's words and tone quickly wiped that expression away. "Leave Iris out of this, Brian. We've got work to do, so let's get on with it."

Iris's hand squeezed his involuntarily as he said her name, and he flashed her a quick affectionate smile.

"Sorry, Iris. I'll see you in an hour, okay?"

"See you soon. Felix?" She pulled him back into her arms for a moment and laid a kiss on him that sent delicious shivers down his back. "Break a leg."

Ignoring Brian's snort of disdain, Felix's grin returned. "Damn right."

CHAPTER SEVENTEEN

IRIS

Iris entered the ballroom from a side door, and looked around in the low light for an empty seat. Despite her encounter with Felix's grumpy boss, she couldn't help herself from smiling non-stop. She was utterly giddy, months of tension boiling out of her system on waves of pure bliss.

As she walked along the edge of the room, she reveled in putting a little extra sway into her hips, and she grinned as she sensed more than a few pairs of eyes in the crowded room follow her. Several thousand people milled around and filled the last of the seats. She was gliding without a care in the world, and settled languidly into the last seat left on the edge of the very last row, a corner shrouded in darkness despite the bright lights illuminating the stage.

As the other con-goers quietly murmured to each other in their seats, Iris reached into her bag and pulled out her phone, texting her aunt.

Iris: *How's the dealer's room?*

Abby: *Having a blast. Some of Angelica's schoolfriends are here, and Tracy found a new Jojo poster for her bedroom. Where have you been?*

Iris chuckled, she could practically hear her cousins correcting their mother in unison, insisting that "It's not a *poster*, Mom, it's a wall scroll!"

Had some cranberry juice with Felix.

I'm at Opening Ceremonies right now.

Abby: *Has he asked you out yet? :D*

Iris: *In a manner of speaking. *^_^**

Abby: *Oh, good! I was hoping he'd work up the nerve.*

Iris: *Real subtle, ditching me like that. :P*

Abby: *It got the job done, didn't it?*

Iris caressed her fingertips across her covered right breast momentarily, hidden in the darkness. Her nipples were still tender from when he'd been nibbling on them earlier.

"Damn right it did, Aunt Abby," she whispered to herself.

Iris: *In retaliation, I think I may end up ditching you all for this guy for the rest of the con. ;) Sorry about that.*

Abby: *Think nothing of it. Good thing you're on the pill, eh?*

Iris's eyes nearly bugged out of their sockets.

Abby: *Yes, I just made an open reference to your sex life. :)*

We're both adults, after all. Have fun!

Iris: *Um. Thanks?*

Iris put the phone into her bag and leaned back in her chair. "What a morning."

CHAPTER EIGHTEEN

RACHEL

Rachel shifted uncomfortably in her seat. "Michelle, why are we at Opening Ceremonies? Nothing happens at these!"

Her friend waved off the objection, gesturing with her hand-held video camera. "*Because* Lazlo Akers is going to be on stage, and I want to get some footage of him!"

Rachel rolled her eyes, adjusting her ruffled Ruby Rose cosplay skirt as she tried to find a comfortable way to sit. "Not only are you going to see your favorite voice actor this afternoon at his own panel, but that'll be better lit, *and* you'll be a lot closer to him. There is no point in being here."

"Ladies and gentleman, welcome to Anime Horde!"

Rachel looked up in surprise, and there was Felix Jackson center stage, warming up the crowd. "I could be wrong."

Michelle turned to her best friend and smirked. "He's the Master of Ceremonies, so of course, our old friend Felix would be here. Shut up and enjoy your sexy crush object. I don't judge you for how you get about your knight in shining armor, so you can't judge me for my Lazlo."

Rachel snorted in annoyance, and settled in. She couldn't really see much of Felix from all the way in the back like this, but the PA system carried that amazing voice of his quite nicely, so she leaned back in her chair to enjoy the moment. As she did so, she accidentally bumped elbows with whomever had sat down next to her a few minutes ago.

"Sorry about that... *Oh!*"

Her neighbor turned out to be a woman with thick curly hair—and in the faint glow of the stage light, Rachel realized her neighbor had very familiar pale blue eyes, and a figure that she remembered very, very well. *Freaking hell, twice in one morning? What are the odds? And she's just as hot as she was last fall, too. Damn, that was a fun con. Snuggling on that couch in the con's Green Room party, and that Truth or Dare game got immediately out of hand, with the whole room cheering as Iris and I made out in front of everyone. The first woman to ever touch my breasts. I'm getting warm just thinking about that!*

She leaned over and whispered, "Iris? Iris Weinberg, right?"

Iris nearly jumped out of her own chair in surprise, and responded in kind with more whispers. "Rachel? You're Rachel from the hotel restaurant this morning, right?"

"I still feel so bad about this morning. Did everything work out?"

Iris leaned in. "Everything's fine. My armor had a bent strut."

"I will totally pay you for the damages."

"Rachel, it's fine. It'll take me five minutes to fix, don't even sweat it."

"You haven't fixed it already?" Rachel raised her eyebrows.

Iris opened her mouth, paused, and then shut it for a few moments before finally responding. "Um. In a weird way, I think I actually owe you one, Rachel." Her eyes narrowed, and she turned to look at Rachel again. "Wait a second. How did you know my last name?"

Rachel pulled off her Ruby Rose wig, revealing her dirty-blonde hair. "GothamCon, last fall?" She moistened her lips. "I was the Spider-Gwen you got snuggly with at the Green

Room party that Saturday night." She tucked a lock of Iris's thick curls away from her face. "You said that I was adorably enticing. Is that still true?"

Her jaw dropping, Iris put a hand over her mouth. "Oh, my *God*. Raye, is that you? Seriously? How have you been? I hate it that I never got your number or email or anything!"

She looked at the stage, and Rachel followed her gaze.

Felix finished his speech and handed the microphone to a tall, skinny fellow with a ponytail, whereupon Felix headed offstage.

"I'm doing good, but not as good as you, it seems. You look great!" Rachel bit her lip for a moment. "Um, can we head out and talk in the hall for a bit? I wasn't expecting to see you here, but now that I have, well, I want to catch up."

Iris nodded. "Absolutely! Now that my boyfriend, Felix... My gosh, I can't believe I'm saying that." She cleared her throat. "Sorry. He can't leave until this is over, so I'm just killing time for the next hour." She stood up and grabbed her shoulder bag. "I'll meet you right outside."

Rachel's thoughts were a hurricane. *Iris is Felix's girlfriend? I don't know if I should cheer or cry or try to kiss her again right here!* She turned to Michelle. "Hey, can you watch my stuff for a bit?"

Michelle craned her neck to watch Iris walk toward the door. "Damn. I overheard. Is that really Iris, that woman from that GothamCon party?" She let out a low whistle.

Standing and smoothing her skirt, Rachel nodded, blushing at the memory of Michelle being part of that cheering party crowd. "Yes, and you're not going to believe what's going on with her. I can barely believe it myself."

Michelle made a wry smile. "I heard, yeah. Felix landed a hot one, good for him. She's got good taste. Just try not to kill her in a fit of jealousy, okay?"

"Jealousy?" Rachel made a nervous frown. "Please, I never had a shot with Felix to begin with. But I sure as hell want to hear about how this happened. Back in a bit."

Rachel stepped out into the deserted, sunlit hotel hallway. Iris was already settled into a padded bench along the far wall. Pausing a moment to inspect Iris under the light of day, Rachel grinned and settled down next to her on the bench, crossing her ankles.

"So, how have you been? You look even hotter than last year, no joke."

Iris beamed. "Thank you, Raye. I am on cloud-freaking-nine right now. Getting to see you again makes everything even better." She gave Rachel a quick once-over. "And you look pretty cute in that red-riding-hood getup."

Rachel gestured with her removed black and blood-red wig, and shook out her natural locks of shoulder-length dark blonde hair. "I swear, this costume makes me look like I'm fifteen instead of twenty. The things we do for show-accurate cosplay, y'know?" She paused, pursing her lips. "This might sound corny coming from someone who you only met once at a party almost a year ago, but I missed you. I thought about that night a lot, and I hated that we lost touch."

Iris scratched her bare shoulder, smiling sheepishly. "Me, too. Although, to be honest, it's probably just as well. Things got really ugly after the con with that guy you saw me with. He wanted me to drag you back to our room for some fun, but it's for your own good I didn't let that happen."

Rachel raised an eyebrow. *Having naked fun with this woman sounds pretty awesome to me, but I do remember the guy she was with being kinda unpleasant.* "That bad, huh?"

"Oh, yeah." Iris scrunched her mouth as if tasting something foul. "Trust me, Raye, the further away you were from that asshole and me over the last year, the better. Thankfully, now that I'm out of New York and living here instead, things are finally turning around."

"Well, I'm glad to hear that last part, at least." Rachel caught herself pulling at the laced edges of her skirt, and clasped her hands together in her lap to stop from fidgeting. "Actually, I don't really go by Raye anymore. That was what everyone called me in high school, and I feel like I've outgrown that. I just prefer my real name, Rachel. Do you go by Iris, then, or...?"

Iris inclined her head. "Absolutely, and let's introduce ourselves properly this time." She took on an outrageously snooty British accent, turning up her nose. "Iris Rebecca Weinberg, Duchess of Manhattan. Charmed, I'm sure." She broke into a quiet giggle as she held out a hand, which Rachel eagerly shook.

"Rachel Galadriel—ugh!—Midnight, Princess of Beverly Hills." She rolled her eyes at the hated middle name. "And before you ask about how weird my names are, it's because my dad's both a pothead ex-hippie and a Hollywood studio executive, who legally changed his last name to Midnight before he met my mom and had me."

Iris's eyes widened. "I wasn't going to ask."

"Yes, you were." Rachel shrugged and laughed. "Everyone does, but it's cool. I'm used to it. Okay, what else?" She furrowed her forehead in thought. "We never really got to know each other at that party, so I want to fix that now. I really do live in Beverly Hills, and it's every bit as shallow and fucked up as you think. Most of my high school classmates were walking, talking, fucking living proof of white privilege, and I got out of town for cons and such every chance I got." She mimed a plane taking off, one open hand skimming off the other. "Might as well put Dad's money to some good use, so I can hang around with people who actually want to exercise some imagination once in a while."

Iris leaned back against the wall and crossed one leg over the other. "I remember you mentioning something about 'still keeping a promise' last year, but you never explained that."

Rachel leaned forward, her elbows resting on her knees. "Yeah. My mom made me promise when I hit puberty to not to let anyone into my panties until I was at least eighteen—a promise I kept! *Probably would have broken that promise if Iris had asked that night, though.* The warmth in her belly was getting hotter. Still have, even though I'm twenty now. But let's just say that there were plenty of things I could do to keep a horny boyfriend happy, even with rules like that. I may be a virgin, but I am not some clueless innocent."

"Do you have a boyfriend now?"

Rachel looked up. "No. *Hell* no. I haven't had more than two dates with the same guy in the last two years because no one measured up." She pointed toward the door they'd come from. "And it's all because of Mister Felix Jackson."

"Wait, what?"

Rachel grinned. "Thought that'd get your attention. So, get this. Two years ago, I'm here at Anime Horde for the first time with three folks I thought were friends, including this guy named Spencer from my school, who I'd been dating for four months." She pushed a stray strand of hair behind one ear. "Long story short, I found out that said friends really only cared about me because I was rich, and because I was gullible enough to pay for everything on the trip."

Iris winced. "Sounds like a heck of a story."

Rachel nodded. "Oh yeah, it's a good one, too. Lots of lies, intrigue, gaslighting, and karma coming home to roost like crazy. And as a subplot to that whole mess, Spencer tried to pressure me into letting him fuck me at the con. When I told him to piss off, he started telling everyone we were hanging out with at the con that I was frigid. That's when I kicked him in the balls, hard."

Iris's face fell, and she put her hand on Rachel's. "Yeah. Wish I'd done that."

"No, it's cool. I'm okay now. It was just..." Iris had gone pale, and she put an arm around Iris's shoulder. "Goddamnit, did someone pull the frigid bullshit on you, too?"

She nodded.

"Pisses me off. If you admit you like sex, then you're a slut, but if you don't want it from the guy begging for it, then you're frigid. Such utter bullshit. But hey, none of that moping. Especially because we both know from GothamCon that you're damn warm and cuddly, right?" She licked her lips. "Now, I'll be honest here. I wanted to get you alone because I want to hear about my favorite Master of Ceremonies suddenly being your new boyfriend."

Squeezing Rachel's hand, Iris slowly brought back that stunning smile. "We just met this morning, so it's new. It's crazy, but he makes me so damn happy. I can barely believe it. So, I'll tell you everything, but first, you need to explain what you meant about your two years of single-ness being Felix's fault."

"You bet. You see, the main reason I came here back then was to compete in the costume contest. I was super wigged out and nervous because I'd just bailed on my asshole ex-friends, I knew absolutely no one else at the con, and I was about ready to sleep on the hotel floor if I had to." Rachel shuddered. "Or worse. There were a few times that day when my mind went to some *very* bad places. The only thing I had left at that point was the contest, so I showed up at their registration desk, and I broke down sobbing right in front of Felix."

Iris squeezed Rachel's hand again. "What happened?"

Rachel squeezed her hand. "Everything that had gone down that day just burst out of me, and Felix dropped everything and sat with me for like two hours while I wept on his shoulder. He listened to my rambling, gave me some great advice, and introduced me to some other cosplayers he knew and trusted—like Michelle, the warm woman I was sitting next to back in the ballroom."

Rachel smiled at the memory, remembering Michelle giving her that first hug as if they'd already been the best of friends for years. "I joined their skit, which worked out pretty well since we all were doing *DragonBall* characters. I did a pretty amazing Android 18, if I say so myself." She rubbed her cheek. "We all ended up hanging out after the costume contest, and Felix was the most awesome gentleman ever." Her face heated. "Even when I threw myself at him. *Especially* when I threw myself at him. I was vulnerable and willing, but he refused to take advantage of that. He turned what could have been the last day of my life into one of the best days. A good man like Felix Jackson was exactly what I'd needed in that moment, and

I've had a bit of a crush on him ever since." She made a show of fanning herself. "He looks good, smells better, and oh man, that voice of his. I could cream from just listening to him read weather reports."

Iris crossed and uncrossed her legs again, looking very thoughtful. "Mmm, I can relate to that, sure enough." She looked into Rachel's eyes. "You said 'last day' back there. Now, I've had some bad times myself, I know how that is, but you're doing okay now, right?"

"Oh, yeah." Rachel nodded. "I ended up transferring to the same college as Michelle, got away from all the toxic mother-fuckers from high school, and life's been pretty great ever since."

Iris raised an eyebrow. "And how is it you're not pissed at me for hooking up with the guy you're crushing on?"

Rachel leaned to one side, resting her head companionably against Iris's shoulder. "Felix is living proof that I didn't have to settle for any old lame-ass boyfriend. In a perfect world, I would love to make another move on him, sure. But he's local here, and I'm west coast. I have no delusions he and I could ever be a couple. So, I'm actually really happy he's met someone here that's cool and hot like you." She turned her head and looked right at Iris's cleavage. "Dear God, you're rack-tacular. Lucky lady. He must've fainted with joy the first time you took off your bra in front of him."

Iris chuckled. "Flattery will get you everywhere, little girl."

That got an amused snort from Rachel. "Little? 34C is not little, Miss Voluptuous. I'm just binding these girls for the cos-play." She rested her head on Iris's shoulder again. "So, yeah. He's my standard of what a good man should be. But now, what I want to hear about more than anything is what happened after you two went back to his room." She grinned. "You don't have to be coy with me."

Iris glanced around. The hallway was still empty, and from the sounds coming from the ballroom, the opening ceremony event was nowhere near finished. "Is it that obvious?"

Rachel nodded, her fingertips skating across Iris's palm. "Even back at the restaurant, it was clear you two were about to get into each other's pants, if you hadn't already. I bet you're just itching to tell someone about it. C'mon, dish. Isn't this what girl-talk's all about?" Rachel whispered into her ear. "After all, I let you take some nice warm liberties with me back at GothamCon. I think you owe me."

"Okay, fair point. I'll tell you everything."

CHAPTER NINETEEN

FELIX

As Felix stood backstage among half a dozen other staffers milling around, listening to the con's myriad guests address the audience, Prowl came up behind him and tapped him on the shoulder.

"Hey, man." He waved to the other staffers, as well, who acknowledged him with nods and returned waves.

Felix turned and gave his best friend a smile. "Hey, hope your morning's been as good as mine."

Prowl shook his head incredulously. "Well, I have good news and bad news for you."

"Bad news first. Spill it."

Prowl grit his teeth. "I need you to take back first shift in the contest office this afternoon. I know I told you I'd cover it, but I got one hell of a phone call this morning."

"Eh, I'll manage," Felix shrugged. "Iris might be cool with just hanging for a bit. So, what's the deal?"

Prowl's jaw ticked. "Bianca's here."

That got Felix's full attention. "That is good news! When did that happen?"

"She said she just moved back to town last week."

"But she was engaged to that asshole from Tampa."

Prowl nodded. "Well, it looks like she finally figured out the asshole part, dumped him, and now she's back."

A huge smile broke out on Felix's lips. "She always told me it seemed like the two of you *should* have been dating."

Prowl nodded. "But whenever she was single, I was already taken, and when I was single, she was taken."

"And now, finally, both of you are single at the same time. Oh, wow. Prowl, that's awesome!"

"See, I dunno." Prowl laughed nervously. "That's why I need you to take the shift, because she and I have a lot we need to talk about, like ASAP, yeah?" He grit his teeth. "Are we cool?"

Felix clapped his hand on his shoulder. "Dude, of course! It's freaking Bianca, man. I'll watch the office with Iris, you and Bianca go walk the con or something."

Prowl almost bent double as he groaned with relief. "Oh man, thank you. I owe you big." He straightened, and looked intently at Felix. "Wait, you said with Iris? What's going on with that? Where is she?"

Felix gestured with an upraised thumb towards the ballroom. "In the audience. I'm meeting her in the back after opening ceremonies are over."

Prowl's jaw dropped. "You actually did it? You asked her out?"

Felix let out a quiet chuckle. "Prowl, my friend, where do I even begin?" He paused. "Let me put it this way. I might need to ask you if she can crash in our room with us tonight."

"Holy shit." Prowl took a step back and looked at his friend in a new light. "Well, I might need to ask the same question on Bianca's behalf, depending how this afternoon goes, you know?"

Felix nodded. "And to think, man. This is only the first day of the con. This year is going to be a whirlwind, I just know it."

CHAPTER TWENTY

IRIS

Biting her lip as she glanced at the ceiling, Iris took a deep breath. "So, we get into the shower, and we start soaping each other all over from the neck down." She smiled. "His hands were so warm, but I had this amazing shiver everywhere he touched me. Then I turned him around, and tried something I'd read about that they do at Japanese soapland parlors."

Felix had stood there motionless in the shower, moaning happily as she'd rubbed her soap-covered breasts against his back. She'd had one hand around his waist, and the other stroked his length, his groin covered with lather.

"Dear God, Iris, that's good. Nice and slow, oh yeah."

She'd bitten gently along his earlobe, her voice whispering in his ear. "Mmm. I love feeling you get hard for me. Look at your hard cock, Felix—I did that to you. Do you like what I do to you?"

Felix barely gasped his reply. "Like is an understatement."

Rachel laced her fingers with Iris's, her mouth suddenly dry. "Broke out the dirty talk early, huh?"

Iris nodded. "I was so goddamn horny, the words just jumped out of me. My thighs were drenched before I'd even gotten near that shower."

Rachel's eyes closed, and she made a murmur of agreement.

"After a little more of that, we rinsed off, and suddenly he was on his knees in front of me."

Iris had run a hand across Felix's temple as he'd leaned in, his nose brushing the ends of her pubic hair. "You don't have to do that, handsome. I haven't landscaped recently."

Felix shook his head, and stroked a line of heat across her thick nest of curls. "I think your body is a work of art, hair included. And whomever gave you the idea that you were ugly needs to be shot." Without further ado, he dove in, taking one of her outer folds entirely in his mouth, his tongue tracing its contours. He reached around to cup her hips, bracing himself as he licked his way across her inner surfaces.

Iris's eyes had rolled back in shock, her knees threatening to buckle as his tongue dragged from bottom to top of her wet opening. When his mouth closed over the hood of her clit, her entire abdomen suddenly was an expanding blossom of welcome fire. "Oh! Lick me, you handsome bastard! Whatever you do, do not stop!"

He looked up, his eyes smoldering, and paused just long enough to say, "As you wish," before returning to his delicious task.

Rachel giggled, covering her mouth for a moment. "I can't decide if I'm amused or incredibly turned on by the idea of a man who quotes *The Princess Bride* while he eats a girl out. Talk about dedication to your hobby."

"That movie was the last thing I was thinking about right then." Iris looked at Rachel. "All I could think about was how good his mouth felt. I mean, he was licking me at least as good as a woman would."

Rachel looked up suddenly, her breath caught in her throat. "You've had women go down on you? Oh, wow." Her grip on Iris's hand tightened.

"Let's just say I experimented a few times in college, and had fun doing it. But my point is that Felix really knew what he was doing. Whoever taught him deserves a medal."

Rachel looked around, probably checking to make sure they were still alone in the hallway. "I want to hear more, but first, you need to understand something." She squeezed Iris's hand. "I am more turned on right now than I have ever been in my life. In. My. Life. More than even when you caressed me so wonderfully at the GothamCon party. She guided Iris's hand to her lap, and then abruptly under her skirt, pressing the other woman's open palm against Rachel's drenched silk-covered mons. "I didn't think it was possible to get this wet."

Iris laughed. They'd been intimate once before, rendering the situation funny instead of awkward.

Wagging a finger reproachfully, but with a smile all the while, Iris pulled her hand gently from under Rachel's skirt. Her smile grew wickedly large as she locked eyes with Rachel and slowly licked drops of the young woman's arousal from her own fingertips. "Miss Midnight, are you trying to seduce me? And with the man we're both wet for not fifty yards away. *Tsk, tsk*. Rachel, Rachel, what are we going to do with you?"

Rachel shivered, her free hand clenching and unclenching on her thigh. "Anything you want."

Iris's eyes were alight. "Do you want to hear the rest of what Felix did to me this morning?"

Lacing her fingers with Iris's again, Rachel nodded. "I'll beg for that if I have to."

"No need." Iris cast her voice in a low husky whisper. "But I'm starting to think it might be fun to make you beg for something else later."

Rachel swallowed. "Well, now I know for sure. I am definitely bi. No question. Please don't stop the story."

Iris smiled. *I can't wait to tell Felix about this girl.* "Well, after he made my eyes cross with a mind-shattering orgasm, I felt it only fair to return the favor."

Iris had loved the sounds he made, his groans of delight as she'd knelt before him under the shower spray, blowing him as her life depended on it. She'd eased back, her tongue sliding sensuously across the underside of his length as his engorged head popped free from her mouth.

"Felix," she'd said with a playful lilt, batting her long eyelashes, "If I swallow your cum right now, do you think you'll have enough strength to fuck me afterwards?"

He'd nodded. "God Almighty, I'll find a way."

She'd grinned, and engulfed him anew, her nose buried in his pubic hair as she'd caressed his length with her warm and wet mouth.

"Iris, I'm close. Don't stop, don't stop…"

Iris gave Rachel a wicked smile. "There are few things that turn me on more than hearing someone scream my name as they climax."

Rachel leaned in, resting her head in Iris's shoulder once more, still holding hands. "Hell, yes. Now I just need to hear my name on the lips of someone worth my time."

"It'll happen. I have no doubt at all." She sighed happily. "But you know what the best part of that shower was?"

"Did he take you right there in the shower? I've had dreams about that."

Iris shook her head. "Nope. After he came, we just spent a few minutes actually getting clean—and I know this sounds odd, but he washed my hair for me, and it was so, so wonderful. That was an experience I will never forget."

As the water cascaded around them, Iris leaned against Felix, sagging bonelessly as he ran his hands through her thick hair, massaging her scalp and making sure to get the shampoo all the way to her roots. She sighed dreamily.

"This feels far better than I would have expected."

He dropped a shampoo-covered hand to one of her breasts, cupping and gently squeezing her. "I could say the same for these, pretty lady."

As he gently pinched her nipple, she gave a small squeak of pleasure. With one arm draped around his waist, she turned her head to the side on his shoulder. "That feels so good, and I love that you love my big ol' boobs, but right now, I really want you to focus on this hair-washing thing. Oh, yeah."

He returned both hands to her scalp. "Where have you been all my life, Iris?"

She shook her head. "You wouldn't have liked me much if we'd met before this year. Hell, I didn't like me much before this year. Meeting you here and now is perfect."

He trailed his fingers down her back, gently squeezed the cheeks of her backside, and then returned to her scalp. "I know that feeling. Last year was a bad one for me, too. But you make me feel...more alive than I've felt in a long, long time." He gently moved her to stand directly under the shower spray, and rinsed her hair clean, continuing the scalp massage the entire time.

After he finished, she kissed him tenderly, their bodies pressed together under the warm shower. "Can I wash your hair next, handsome?"

"I'd love nothing more."

As she worked the shampoo into his hair, she spoke up again. "See, that's the thing. Last year, I wouldn't have bothered to do this for someone else—I just wanted it to be all about me. God, I was an idiot."

He leaned his head forward, letting her reach everywhere on his scalp. "It's an easy trap to fall into."

"I'm just glad I pulled myself out of it." She paused. "Felix, are you okay with all this? This day feels like it's been this amazing eternity, but it's only been one short morning. You don't think any less of me for moving so fast, I hope?"

Rachel hit Iris on the shoulder. "What on earth did you say that for? You might have ruined everything!"

"Thankfully not."

"Not a chance, beautiful." Felix shook his head vehemently. "Everything about this morning just feels right. And I'm moving just as fast as you. If we're making a mistake, and I'm positive

we're not, then it's on both of us." He traced a fingertip across the line of her chin. "I do have a question, though."

She took his finger in her mouth, playfully licking it. "Ask away."

"Do you live in town?"

"Sort of. I moved here from New York in January, and I'm staying with Aunt Abby and Uncle Marcus. We're about twenty minutes east of here. They've got a little carriage house out back I've taken over. Why?"

He looked right into her eyes, caressing her cheek. "Because in a moment, we're going to dry each other off, and then I'm going to take you to bed. And I really, really don't want this to be a one-time convention fling. I don't want you to disappear. I want to be your boyfriend." His lips pinched nervously.

"Aww. He's so sweet! You *did* say yes, right?"

Iris nodded. "He was so terrified I might bolt on him, I could tell. But he really nailed it when he said everything that's happened so far just feels really right. So, of course, I said yes, on the condition that he started telling folks that I was his girlfriend in return." She smiled happily. "I have a boyfriend, all out of the blue, and I couldn't be happier."

"What did he say to that?" Rachel pulled a water bottle out of her bag, and took a sip.

Felix listened to her words, and then straightened as the last of the shampoo rinsed out of his hair. "There is a God." And then he kissed her again. "I'm your boyfriend. Yes."

Rachel swooned.

CHAPTER TWENTY-ONE

FELIX

Prowl hit the End Call button on his smartphone. "Okay, I just told Bianca where we're at. She should be here shortly."

Felix shifted from foot to foot, staring impatiently at the other staffers and guests making endless speeches onstage. "Dammit, this stupid opening thing is taking fucking forever."

Prowl laughed. "Dude, chill. She'll be back there when it's over. I'm sure of it."

"I'm not worried about that." Felix massaged the back of his neck. "I'd just rather be with her than waiting on Grand Warlord Brian the Windbag drone on and on about how great he thinks the con is going to be."

Prowl chuckled. "I can't help but laugh at this, you know? The instant you finally calm down and decide not to worry about meeting women, you meet one hell of a someone."

"I know, right?" Felix threw up his hands in amazement. "I'm the boyfriend of a woman who is more than I possibly could have dreamed of. We've barely scratched the surface of all the things we have in common. She's funny, she's romantic…"

Prowl snickered. "She's hotter than the fire of a thousand exploding suns. Can't leave that out, eh?"

A new woman's voice appeared behind the duo. "Oh Prowl, you do know how to compliment a girl."

"Bianca!" Felix rushed past Prowl to greet their long-absent friend, giving her a huge hug, and then stepped back to have a laugh at her outfit. "Prim and frumpy as ever, I see."

Bianca Torres was a tanned beauty of Filipino origin, six feet tall and expertly toned from years of calibrated exercise. She wore nothing but a pair of sneakers, socks, a purse over one shoulder, and a red one-piece swimsuit straight from the opening credits of *Baywatch*, the thin fabric straining against her ample bustline.

"Hey, nothing wrong with wanting to look pretty now and then. Isn't that right, Prowl?" She ran her fingers through her solid black hair, pulling it back into a ponytail.

Prowl's cheeks glowed like a red-nosed reindeer as he fought a losing battle over keeping his eyes above Bianca's neck. The ponytail motion caused some very interesting movement in her shoulders and chest. "Uh-huh." She was as supremely confident as Prowl remembered, standing proud as more than a few eyes around them backstage took in the sight of her.

Walking over to her favorite northerner, Bianca traced the back of her hand gently across Prowl's cheek. "Sorry, Prowl—I'll tone it down a bit." She turned to Felix. "But *you*, Felix, what's your story? You know I love you, but I usually have to scoop your eyes back into your head when I dress like this. But today? You're just mellow and happy, not staring at all."

Felix shrugged and opened his mouth, but Bianca interrupted him, stepping closer to him and squinting. "Did you get laid recently? Is the dustbowl-dry-spell-of-doom finally over? Can women across the nation finally breathe a sigh of relief?"

He held up one hand in surrender. "A hit, a most palpable hit! Heh. Yeah, I met someone, and it's been a pretty intense day so far."

Bianca leaned back, one eyebrow raised. "If she's here at the con, then Big Sister Bianca will need to have a word with her, you understand. To make sure she's not another psycho, like that bitch Tia. Man, that woman messed with your head."

Prowl stepped in. "Bianca, be nice. I was there when they met this morning, and they're incredibly cute together. They're like a little pair of Ewoks, rubbing noses and planning the murder of stormtroopers together."

"Ewoks? Really?" Felix put his hands on his hips indignantly.

Bianca laughed. "How many overused Monty Python quotes did they throw at each other?"

"Hey!"

Prowl shook his head. "None, believe it or not. She actually recognized the artwork from his con badge, and it was all down-hill from there."

Felix coughed. "Her name is Iris, and she's amazing. In all seriousness, Bianca, please don't mess this up for me. I've got a really good feeling about her."

She smirked. "You just met her this morning, and you've already bumped uglies, so I bet that *something* felt good, mmm-hmm."

Felix frowned silently, crossing his arms over his chest.

Prowl blinked in surprise, and stepped away. "Hoo, boy."

Bianca put a fingertip to her lips, watching her 'little brother' react so strongly. "You're serious. This isn't just a hook-up, is it?"

Felix shook his head, not blinking.

Bianca tapped herself lightly on her check, miming a slap. "Then this is where I apologize. Felix, I'm really, really sorry. You would not believe the bullshit I just escaped from, and I think it's made me a little cynical. I'll be nice to the new girl."

A long slow exhale, and Felix closed his eyes for a moment, and then opened them again. "Thank you. Apology accepted." The two shared another hug, this one a bit more somber.

Prowl wiped the sweat from his forehead as he stepped back. "Is it safe to approach yet?"

Bianca pulled Prowl back into arm's reach, and the three shared a familiar group hug. "Damn, but I missed you two boys."

Prowl harrumphed comically. "*Men*, thank you very much. But hold on a sec. You said you *escaped*?"

Bianca crossed herself fervently. "Uh-huh. So, time for me to apologize again. Remember when you two tried to warn me the spring before last that Richie was an asshole, and taking his ring and moving to Tampa was a bad idea?"

The two men nodded in unison.

"You had it right, and it was actually worse than you could have imagined. I am so sorry I doubted you." She frowned, and mimed spitting on the ground. "Let me put it this way. I'm about to file a restraining order against him."

Prowl's eyes suddenly went very large, and his voice very quiet. "Where is he right now? If he put one hand on you—"

Bianca leaned forward and kissed Prowl's cheek. "Down, Viking. He never hit me. That would've been easier to deal with, I think."

Felix nodded. "You would've caved his head in if he tried that."

"Oh, boys—sorry, *men*—you just don't know." Her face scrunched as if she'd bitten into something rotten. "Here's the abridged version. He wouldn't let me get a job because he said his pride as a man demanded he would support me."

Prowl frowned. "Wouldn't *let* you get a job?"

Bianca poked him in the shoulder. "Don't interrupt, but I was in love, and at the time, it seemed all romantic and sweet. Then he said I had to stop my Taekwondo classes because he couldn't afford the fees. Then he asked me to stop talking to folks on Facebook and such, because he felt like I was spending more time on that than with him."

"That explains why you dropped off the net all of a sudden," Felix noted. "I was a little worried about that."

"And you were right to be. But I obeyed him, because he made a strong argument, or so it seemed then, and I didn't want him to feel jealous of ex-boyfriends or whatnot." Bianca shook her head. "It's all so obvious now. But the real eye-opener was when he'd tried to cut me off from talking to my family."

Prowl and Felix's faces both grew dark.

"He shows his face around here," Prowl promised, "he crawls home to Florida with two broken legs."

Felix's jaw ticked. "I wish you'd called us or emailed us, or something. We would've been down there faster than a falling meteor, you know that." He glanced back towards the stage, frowning.

Bianca nodded. "I know, 'all for one, one for all,' and I love you two for it. But it was my mistake for falling for his bullshit in the first place, so it was my job to clean it up. I cleared out my savings, which he couldn't touch, I packed my bags while he was at work, I took the car that was still in my name, I threw his ring in his ugly cat's litter box, and I got to a shelter. Stayed there just long enough to get things taken care of, and then drove the hell back here to my real home. I am not some fucking damsel in distress who needed a rescue. It was my shit, and I handle my own shit."

Prowl held up a finger. "Agreed, and clearly you did handle it, and I'm glad. But if something like that was to happen down the line, and you did need help, please don't let that pride of yours tell you not to come to us if things go cock-eyed. We care, and we love you."

Bianca grinned, took Prowl's outstretched finger in hand, and suddenly started sucking it suggestively, her eyes never leaving his. After a long moment, she relinquished her mouth's grip. "I love it when you say things like that, big man."

"Down, Bianca." Felix rolled his eyes. "He's got steam coming out his ears. Prowl's just glad you're safe. Aren't you, bud?"

Prowl swallowed, his voice cracking a higher octave than usual. "Whatever happened to *sorry, Prowl, I'll tone it down?*"

She just smiled.

Felix looked back to the stage again. "My cue should be any second now."

Moments later, Brian announced, "I now declare Anime Horde officially open!"

Leticia, the stage manager for this event, walked over to Felix. "I thought Brian was supposed to call you back onstage to do that part?"

Felix gave his colleague a nod. "That was the plan, but I guess Brian's not done being a grouch. Lovely." Felix sighed, and made a rude gesture in the direction of the stage. "Whatever, asshole—and thanks Leticia, sorry for the trouble."

She clapped him on the shoulder with a smile, and he turned back to Prowl and Bianca.

"Anyway, let's give the crowds a couple minutes to thin out, and then I'll take you to meet Iris." He pointed at each of his two friends. "And then you two will need to get going. You've got a lot to talk about."

Bianca reached around and goosed Prowl's butt, causing the man to jump in surprise. "Damn right we do, but first..." She produced a smartphone from her purse, and pulled her old friends in for a photo. "BFF selfie!"

A moment later, she tapped at her phone screen, and then held it up for them to see the picture on her Facebook wall. "Bianca Torres has now officially checked in at Anime Horde. Now, let's go meet this new fan of yours, Felix."

CHAPTER TWENTY-TWO

IRIS

Rachel took another swig from her water. "Okay, so you two got out of the shower, and rubbed each other down with towels to dry off, which I'm sure was fun, and then what?"

Iris idly toyed with the shoulder strap of her tank top and bra. "We climbed into bed, and just kissed and cuddled for what felt like a really wonderful forever."

Her hair spread out across the pillow like a fan, her eyes glassy with overwhelmed emotion as Felix's mouth explored a gentle trail from her neck to her breasts. "God, yes. Give the tips a pinch, I love that."

Felix bit down very gently on her right nipple, and then soothed it with a swirl of his tongue. He seemed hypnotized by the sight and feel of her exposed breasts. "You just tell me if I'm being too rough, beautiful."

"If anything," she happily replied, "you're being too gentle. I'm not made of glass, you know." She pulled him upwards, snaring his mouth in another long and soul-burning series of kisses.

She indulged in a small moan as she gave one of her own nipples a hard squeeze through her blouse and bra, the stiff points holding Rachel's gaze like a magnet. "I won't bore you with the nitty gritty, but we talked a little about how neither of us had been with anyone in months, and we'd both been tested clean since then. In any event, it was time to get him ready."

Iris curled up on her side, her face level with Felix's hips, his half-hard length cupped in her hand. "A handsome man all over. I can't wait to have this inside me, Felix." She shifted her hips so that her open thighs were pointed towards him. "Enjoying the view?"

His shoulders were propped on a small pile of pillows, so he was halfway sitting as he watched her go to work on him. "Enjoying every moment of you, Iris. Want to sixty-nine for a bit?"

She shook her head as she dragged the tip of her tongue across his length. "Maybe next time. Right now, I want to get you nice and hard for me, and I'd hate to accidentally bite you because you hit something sensitive." With a twinkle in her eye, she guided his hand between her legs. "But I'd love it if you just played a little. I want to feel your fingers all over me."

He obliged her by slipping a finger just a little ways inside her, causing a small flood of wetness to spread across her opening. "Oh, that's perfect, Felix. Keep that up while I take care of you, lover boy." Without any further ado, she lowered her face, and his moans echoed across the room as his cock grew inside her mouth.

As her loving ministrations restored the energy he'd spent in the shower, his fingers slid back and forth between her folds, everything coated with the wet proof of her eager libido. She closed her eyes as she massaged his cock with her tongue, inhaling his clean scent and imagining what this would feel like between her thighs.

Suddenly, her eyes shot open as she felt something brand new—a warm and wet fingertip gliding along the tiny bud of her back door.

"He put his finger in your ass?"

"No, just touching along the outside. Still, that's new territory for me."

His warm hands were as nice as ever, no question about that. And if nothing else, she was certainly clean after the shower they'd just taken. "That's...different." She turned her head to look at him. "You like my ass, handsome?"

Felix grinned. "Sorry, couldn't resist a little tease there. I'll be good."

Her mind racing, she purred as his finger moved from her ass and slipped back inside her pussy. "Y-you...you can be the first man to put his cock there, if you want."

Rachel's eyes went wide. "Whoa, wait. You'd never even had a finger before, and all of a sudden, you were offering him your butt-virginity?"

Iris ran a hand through her hair. "I panicked. It sounds so stupid now, but right then, I was terrified if I didn't pull out all the stops and let him do anything he wanted with me, he'd suddenly call me frigid and leave me high and dry."

Leaning in, Rachel gave Iris a peck on the cheek. "There's that f-word again. Someone used that to really hurt you, huh?"

"Sure did." Iris grimaced. "Thankfully, I now have this new amazing boyfriend instead, who thinks I'm awesome."

Felix shook his head. "One step at a time, beautiful. We can do that another night, if you want, but right now, I just want to take things simple and sweet. Sorry if I got too playful back there."

"I wasn't expecting it, but it was kind of nice, actually." Her face heated. "I want to get back to what I was doing, but I'd like you to keep touching it. My ass, I mean." She laughed. "I feel weird just saying that—'I want you to touch my ass'. Please?"

As she took him into her mouth again, he thrust two fingers into her pussy, and then spread the slippery honey between the cheeks of her backside, teasing her tight rear entrance.

"Your wish is my command, gorgeous. Besides, you really don't want to try anal unless you've got some lubricant handy. Did that once back in college—trust me, it didn't end well."

Rachel was on her back across the bench, her head resting on Iris's lap as she looked up. "You know, I have a bottle of lube in my suitcase upstairs. You could borrow it if you want."

Iris lightly tickled Rachel's stomach through her costume blouse. "Why on earth did you bring that?"

Rachel smiled. "Because I also brought along my favorite dildo, and planned to take some time for myself in my hotel bathroom this weekend." She licked her lips. "Might have to do that sooner than I thought now. But don't stop, I want to hear about him spreading you open with that rod of his."

"We're getting there, Miss Midnight. Don't get your wet little panties in a bunch." Iris leaned back, closing her eyes as she recalled the moment. "I had him roaring to go in short order, and soon, we were cuddling under the covers again with every inch of him pressing into my thigh like a steel bar."

Felix purred, nuzzling her neck. "I just want to touch every last part of you, Iris. I want you. I have never wanted anyone like this before." He threw back the covers, and reached down between her legs, two fingers slipping easily into her drenched folds.

She gasped, looking at her own spread thighs, watching this man's warm hand reach into her. "I need you, too, handsome. I want to come all over your beautiful shaft, and I want to hear you whisper my name in my ear as you fill me. I want it so bad, Felix."

He slithered down the bed, kneeling between her open legs. He moved forward until the underside of his shaft was rubbing back and forth along the tip of her clit, exposed from under its hood and glistening with wet heat.

"You're amazing, Iris. Are you ready?"

She nodded, and he leaned forward, covering her body with his as he shifted position. The swollen tip of him pressed against her for a moment, and then slipped past her soft lips and into her.

They gasped in unison, her arms wrapping around his shoulders.

Already breathing heavily, he slid deeper inside her, his lips whispering in her ear. "Make love to me, Iris. Show me your heart. Don't hold back."

Rachel's hands went to her bright red face as she looked up. "I can only hope my first time will be at least half this special."

Iris ran her fingers idly through Rachel's wavy hair, her story paused as Iris pursed her lips in thought. "You only have one first time, true enough. Mine was the summer before my senior year of high school, and it wasn't bad, but it wasn't...special. You should definitely have something special."

"I really appreciate that, Iris. If anything, you're just as sweet as your beautiful man, you know that?"

Iris grinned, and checked the time on her phone. "Well, let me wrap up this story, because I think the opening ceremony is going to be over soon."

Nodding eagerly, Rachel snuggled in, looking at Iris happily from where her head rested on her lap. "Go on, then."

Felix's length was so deliciously warm inside her, and she couldn't help but moan as his chest rubbed against her full breasts and rock-hard nipples. "Grind it into me, handsome. Make love to me."

Propping himself up for a moment, his hands on either side of her shoulders, he looked down at her. Her damp hair had spread across the pillow again.

"So tight. And perfect. You set my senses on fire, Iris. And you're so, so beautiful."

She pulled him close, her tongue teasing across his ear. "And you're my dear boyfriend, Felix. My darling, considerate, handsome hunk of a boyfriend." She shifted her weight and rolled him onto his back. He slipped out of her in the process, but she wasted no time in reaching down and guiding him back inside as she sat on his hips. "Mmm, there we go."

Playfully struggling against her hands on his shoulders, he looked up into her eyes. "Ooh, am I your prisoner now? You going to have your way with me?"

She flashed another brilliant grin. "Uh-huh. I'm going to use this handy piece of yours to fuck myself senseless. You're permitted to lick my nipples in the meanwhile." Her giggles turned into another gasping moan as she widened around him and descended.

He indulged in this permitted activity with a throaty laugh, craning his neck to taste her luscious breasts. "Such a naughty girl, taking advantage of poor little me. Do you like being a bad girl?"

Tossing her head so that her face was half-obscured by a cascade of auburn curls, she lowered her voice to that throaty alto growl that made his toes curl with arousal.

"Oh, Felix—I'm not bad, I just fuck that way." She bucked, and Felix shuddered in pleasure.

He grabbed her hips, thrusting upwards to meet her movement. "You're gorgeous beyond words, Iris. And for the record, if you ever decide to cosplay as Jessica Rabbit, be warned that you might never get to leave your hotel room because I'll be too busy lifting that skirt and fucking you non-stop."

Iris grinned. "You liked that, then? Pity I can't really pull off that look."

He grabbed her shoulders and rolled her onto her back, kneeling between her legs. His cock pulsed with his heartbeat, glistening with her wetness and eager to be buried inside her once more. "You can, and you just did, and you're about to feel just how turned on I am right now." Holding her by her ankles, he held her thighs apart and speared into her, driving his cock deep within, savoring her impossibly sensual and soft grip around his erection.

Gasping his name between thrusts, she grabbed the sheets and held on for dear life as he spread her sex wide open with each drive. His hands slid down her thighs, grabbed hold of her waist, and pulled her up towards him to meet his thrusts, pushing his length even deeper with each motion.

"I'm close, Iris. So close, so tight. Iris, Iris, Iris..."

As he rubbed hard against her clit on each new entry, as the sound his voice moaning her name echoed across her ears, and as the day's events flashed before her eyes, she welcomed the rush of heat as it flashed from her neck to her toes, and then back up her inner thighs to pulse between her legs.

"Come with me, Felix—no one's ever made me come like you have." She grabbed his hands, holding his grip to her hips. "Come inside me, I need to feel you inside me..."

He was nearly out of breath, but her words seemed to drive new life into him, and he thrust his cock home again and again. "I will, I promise."

Her climax triggered first, causing her walls to clamp even tighter around his hard flesh. In turn, it pushed him far over the edge and into sweet gasps of bliss from his lips.

No more words now, they simply clung tightly to each other as he filled her body, and as she squeezed every last drop out of him.

"Felix?"

"Yes?"

"This is crazy how perfect this is. How perfect you are. How perfect you make me feel."

He nodded. "Likewise, and I'm not questioning it for a second. I'm reveling in it."

As she nodded agreement, he curled up close. "I want to share everything I can with you. I want to know everything I can about you."

She kissed him again, savoring the taste of his lips. "You will, and I want all that, too." She glanced at the clock on the night-stand, and her eyes went wide. "But at the risk of ending this amazing moment—didn't you say you had to be at Opening Ceremonies by noon?"

His eyes shot open, and he sat up. As the clock's implications hit, he pulled the sheets away and worked to untangle himself from them. "Oh man, the Chair's going to kill me if I'm late! Okay, if we jump into the shower—for real this time, no hanky-panky—we can rinse off, get dressed, and get to Main Programming in time." He held out a hand. "Care to join me?"

She stood. "Always."

"And that, Rachel Midnight, is the completely true story of the first time Felix Jackson made love to me. And if there's any justice in this world, it damn well won't be the last time."

Rachel sat up, smoothed her skirt, and sighed happily. "I don't think you understand just how much this meant to me, Iris. I mean it. I owe you something so precious that I don't know how I can ever repay it."

Iris rose and pulled Rachel into a hug. "You don't worry about that. You just leave everything to me."

Rachel blinked. "Leave what to you?"

Iris just grinned. "Come on, they're wrapping up in there. Let's go wait for him inside."

CHAPTER TWENTY-THREE

MICHELLE

As the considerable crowd for opening ceremonies thinned out, Michelle Liang found herself waiting on Rachel, along with three of their mutual friends. The group had all agreed to do *RWBY* cosplay this year, so Michelle had chosen the white-garbed and rapier-wielding Weiss Schnee for her character. She'd even spray-dyed her normally black hair a glowing platinum white for the purpose.

Right before Rachel had suddenly run off with that Iris woman after the start of Opening Ceremonies, she'd promised Michelle she'd meet up with everyone in the back of the room, and Michelle suspected that she was going to get one hell of a story later on about all this. She'd overheard enough of Iris and Rachel's whispers, not to mention witnessing the missile scythe incident earlier that morning, to tell Iris was Felix Jackson's new girlfriend, and that was more than enough to explain why Rachel was so intent on talking to this beautiful woman.

"What the hell, Michelle? I can't believe she ditched us."

Michelle turned and looked at her friend, Edie Vasquez.

"I thought we're all going to spend the whole con together, you know?" Edie was tall, blonde, and the walking epitome of a California Girl, for good and for ill. She had cosplayed as the statuesque Yang Xiao Long, and was just as impatient as her favorite character.

"Edie, she promised she'd be back here afterwards, and the show just ended, so give her a chance to show up, okay?" That was from Adelaide Devereaux, a tiny Black woman dressed as Blake Belladonna, looking up from her smartphone. "Besides, I needed a minute to post all the pictures I just took."

The last member of their group chimed in as he adjusted the straps on his shield. "I hear what you're saying, Edie, and I'm not crazy about Rachel running off, either, but sometimes we just need to be flexible, y'know? I'm sure she had a good reason." Raeshawn Freeman had gone in drag this year as Pyrrha Nikos, and his costume was absolutely flawless. His flawless brown complexion somehow helped everything look good on him, and Michelle found it amusingly unfair that he could walk better in heels than any of the women in their circle of friends.

Edie paced with frustration. "Michelle, why did she bail, anyway?"

Checking the battery on her pocket-cinema camera, Michelle smiled. "Two words, Edie: Felix and Jackson. Let me put it this way—you've got a crush on Idris Elba, right?"

"Who doesn't?" Edie pulled off one of her gloves, flexing her fingers a bit. "And what's your point?"

Michelle smiled. "I'd like to think that if you suddenly had the chance to hang out with your favorite movie star, you'd bail on us immediately, and that we would totally understand. Same thing."

This got a knowing smile from Raeshawn, who'd been there when Felix had put Rachel in Michelle's orbit.

"But she didn't leave with Felix," Adelaide pointed out. "She left with some curly-haired white girl."

"Uh-huh." Michelle grinned as she spotted Rachel and Iris entering through a door about thirty feet away, and she immediately turned on her camera and activated its zoom. "Who happens to be Felix's new girlfriend. Hang back for sec, people. I want to see where this goes."

CHAPTER TWENTY-FOUR

FELIX

Felix's face lit up as Iris walked through the door, and he headed right for her, leaving Prowl and Bianca behind as he sped forward. A few convention staffers were lingering at the tech station at the back of the room, getting ready for the next event. They waved to Felix as he passed by.

Felix immediately laced his fingers with hers. "Sorry to keep you waiting, Iris. I hope the opening ceremony wasn't too dull?"

"Not at all, handsome. You looked and sounded great up there." She leaned in for a quick kiss. "Mmm. But as it happens, I ran into someone you know." She turned and gestured behind her, where Rachel was standing.

Felix leaned to one side to the young woman who'd gotten him splattered with juice that morning. She was still wearing that cute Ruby skirt, but had removed the wig to reveal a head of dark blonde hair.

"Oh yeah, Rachel, wasn't it?" Before she could answer, his face lit up as his memories clicked into place. "Oh, my God! Rachel *Midnight*! It's been too long. How have you been?" He put a hand on her shoulder. "I didn't recognize you with the wig before, you look great! Believe it or not, I was thinking about you yesterday. I'm so glad you're here. How is everything? Did Michelle and Raeshawn come with you this year?"

Rachel's breath seemed caught in her throat. "I...uh..." She grabbed his hand, keeping his on her shoulder, and then clasped Iris's with her other. "I'm...I'm..." She took a deep breath. "I'm doing really, really good. Thank you. I was, uh, thinking about you, too." She bit her lip. "And yes, they're here, too. Sorry about this morning, though."

"Nothing to apologize for, it all worked out really well." Felix laughed. "Would it be too forward to get a hug from an old friend?"

Rachel wrapped her arms around him, her cheek pressed against his chest.

As he stepped back from the hug, Rachel put her hands to either side of his face. "Felix, I'm sorry I didn't keep in touch, but now that you're here, I need to tell you something." Before he could respond, she continued. "You saved my life two years ago. I will never, ever forget you, and it isn't nearly enough to just say thank you."

She lunged forward and kissed him full on the mouth—a hungry, needful kiss.

Felix was so overcome with surprise and the primal pleasure of this young beauty pushing her tongue into his mouth that he couldn't help but respond in kind for a moment, his senses lost in the face of her intense need.

Iris just grinned.

The spell abruptly broken, Rachel broke off the kiss. Her eyes locked with Felix's, a seeming eternity passing between them before she spoke. "I'll never be sorry for that," she said quietly. She turned, suddenly caressed Iris's cheek, and gave her a brief but equally passionate kiss. "Be good to him." Then she bolted.

Felix watched her go as she ran past her friends, who then followed her out into the hall. He touched his lips, and then, suddenly reality came crashing through.

"Did that just happen?"

Iris clasped his hand tight, and stepped in for a long and sensuous kiss of her own, the fingers of her free hand caressing his neck. "Sure did," she said as their lips parted. "She's got a lot on her mind right now, and it looks like both of us figure into that. She and I had quite the talk over the last hour."

Felix could only stand there dumbfounded—and more than a little aroused.

"Felix, any chance you could bring your friends up to speed here?" Bianca stood a few feet behind him, arms crossed.

Prowl stepped forward. "Iris, lovely to see you again. Since your new boyfriend is having a bluescreen moment right now, allow me to introduce a friend of ours from college." He gestured to his side. "Iris Weinberg, this is Bianca Torres. Bianca, this is Iris."

Bianca nodded in greeting. "You seem pretty happy with our boy here."

"It's been a crazy morning, but I've never been happier." Iris brushed a lock of curls out of her face. "As far as I'm concerned, any friend of Felix is a friend of mine."

Bianca gestured with a thumb in the direction that Rachel had gone running. "Does that include Miss Miniskirt back there?"

"Oh, God, yes. She needed to kiss him like you and I need air or food. I knew she was going to do that before she did, although I wasn't expecting her to also kiss me." She gave Felix a quick peck on the cheek. "You okay with everything, handsome?"

Closing his eyes and taking a deep breath, Felix shook himself back into a functional mental state. "Yeah. I'm good. If you're good, I'm good."

Iris squeezed his hand. "Don't worry, I'll explain everything in a bit."

"As much as I'd love to hear this story, I suspect you'll want some privacy for that one," Prowl noted. "And at any rate, Bianca and I need to head out for a bit ourselves."

Bianca shook Iris's hand, looking right into her eyes. "True, but before that, I want to say one thing." She leaned closer her ear. "Please understand that I'm saying this with an affectionate smile, but that I'm still saying it: You break his heart, I'll break your face."

Iris nodded. "Please do. If I mess this up that badly, I'll deserve it."

Bianca smiled as she stepped back. "You two have a nice afternoon, then. Prowl, let's get going."

"Oh, before we go!" Prowl handed a card key to Felix. "This is for the contest office. The forms are on the table, and I left a cooler in there with a bunch of my sandwiches. You two help yourself to anything in there. I made plenty. See you in a couple hours!"

With that, Felix and Iris were standing alone in the ballroom, empty but for a few staffers working to change the stage set-up, watching the tableaux from a safe distance.

He turned to her, squeezing her hand again. "I'm pretty damn happy right now. Care to keep me company for a bit longer?"

Iris snuggled in as they started walking. "Mister Jackson, they'd need a tractor beam and high explosives to keep me out of your arms right now. Lead on, handsome."

CHAPTER TWENTY-FIVE

PROWL

"Come on, we'll take my car. I've got a shirt and shorts in there I can throw over the swimsuit." Bianca led Prowl through the parking lot, playfully pulling him by his necktie.

He gave a half-hearted chuckle, but after a few moments, he undid the knot and let the tie slide from his neck as she tugged on it. "Bianca, seriously. Tone it down a notch."

She turned around, wrapping the loose tie around his shoulders, pulling him close. She hugged him tight, pressing her exceptional breasts right against him, and giving him one hell of a view as he glanced down at her cleavage.

"Aw, I know you like it when the ladies come on strong. I've seen what happened at all those parties, and now, I finally get a chance to play."

He sighed, and was peppered with a series of brief kisses as he tried to talk. "Bianca, I'm not a playthi—Bianca, stop!" He put up a hand between her mouth and his. "Stop for a second. Let go. Please."

She hesitated, but then stepped back, a worried frown on her face. "What's wrong?"

Gesturing to her nearby car, he adjusted his glasses that had been knocked off-kilter by her kisses. "Several things. If you'll unlock your car, we can get going, and we'll talk."

She hit the unlock button on her keychain, and walked around to retrieve her gym bag on the driver's side. "Are you upset?"

He held up his hand. "Not yet, but the day's still young. We've got a lot to talk about, and there are some assumptions you're making that...that you really, really shouldn't."

Slipping on a pair of soccer shorts and a t-shirt, she dressed in silence, and then climbed into the driver's seat.

"Where to?"

"Let's hit the Brazilian place. The lunch buffet is a decent price, and I'm starving. I'm going to need a lot of protein to get through this weekend."

She offered a devilish grin. "Damn right, you're gonna need all your strength for what I've got in mind."

"Goddammit." He slapped his forehead. "Bianca, *stop*. I asked you to ease up, and I meant it. *Please*."

Cursing under her breath, she nodded. "Sorry."

"Apology accepted." There was a minute of silence as she pulled out onto the road

"Look, you weren't here last year, so there's a lot of heavy stuff you missed. While Felix was going out of his mind trying to hit on everything in sight with a vagina and a pulse, I walked into my hotel room on Saturday morning to discover Natalie was cheating on me with Mikhail Yemelin, and it turns out, she'd been fucking him for something like nine months."

Her jaw dropped. "She *what*? I heard that you two broke up at the con, but seriously?"

"Yeah. Seriously." He turned to look at her over the rim of his glasses. "And you might recall this isn't the first time someone's pulled that shit on me."

"Danica Blakeman. I remember that bitch. Junior year." She smiled. "I never told you this, but I punched her face after she cheated on you."

"Wait, what?"

"God's truth, may He strike me down if I lie. After I heard about her sucking off that teaching assistant and throwing it in your face afterwards, I marched right down to her room and punched the shit out of her. I told her that if she even so much as said an unkind word to you again, that I'd come back and break her in half." She snorted in satisfaction.

He sat back in his seat. "I wondered why she transferred out."

"Good riddance, I say."

"Well, my point is, after Natalie's affair and the nuclear drama fallout afterwards, I realized something." He pulled off his glasses and rubbed his eyes. "I had a bad habit of dating women who took me for granted, who didn't respect me."

Bianca furrowed her brow. "I respect you."

"Yeah, but with an asterisk." He looked away, watching the trees go by as they drove. "You've always treated me like your puppy, but you were hardly alone there. And I'll cop to it, I used to like it." He released a long, tired sigh. "Puppies get attention, they get petted. Girls think puppies are cute. I liked being cute." He turned back to face her. "But after Natalie, I decided I was tired of it. I'm tired of fetching, I'm tired of being told to heel, and I'm tired of being trained to be an obedient boyfriend and being ordered around. I'm just tired."

Bianca drove in silence.

"So, I need to be up front with you, Bianca. I can't be treated like your backup dildo. You can't just drive back into town and assume that just because we're finally both single at the same time, that I'm going to just...jump into bed with you and be your boytoy." He ran a hand through his hair. "I'm not a lapdog anymore. I'm a human being, same as you, and, well—I need to be treated like one."

As they stopped at a red light, she put her head on the steering wheel. "I'm sorry, Prowl. I shouldn't have come back. I already pissed off Felix with his new girlfriend, and now I've fucking ruined it with you." She leaned back, and a tear streaked down her cheek. "Look, I'm sorry. I'll take you back to the hotel. Let's just forget this."

"*No.* Hell no." He reached over and put his hand on hers. "You haven't ruined anything, and Felix accepted your apology, remember?" He squeezed her hand gently. "And you apologized to me just now, and I'm accepting that, too."

"But you just said I'm horrible to you."

"Hoo, boy." He took a moment to gather his thoughts. "Okay, let me say it this way. I don't think you're horrible. I never have. You're one of the most important people in my life, after my family. Heck, you almost *are* family to me. And I've been crazy about you ever since we met at freshman orientation, you know that."

She drove onward as the light changed. "Pity that I was still with my high school beau at the time."

"Story of our life, Bianca, but that's water under the bridge. So's Richie. So's Natalie. So's all that." He squeezed her hand again. "The bottom line is this: I'm still crazy about you. That never changed. And I do want to see if this can work. We've waited eight years for this chance, after all. But if it is going to work, then I have to set some ground rules for my own safety. And I'll be honest, so should you."

As they pulled into the restaurant's parking lot, she frowned in thought. "Ground rules? Prowl, I can't be ordering you around, that's how I nearly fucked this up to start with."

"Nuh-uh. Not the same thing." As she parked the car, he undid his seatbelt, but made no move to get out of the car. "Is it fair to assume you don't want me pulling the same shit Richie pulled?"

"You wouldn't do that!"

"Damn right, but the point is, you know where your limit is because of him. He did things you never want to have happen in a relationship again, and it's fair for you to tell me what those are. And if I fuck up and cross those lines, then I have to face the consequences." He held out his open his hands. "We both get to draw lines in the sand and say, 'These shitty things don't happen if this is going to work', and we take it from there. You start. What's one thing you really don't want me to ever do?"

She took a deep breath. "Okay. Don't ever try to say I can't talk to people I want to talk to, especially family. That's what broke the camel's back with Richie."

He nodded. "Done. Here's mine: don't take me for granted, and here's a specific thing with that." He leaned over, and kissed her cheek. "I want you to charm me. Woo me." He sat back. "Call me corny, but no one's ever done that before, not to me. Everyone's just walked up, pulled me into being their boyfriend, and assumed, correctly as it turned out, that I'd go along for the ride." He rubbed his forehead. "Just once, I want to be with someone who makes me feel special. Who makes me feel wanted rather than just being handy, useful, and available."

She wiped the tears from her eyes. "I'd like that, too. Richie did a number on me, made me feel ugly, like he was doing me a favor by proposing to me, because no one else would want some crazy bitch like me."

"Oh, man." He stroked her dark hair. "That explains a lot. So yeah, to hell with him, and to hell with the cheating bitches of my past. Let's you and me charm the hell out of each other. Let's give each other a real reason to want to be dating, besides it just being convenient timing and maybe getting our rocks off."

She smiled and nipped playfully at his hand, which he withdrew with a chuckle. "Am I allowed to try and seduce you?"

"By all means, Bianca." He held up a finger. "Just don't go from zero to sixty in two seconds on me. Give me a chance to warm up first."

She leaned forward, and gave the tip of his finger a dainty kiss. "I can do that."

CHAPTER TWENTY-SIX

IRIS

"Felix, why are you staring at that cooler like it's the Ark of the Covenant?"

Felix looked at her, a smile across his face. "Iris, sweetheart, you just don't understand yet." Kneeling in front of the giant blue and white plastic box, he reverently lifted the lid, and inspected the contents. "Dear God, there must be three dozen sandwiches in here. Way to go, Prowl."

Iris looked around the Costume Contest office. It was a converted coat-check room, about forty feet to a side and mostly empty space, although there were some plastic storage tubs and a large electric box fan against one wall. The only furniture was one large and long banquet table near the back, covered with a floor-length tablecloth and skirt, and several wheeled office chairs behind it. The table had a stack of freshly printed forms on it, a pile of clipboards, and the cooler in the corner had completely taken hold of her boyfriend's brain.

"So, Prowl made sandwiches. Why is this such a big deal?"

A row of four immaculately sealed plastic bags were placed reverently on the table. "Because, my dear," he said with a twinkle in his eye, "Prowl is a freaking prodigy genius with these things. Everyone keeps telling him he should open a restaurant, but he keeps saying it would take all the fun out of his cooking." He met her gaze. "I am giving you first pick of these, and once you've eaten one, you will be enlightened." He glanced downward at the bags. "Choose your destiny."

She sat in one of the chairs, one eyebrow highly arched. "Now you're just messing with me."

Eyes wide, he shook his head with all the solemnity of a high priest. He gestured again to the sandwiches.

"All right, all right. I am hungry, so let's see what we've got." Each bag had been clearly labeled with Prowl's very neat handwriting. "Wait, that can't be right. Black pepper French dip with provolone. A cold French dip? I thought they were served hot?"

He nodded. "Not this one. The bread's carefully soaked with just the right amount of au jus, and chilled to perfection."

"Maybe another time. Canadian bacon on Ezekiel bread, toasted. Hmm. Grilled corned beef and salami on rye with Tzatziki sauce—the stuff they put on gyros?"

"Oh, yeah. Prowl made that one as a joke at first, but it turned out better than anyone expected."

She looked at the last bag. "This one looks normal enough. Chicken salad on honey wheat. I guess I'll have that."

He slowly nodded, returned the other three bags back to the cooler, and then retrieved another sandwich identical to the one Iris had selected. "To quote the third *Indiana Jones* movie, 'you have chosen...wisely.' And it's a damn good thing Prowl made a whole pile of each kind, because otherwise I'd kind of insist we share yours."

She opened the bag, and picked up one of the sandwich halves. "It's just chicken salad, what's the big deal?"

"Famous last words. *Bon appétit.*" He watched her carefully as he opened his own bag.

She propped her elbows on the table, took a bite...and the world stopped.

He grinned. "Now you understand, right?"

She took a deep breath through her nose, and took another bite. She chewed for a few silent moments, her eyes as side as saucers. Carefully, lovingly, she swallowed. She placed the sandwich back on the plastic bag, swallowed again, and whirled on Felix.

"Oh, my God!"

"I told you!"

"It was spicy, but it was bold, it was—Felix, what the hell did he do to make this?"

He took a moment to take a bite of his own, his eyes closed as if in contemplation of holy mysteries.

She followed suit, doing her best to resist devouring the entire rest of the meal in one ravenous swallow.

While she savored each bite, Felix answered her question. "He came up with this right after we graduated from college. We went to this con in Denver, ate at this amazing Japanese *yamagoya*-style restaurant there, and one of the things they served was a spicy cold chicken stew. It was just amazing, and Prowl swore that he would recreate it. But if anything, I think he surpassed the original."

"Is there bacon in this?" She was looking at the chicken salad from different angles, as if it was a vital clue on a police procedural.

"Just a tiny bit for seasoning and a bit of smoky flavor. There's a spice mix that doesn't seem like anything special when you see the ingredients, although he measures each part super carefully. But the real secret is the mayo he uses. He absolutely refuses to tell anyone, even Bianca and me, where he gets it. Our friend Barry, who you'll meet sometime this weekend, thinks Prowl goes on some secret pilgrimage up north for it from some obscure dairy farm, but I think he makes it himself. The stuff is liquid gold. It's freaking unreal." He gave a happy sigh, and indulged in another bite.

She leaned back in her chair to eye the cooler thoughtfully. "Are the other kinds just as good as this?"

"Almost." He smiled. "They're all delicious, but the chicken salad is unquestionably the best. Needless to say, Prowl's a popular man to invite to potluck dinners."

She gave a low whistle. "I have to tell Aunt Abby and Uncle Marcus about this. They both pride themselves on being great cooks, but damn, this is on another level. Abby's going to be so jealous."

They finished eating in companionable silence, and after a while, Iris got up to pace around the room, stretching her legs.

"I'm surprised no one's showed up to register."

Felix shook his head. "Nah, this is typical. Most people wait until tomorrow to sign up, but we keep the office open on Friday afternoon, just in case." He paused, and looked at her thoughtfully. "Hey, did you want to enter? I've seen a lot of costumes up close over the years, and I have to say, your Bronwyn DKD armor is top-tier stuff, seriously."

She grinned, stretching her arms behind her for a moment to work out some stiffness, enjoying the sight of Felix watching her body. "Nope. I like walking the halls in costume, and I am proud of getting all the details from DKD right, but competing for prizes brings out the worst in me, and that ends up killing the fun." She sashayed over towards where he was sitting and leaned down to give him a long kiss. "Besides," she winked as she stood, "I'd have an unfair advantage, seeing as how I'm sleeping with a certain sexy Contest Department Head." She walked around behind him and sat back in her chair.

"I'm the host, sure, but I don't sit on the judge's panel. But I hear you, no worries." He pulled the back of her hand to his lips for a kiss. "You know, speaking of *Damashii Knights Daitai*, back when we were talking towards the reg desk this morning, we were talking about the DKD dub, but we got interrupted."

She tensed a bit, but tried not to react beyond that. "What about it?"

"Well, it's really cool that you cosplayed Bronwyn, because she's honestly my favorite character in the show." He gave her a smile, then turned to look over the contest forms.

"You're just saying that."

"No, seriously! I think her relationship with Li Shan is really sweet, sure, and I really love it that she's a fully fleshed-out character with a real agency." He opened a box of pens, and set them out in a row along the table. "Even when Li Shan is kidnapped and brainwashed, she never once lets anything stand in her way of saving him, never takes any crap from anyone, and I found it really refreshing."

She bit her lip, waiting uncertainly.

"But I digress, we were talking about the English dub." He fiddled more with the forms, separating them into smaller piles. "Normally, I prefer subtitled stuff, but the DKD dub really blew me away, and made me like Bronwyn even more, which I didn't think was possible. The voice actress for that role, Melanie Manson, really did her research. I mean, Bronwyn's supposed to be from Wales, and Manson gave her this beautiful Welsh accent that really elevated what was already a fantastic performance. The olden times monologue at the Grand Melee arena, especially. Pity that she hasn't been in anything else, yet. I think that was her first dub job."

Her throat grew tight and her sinuses stung.

He blinked, probably realizing she had been strangely silent, and looked up.

She was staring right at him, her mouth open in disbelief, tears streaming down her cheeks.

"Iris, what's wrong?" He reached for her hand.

She took a deep breath, and stood. She wordlessly took his hand and pulled him to stand before her.

He opened his mouth to speak again, but she put a finger to his lips. She looked him up and down, and then pulled him into a sudden kiss that eclipsed even the intensity they'd shared in bed earlier that morning.

She clasped him to her as if to save herself from drowning, and after a moment of startled confusion, he returned the kiss in kind. After she reached down to grab the cheeks of his backside, pulling him even closer, he gently palmed one of her breasts through her shirt in his warm hand. The kiss continued for a long moment, but eventually they parted, breathing deeply as they stared into each other's eyes.

She spoke first, her eyes still damp. "You can't be real. You just can't. I must be at home, in my bed, dreaming, wishing, masturbating...something. I can't possibly be really living this. How can you be real? How in the world did I find you?" Tears fell again, and she threw her arms around him, her face buried in his shoulder.

"I'm real. I swear to everything holy, I am really here." He hugged her tight, and gently lifted her face to look her in the eye again. "If anything, you're stealing my line, pretty lady. I'm still in shock I found someone as breathtaking and wonderful as you. But what just happened?"

She half-collapsed back into her chair, wiping her eyes. "You might not believe this, but I'm Melanie Manson. That's the stage name I took for my one and only professional dub performance." She cleared her throat and switched to Bronwyn's working-class Welsh accent, looking at Felix. "'The legends and tales of olden times, they never did bring us any such as you, love.' Episode Nine, exactly ten minutes in."

His jaw dropped. "I had no idea that was you."

She nodded. "I know you didn't. The studio was too cheap to put photos of anyone in their press releases, so no one outside of the crew ever knew what Melanie Manson looked like."

"I meant every word of what I said before. I'm serious."

"And you have no idea how happy that makes me, Felix. I wanted that role so badly. I did absolutely everything possible to get it, *everything*, and then I got it for my first pro job. I worked so damn hard to make it the best performance I possibly could..." She clenched her eyes tight, and her voice was a tightly controlled monotone. "And I haven't been able to bring myself to watch it since, because whenever I do, all I can think about is that shit-licking, goat-fucker of a director, William Worchester. He used me like a goddamn gym sock, and then threw me in the trash the instant I showed a hint of backbone."

He sat beside her, clenching and unclenching his fists. "This is the part where I threaten your ex with bloody violence. I am so sorry anyone ever treated you like that."

"Thanks, handsome." She scooted her chair closer to him, and rested her head on his shoulder. "I was this prima donna idiot, convinced she was God's gift to the future of the anime dub industry. I was ready to take the world by storm, and I decided I would make my name at the smaller studios first. The idea being, my *obviously superior* performance would stand out more among lesser actors. God, I was a stuck-up bitch. I'm so glad you didn't know me then."

He took one of her hands in his. "Likewise. At last year's Horde, I was so bloody desperate and lonely, I made passes and got into the personal space of nearly every woman in sight, and got rightfully shot down each time. I'd hate to think what would've happened if I'd met you for the first time back then. But I'm interrupting you, so go on."

She nodded. "So, I met Worchester at a con in Pennsylvania early last year, and he was talking a big game about how he's going to make his new company, Downtown Dub-Media, the new industry leader, buying up obscure anime on the cheap, like DKD, and elevating them so fans would shell out big cash." She sighed. "I decided DDM was going to be where I made my name, so I started flirting with him big-time. I assumed that casting couches were how things got done, and that maybe I could wrap him around my finger to get all the best roles." She sniffed. "Like I said, I was seven kinds of horrible."

She straightened, her hands trembling slightly as she fidgeted with one of the pens. "A few weeks later, I moved in with Worchester, and in return for being his fuck-toy, he promised me Bronwyn in the DKD dub. I thought I was manipulating him, but really, he had all the power in that so-called relationship. Then the recording started, and things got weird."

"How so?"

"Well, I was doing my serious artist thing, researching accents, going over the original material like a Talmudic scholar, writing emails to the Japanese voice actress and asking for advice, which she never responded to, but that's probably just as well. Then, when I got into the recording booth for the first time, Worchester and his crew laughed at me."

He blinked. "Because you were taking it seriously?"

"Bingo." She leaned over and gave his earlobe a playful nibble. "One of the things I already adore about you, Felix, is that you get it. It's like you automatically understand where I'm coming from on things, and I want you to know how much I appreciate that." A long sigh. "Unlike certain people in my past."

She continued. "So, I'm in the booth, opening the metaphorical vein all over the microphone, remembering every last bit of acting technique and lore and using every trick I can think of to make Bronwyn live through me, and then he cuts me off mid-line." She pitched her voice to imitate a nasally male New Yorker. "What the hell you doing in there, Mel? This isn't fucking *Shakespeare in the Park*. Just read the lines, we'll crank this bitch out, and then we'll move on to the next show. Stop making a production out of it."

"Said the man running a production." He shook his head. "Unbelievable."

"I know, right?" She resisted the urge to growl. "Like, how dare I try to actually act and make something good. I pushed through as best I could, trying to get some decent takes in despite his rush. And then I made the mistake of talking to the other voice actors."

"How was that a mistake?"

"Well." She gave a resigned sigh. "Everyone records their parts alone, one person in the booth at the time. But I was in the studio every day since I was Worchester's pet pussy, so I got to talking with everyone else in the dub. I talked up about how excited I was for the show, and I really wanted to make this a project that would make us all big names, and it seemed like my enthusiasm actually started rubbing off on everyone. The rest of the cast started bringing their A-game in spite of our illustrious director's low standards, so by episode three, you could really tell the difference in people's performances."

He nodded. "Indeed, you could, I remember noticing the big improvement. So, I'm guessing that Worchester got pissy about you undermining his authority or something?"

"Got it in one again, smart guy." She leaned over to kiss him again. "So, it's weeks later, we're on episode eleven, we're nearly wrapped, and suddenly, Worchester finds out I've been comparing notes with the other actors, and doing my whole *we happy few* bit to get everyone to step up. I didn't think I was doing anything wrong, but he didn't see it that way, especially after I stood up for myself and took credit for the dub being as good as it was." She rolled her eyes. "Again, me last year was a seriously stuck-up bitch. After that, he got mean and cruel in bed. Rough, rude, crude, basically treating me like a piece of meat, never mind if I ever got anything out of it." Another kiss. "Unlike a certain wonderful someone."

He smiled, running his fingers through her hair. "Flattery will get you everywhere."

"Oh, my..." She suddenly remembered using that very same line with Rachel earlier. "That reminds me, I need to tell you about something, but let me finish this first." She leaned in close, her hand gently gliding back and forth along his clothed thigh. "After a couple of days of him being an asshole in bed, I started pushing back, trying to assert what I wanted out of sex and what I didn't, and just flat-out refusing to spread my legs for him at times. I'd never refused him before that." She took a deep breath. "He started calling me..." She paused. "Frigid. Not just in private, but in front of everyone at the DDM offices, including the other actors."

"He was trying to hurt you. I will never, ever do that. I swear."

"Oh, he succeeded. That word still tenses me up inside." She leaned forward and kissed him on the cheek again. "Although, you've already helped quite a bit in that regard, my hero."

She bit gently on his earlobe. "Now comes the final act of this little drama. On the day after I wrapped my last scene as Bronwyn, I walk into Worchester's office, and he's got some little firecracker bent over his desk with her pants around her ankles, and he's just ramming her—exactly the same way he had fucked me in that office earlier that morning."

He winced. "Fucking hell. Prowl went through something like that last year with his last ex, so I have an idea of what that feels like."

"Be glad you've never been there firsthand." She continued lightly tickling along his leg. "All I could think about in that moment was, thank God I always used condoms with him. He looks up, holds out his hand, and says," she shifted to imitate a man's voice, "give me your key, you frigid cunt. You're out on the street."

"While he's still fucking this new girl? Right in front of you?" He was incredulous.

She nodded. "Kinda sums him up, really. I ran out of there like a bat out of hell without another word, key in hand, got to said apartment, and packed up everything I owned. I took a taxi to Madison Square Gardens. I found out later the new girl he was banging replaced me in more ways than one. She got cast in a role that was intended for me."

"A real charmer, this guy. So why did you go to the Gardens?"

"This is where Uncle Marcus comes in." She smiled, her hand sliding a little higher up Felix's leg. "I knew he was in town on tour, so I met him and his girlfriend, Dipa, backstage, explained the situation, and he drove me back home to Abby and the girls at the end of the week. That was this last January. I've been living there ever since." She looked at his face, and grinned. "I know what you're going to ask next."

"You mentioned Marcus having a girlfriend?" He scrunched his face. "Since you said it so matter-of-fact, I'm guessing your aunt and uncle have an open marriage?"

"Yeah, they're polyamorous. I've been in some poly relation-ships myself awhile back. It's nice, as long as everyone's honest and open about what's going on." Her fingers were now tickling across his zipper. "That doesn't bother you, does it?"

He gave a happy purr as her hand closed around his clothed crotch. "Not at all. I've never been in that situation myself, but a surprising number of folks in the local fandom here are poly, so I've heard a lot about how that can work." He watched her lower his zipper, and caressed the curve of her breasts. "I have three more questions."

She paused to pull her tank top and bra up over her head, and dropped them in her shoulder bag, leaving her wearing nothing but her shoes and a pair of jean shorts. She returned to fishing his length from his open zipper.

"Do you now? Go on.".

He shifted in his chair. "First, is Marcus in a rock band or something? Second, might I ask what's got you all hot and eager all of a sudden? Not that I mind, of course." He gestured to the unlocked door. "Third, are you sure you want to do this right now, when someone could walk in at any minute?"

Her hand sliding up and down his circumcised shaft, she licked her lips with anticipation. "He's not a musician. He's a professional wrestler. You mentioned you were into wrestling, so you've probably seen him on TV. He uses the name Brimstone in the ring. That's why he wore the wig and the facial appliances for his cosplay, so he wouldn't be recognized."

Giving one of her bare nipples a playful pinch, Felix nodded. "I know that name well, and as it turns out, he's one of my favorites. I'll do my best not to have a fanboy moment the next time I see him, then. God, I love how you touch me. And the rest?"

Sliding down to kneel on the floor, she hit the lever on the side of his chair so that he was as low to the ground as possible, and then moved underneath the large sign-in table, the floor length table skirt hiding her from anyone walking into the room. She pulled Felix toward her, his crotch now hidden below the edge of the table, and continued rubbing his length.

"Thinking about how much better a lover you are than my last ex, or anyone else I've ever been with, got me seriously wanting more. I was already simmering and getting wet from Rachel ravishing us both back there. But right now, I want to take my time and suck you off, nice and slow." She gave the tip a playful lick. "Finally, let's just say I'm feeling adventurous, and the idea of blowing you while you sign people in, with no one knowing what's going on, has my panties completely soaked through." Another lick all along his length, slow and wet. "Do you want me to stop?"

He choked. "You're kidding, right? Wow, scratch one off the bucket list."

She happily lowered her mouth over his fully erect length, and worked carefully to make the next few minutes a silent heaven for his senses. As her head slowly bobbed up and down, he visibly relaxed, as if every possible care and worry in his mind just faded away to smoke.

But a moment later, his eyes flew open again when there was a knock on the door, and she continued her steady sucking without missing a beat.

"C-come in," he managed to stammer.

Rachel's elfin face peered around the edge of the door as it opened. "Um...hi? I hope this isn't awkward or anything."

Iris immediately shoved a hand down the front of her un-buttoned shorts, furiously rubbing her clit as she swallowed the entire length of Felix's cock under the table.

He gasped. "Rachel! No, it's fine. Come on in."

CHAPTER TWENTY-SEVEN

MICHELLE

As Rachel ran from the main programming ballroom, Michelle and her friends ran after her. "Rachel! Slow down! Wait!"

Instead, Rachel veered left, darting into the women's restroom.

Michelle slowed to a walk, and turned off her camera. "This is going to be interesting." She turned to the others. "Edie, Addie, Raeshawn, I think I should handle this. Can you wait here?" She spotted Rachel's Ruby Rose wig, accidentally dropped by Rachel mid-run, and picked it up on her way into the restroom. "Rachel?"

Standing at the far end of the line of sinks, Rachel was splashing water on her face, then stared at herself in the mirror.

Michelle walked closer, holding her camera in one hand and the wig in another, both of which got carefully deposited on a dry section of the counter next to Rachel. "Hey, Rach. You're safe, it's okay. I've got you." Michelle put her arms around her friend, and gave a warm hug from behind. "Quite a morning, huh?"

Rachel gave her arm a grateful squeeze. "More than you know."

Michelle bent down for a moment, checking to see if anyone was in any of the stalls. "Looks like we're alone in here, for the moment. Want to talk about it?"

Rachel nodded, still leaning forward against the counter. "In short, I realized Iris, the woman back there with Felix, had just come from having sex with him, and I somehow badgered her into telling me about it out in the hall. I shared a lot of myself in return, and the two of us had a few, ah, moments out there that were pretty intense."

"Uh-huh." Michelle reached out and smoothed out a few of Rachel's stray hairs. "Edie was pretty pissed off that you bailed on Opening Ceremonies. She's all in this group experience mode today."

"Oh, please. Miss I-Won't-Shut-Up-About-Idris-Elba can bite me. If her crush had come walking along and snapped his fingers, she would've done the same." Rachel looked at her reflection again, and wiped away a tiny streak of supposedly waterproof eyeliner that had made a small smudge.

Michelle laughed. "My words almost exactly. Don't worry, it's okay."

Rachel glanced around, confirming they were still alone. "Michelle, I need to tell you something." She hung her head for a moment, and then looked up again into the mirror. "I'm bisexual. I really, really hope that this doesn't make things weird."

"I knew that already, Rachel." Michelle picked up her camera, and carefully replaced the lens cap. "I've known that for a long, long time. And it doesn't bother me in the slightest, why should it?"

"You what?" Rachel turned her head to look at her friend. "Wait, how? I just figured that out less than an hour ago!"

Hooking on the camera's strap, Michelle swung the device over to hang from her shoulder. "Lots of little things. Your little GothamCon misadventure, for one thing. For another, when we were getting dressed this morning, you noticed my lacy underwear a lot more than a straight girl would."

Rachel blushed as red as a rose, and Michelle continued.

"To be fair, I was being a horrible tease at the time. When I was slowly pulling up my panties, I deliberately bent over in front of you, just to hear your reaction, and your intake of breath at seeing my naked parts has had me giggling inside for hours. You're kind of adorable." Michelle smiled and patted Rachel's shoulder. "I'm happy for you that you figured this out for yourself."

"Well, now I just feel silly for making a big deal out it."

Michelle shook her head. "Don't. It is a big deal, and I'm very honored that you came out to me."

Rachel stood straight, smoothing her skirt. "What about you?"

"What about me?" Michelle rolled her eyes with a smile. "Are you asking if I'm gay, Rachel?"

Rachel smiled uncertainly. "Well, I know you were dating and sleeping with Randy last fall, but that doesn't necessarily mean anything."

"True enough, he could've been a beard for all you know." Michelle laughed. "But he wasn't. I look at it this way. I do think some girls out there are pretty hot, but I think a lot of boys are hot, too. I'm not interested in dating any women right now, but then again, I'm not interested in dating any guys right now, either." She paused thoughtfully. "Except Lazlo Akers, of course, but he's firmly taken, alas." She held up her camera. "Honestly, I'm too focused on my art right now to really give any time to a boyfriend or girlfriend. But who knows what'll happen on campus this fall? I'll just take things as they come, you know?"

Rachel let out a long breath. "You're far more Zen about this than I could ever be. I'm super jealous."

"Hon, think about it." Michelle handed over the black wig. "My other best friend is a baby drag queen, my dad is transitioning into becoming my mom, and I live in San Francisco. I'd like to think I'm pretty hard to shock—although those kisses you planted on those two back there were a damn hot surprise, I'm just saying." She held up her camera again. "If you're interested in seeing what you look like when you're in heat, I got it all on here."

Rachel blushed anew, her hands straightening the wig. "Please tell me you're kidding."

"Nope! But I promise it'll stay on my private not-net-connected storage drive."

Rachel sighed. "I'll hold you to that." She took another deep breath, checked her wig in the mirror one last time, and then turned back to face her friend. "Okay, sanity restored for now, I think I'm ready to face the con again. What next?"

Michelle flashed an almost predatory grin. "If you'll recall our discussion over breakfast, right before your scythe went off and launched Iris into Felix's arms, we were going to sign up for the Costume Contest right after we have lunch. We won't have time to register tomorrow, so we have to do it this afternoon."

Rachel's eyes went wide with terror.

CHAPTER TWENTY-EIGHT

KALLI

Kallista "Kalli" Calderon walked into the Security dispatch office, fanning herself with her cap. "Hey, folks. It's not as bad as last year, but man, every now and then, you turn a corner, and you walk into a cloud of fanboy-funk. Someone needs to hose down the crowd over by the videogame room." She paused, suddenly realizing the entire room was silently staring at her. "What?"

A dozen faces all turned to look at each other nervously, no one wanting to be the first person to speak.

"Oh, for heaven's sake." Kalli walked right up to Megan at the radio desk. "Megan? Care to explain why everyone is afraid I'm going to produce a grenade launcher?"

Megan's grin was a toothy rictus, a drop of sweat trickling down one cheek. "It's nothing! Honest! Really! We were just all, uh, talking about that weirdness at the swimming pool last night, yeah!"

"*Megan!*"

Another security staffer, a stout Black man with a nametag that read "Harbinger," stepped forward. "We might as well tell her, Megan. Half the staff has heard about it by now."

Kalli's eyes narrowed. "Yes. *Do* tell me. Please."

Harbinger scratched his beard. "Um. At the end of Opening Ceremonies, a report came in that Felix Jackson was standing around with Prowl and some other folks, and he was with two women, one curvy lady with dark curly hair, and one in a black Ruby Rose cosplay skirt. They both shoved their tongues down his throat, then kissed each other for good measure."

"Dark curly hair. Curvy." Kalli slapped herself on the forehead, hard. "*Demasiado lento, maldito idiota!*"

Megan was still grinning nervously. "Well, at least you don't have to worry about Felix making another mega-awkward pass at you or anyone else this year. So, that's nice, right?"

Harbinger was waving his hands in a frantic negative to Megan as she said this, then just covered his eyes.

Taking a deep breath, Kalli walked back to the door, her right fist clenched and trembling at her side. She raised that fist, and for a moment, looked as if she was going to punch a hole through a nearby wall, but relaxed it and gave a resigned wave to her colleagues. "I'll be patrolling the panel rooms if anyone needs me."

CHAPTER TWENTY-NINE

FELIX

"Umm...hi? I hope this isn't awkward or anything." Rachel waved nervously from the contest office doorway. "We, ah, need to register. For the show."

Adelaide gave Rachel a gentle shove. "Blocking the doorway, Midnight. In you go."

With a small, forced laugh, Rachel stepped into the Costume Contest office, followed by her four friends. "So. Um. Forms?"

Michelle walked past Rachel and picked up five forms and pens from the piles laid out in front of where Felix sat at the table. "Hey, Felix. Great to see you again. Same procedure this year?"

Felix nodded, leaning back slightly in his chair, a wide, tight-lipped smile on his face. "Yes, indeed, Michelle. Same old forms." He nodded a greeting to the others. "Addie, Edie, welcome back. Raeshawn, always a pleasure to see you. You outdid yourself this year." His eyes fell on Rachel, and he gave her a warm smile. "Good to see you again, Rachel."

Before Rachel could respond, Raeshawn stepped forward. "If I'm gonna keep winning prizes, I gotta keep stepping up my game. What can I say?" Adjusting his bustier, Raeshawn glanced around the room. "Speaking of game, I think we're all wondering, where's this new girlfriend of yours?"

Felix gestured in the general direction of the door. "She, ah, stepped out for a few minutes. Said she'd be back pretty soon, though."

Under the table, Iris increased her ministrations with some especially strong suction on his length.

He about swallowed his tongue, insanely turned-on, yet trying to maintain decorum.

The group took a few minutes to fill out the forms, each one taking a clipboard.

Michelle finished hers first, setting the clipboard in front of Felix. "What are you doing later today, Felix?"

Felix glanced down, then quickly back up. "Honestly, I haven't thought that far ahead. I'll be in here for another couple of hours, then Prowl takes over for a shift. I've got the rest of Friday wide open, except for a dinner staff meeting." He shifted a bit in his chair, carefully gathering his words. "Iris doesn't really know anyone in town yet, so I figured I'd introduce her around, do my dinner staff meeting thing, then maybe we'd catch something in one of the film rooms. We'll play it by ear. Did you have something in mind?"

Michelle shrugged. "Well, we're shooting a bit for Journey in one of the panel room's that's not getting used this afternoon. Your friend Dory in Live Programming set that up for me. Thanks again for that. It won't take too long, so I'll text you or something in case inspiration strikes afterwards. I really want to meet this Iris lady. You totally deserve to have someone nice in your life."

"You're a sweetheart, Michelle, thank you. And I'm always glad to help with your show, you know that." He shifted a bit in his chair, wondering what Michelle would think if she knew what was going on inches away from her. "Are you all doing a skit this year, or just presenting the costumes?"

Edie struck one of her character's fighting poses. "Nothing fancy. We get on stage, pose a bit, basically let the costumes talk for us."

As everyone finished up, Rachel tapped Michelle on the shoulder. "You're going to the Lazlo Akers panel next, right?"

Michelle grinned. "Of course. Why?"

Edie slapped her forehead. "Oh for—Rachel! Are you ditching us *again*?"

"Let it go, Edie. Rachel and Felix probably need to talk out a few things. Am I right?" Adelaide adjusted her hairbow as she gave Rachel an inquiring look.

Rachel returned a forced toothy grin. "Yep. Definitely need to talk. About...stuff. Yeah." She turned to face Felix. "If that's okay?"

Felix bit his lip, unsure at first how to answer this, until Iris suddenly deep-throated the entire length of his hard shaft below the table. "Absolutely okay. No question about it."

Rachel clapped her hands once. "Okay, I'll meet you all at the panel room in an hour then. Thanks, everyone." As the rest of the group filed out, Raeshawn shot Felix a discreet thumbs-up gesture while looking right at the table, and then left with a broad smile on his face.

Rachel stood by the door, turned the Costume Contest Office sign around to show that no one was on duty, and then closed the door and locked it.

She turned around and pulled off her wig once more as she walked back to Felix's table, smiling all the way. "You two are so unbelievable." Without warning, she stepped around to Felix's side of the barrier, and pushed the table aside to reveal a near-naked Iris on her knees, happily inhaling his erection.

Felix shrugged in response. "Entirely her idea, not that I'm complaining."

Iris let his length fall from her lips, and she looked at Rachel with a heavy-lidded gaze. "Going to tell us what's on your mind, Rachel?"

Rachel seemed unable to look away from the nakedness on display. She licked her lips. "I need to say something. Something crazy. Please hear me out."

"I'm listening," Iris murmured happily, and then returned to blowing Felix in a slow rhythm, angling her head so that Rachel could see every detail of his length as it disappeared, inch by inch.

He nodded agreement, rendered unable to speak by Iris's playful tongue.

Rachel tossed her wig onto the table. "I was telling Iris earlier that I have no illusions about ever making a relationship work with you, Felix. I live in L.A. right now, and I'm going to college with Michelle and Addie in San Francisco in the fall. More to the point, I sincerely don't want to come between you two."

She stepped closer, putting her hand on Felix's shoulder. "But, if I'm going to be completely honest with you and with myself, then I can't deny that I want you. I want both of you."

Rachel reached out to caress Felix's cheek. "After you saved me two years ago, I couldn't stop thinking about you. I avoided you last year because I was still too young, and because I was scared. I even asked Michelle not to mention me when she saw you. But now I'm nineteen, and I can make my own decisions." She reached under her skirt, and slid her red silk panties down her legs. Straightening, she placed them in Felix's hand, the sleek underwear clearly drenched with her arousal. "And what I want is the both of you. I want you two to let me join you in bed tonight. I want you, Felix Jackson, to be the first man I make love to."

Iris looked up, a wide grin on her face. "If you're worried about my reaction, Felix, don't be. As long as I get to play, too, I'm all in favor."

"Oh, wow." He caressed the expensive silk between his fingertips, and while keeping eye contact with Rachel the entire time, he lifted the wet fabric to his nose and inhaled deeply, savoring her lustful aroma. "Rachel, you're a beautiful woman, and I'm honored. If you want me, if you want us, then I want to do anything I can to make your first time as special as possible."

He pulled Rachel closer, and their lips met for the second time.

As Felix and Rachel kissed, Iris squeezed Felix's length approvingly, and spoke with a voice dripping with lust. "And again, Felix, you get it. I love that. Rachel, we're going to make you gasp our names tonight, and I'm really looking forward to it." She returned her mouth to his body, purring happily. As her tongue slid all along his length, his kiss with Rachel intensified.

Rachel broke the kiss, her cheeks flushed with desire. She looked at Iris. "Make room down there, Miss Voluptuous. And get those pants off of him." She looked back into Felix's eyes. "I might be a virgin, and I'm not ready to change that until this evening, but like I told Iris this morning, I'm no innocent. Let me show you."

As Felix obligingly lifted his hips, Iris helped him slide down his slacks and boxers.

"Aren't you all take charge now." Iris gave Rachel a mischievous smile.

Rachel brushed a stray strand of hair out of her eyes as she knelt between Felix's open legs. "Like I said, I know what I want." She looked at him, taking his cock into her hand. She could feel his warm pulse as she held him, and she shivered as she watched one of her closest-held fantasies turn real. She was about to suck the cock of Felix Jackson, the man who'd saved her, who'd held her, who'd turned her world upside-down when she'd needed it the most.

Iris was kneeling next to Rachel, and watched as she leaned forward, taking her first tentative taste of him, her lips pursed around his engorged tip.

"Make sure to get every last inch inside you, Rachel. He loves that."

Rachel paused, and turned to look at the auburn-haired beauty beside her. Iris was still wearing nothing but a pair of half-unbuttoned denim shorts, and Rachel couldn't resist reaching out to pinch one of this woman's hard nipples. "And I remember you saying how you loved it when he gave these a hard squeeze." Her palm opened to caress the soft breast, and Rachel smiled as Iris's eyes closed in pleasure. She turned back to Felix, still stroking him all the while. "Felix, I want Iris to be the first person to finger me. Do you mind? You'll still be the first man inside me tonight." She reached behind herself, lifting the back of her skirt and tucking it into her belt.

Felix ran his fingers through Rachel's wavy hair, his deep voice purring with approval. "I'd love to see that, oh yes." He raised an eyebrow with a smile. "Iris, did you tell her about all we did this morning?"

Iris gave a playfully guilty nod. "Didn't I say I had something to tell you? I ran into this little fox again by pure chance. She could tell I'd just been gloriously fucked by you, and begged me for details." She reached down, squeezing the cheeks of Rachel's slender ass, who lifted her hips obligingly off her heels to give Iris better access. "How could I resist?"

Laying a trail of kisses along Felix's inner thigh, ending with a gentle caress of his balls with her lips, Rachel rocked her hips back and forth in anticipation. "I want you to look me in the eyes while your girlfriend fingers me, Felix. Watch me. Please."

Recognizing her cue, Iris let her hand drift between Rachel's kneeling thighs. The woman's folds were shaved bare and smooth, save for a small soft patch just above her clitoris, and Iris's fingers lightly danced across all of it. Rachel moaned at the intimate touch, eyes locked with Felix as she stroked him.

"You know I'm wet enough, Iris. Don't make me wait."

Iris leaned in, her chest rising and falling with heavy breathing, her voice low and growling with lust. "I told you, Rachel, one of these days, I was going to make you beg, and that moment is now." Her finger glided across Rachel's inner lips, teasing them open. "Keep your eyes on our man, now, but let's hear what you have to say to me."

"Dear God." Felix felt like he was under a spell. He couldn't look away from Rachel's brown eyes even if he wanted to. She was looking at him as if this was the greatest moment in her life, and he knew that he would do nearly anything to return her lust in kind. "I must have done something right with my life to deserve this."

Iris brought a finger to her lips. "Shh, lover boy. I think Rachel needs to tell me something." Her other hand was still between Rachel's legs, gently squeezing her outer lips, causing Rachel's opening to spill forth a new layer of slick wetness. "Speak up, princess."

Rachel indulged in taking the first two inches of Felix's shaft into her mouth for a moment before regretfully letting him fall from her lips. "I want your fingers in me, Iris." She stared adoringly into Felix's eyes. "I want you to spread me open right now, like this beautiful rod is going to spread me open tonight."

Shaking her head and making *tsk* sounds, Iris withdrew her hand for a moment, and delivered a playful swat across the cheeks of Rachel's naked ass, causing the blonde to gasp in surprise and obvious pleasure. "Not even close to good enough, Rachel. I said I wanted to hear you beg. Beg me to take your wet pussy. Beg me to make you come in front of your hero. Beg me for the privilege of fucking my boyfriend." She threw Felix a quick wink. "I want to hear the need in your voice. You've been masturbating while thinking about my boyfriend for two years, I bet. I want you to remember every time you came on your favorite dildo, pretending it was Felix giving it to you hard, and I want you to put that need into your words right now. Rachel Midnight. I want you to tell us what you want, you need, with everything you've got."

Rachel nodded, her hands gently caressing his length as she knelt before him. "Every night for the last two years, I've wondered what it would be like to kiss you, to taste you, to suck you, to fuck you. I wanted to hear you say my name, I wanted to hear you whisper and moan my name in pleasure." Her voice quivering, she paused to take another suckle at his tip. "Oh God, you taste so good. I never thought this would really happen, but now that we're here, I will do anything for you. I need you."

Still staring into his eyes, she continued. "Iris, when I met you this morning, it was clear you and Felix were meant to be together, and I was shocked to realize I wasn't jealous. I was incredibly happy. Then you willingly shared so much with me, and I witnessed your beautiful spirit and your eyes and your voice, and that divine body of yours. Everything about you made me realize things about myself I was afraid to see before. And I want you just as much as I want your boyfriend. I need your fingers inside me right now. Please, please..."

Licking her lips, Iris obligingly slid two fingers partway into Rachel's virgin opening.

As Felix watched, Rachel's eyes teared up, obviously completely overcome and overwhelmed with pleasure. "Thank you. Oh, thank you." Gasping, she rocked her hips, seemingly trying to take even more of Iris's fingers inside her.

Iris leaned forward to kiss the top of Rachel's head. "You're welcome, princess. Keep going, tell us everything, and I'll give you even more."

Rachel nodded, swallowing as she seemingly tried to collect her thoughts. "Iris, I want to taste my first pussy tonight while Felix takes me from behind. I want him to bend me in half to drill me hard, my ankles on his shoulders while you touch me all over. I want Felix to lick my slit until I scream. I want you to make love to me with my dildo while Felix watches. I want to watch while you wrap those breasts around his rod. I want..." She shivered. "I want Felix to rub the lube in my room all over his length, and...and I want to feel him in my ass tonight. I need him, Iris. I need you, Iris. Please let me into your bed tonight."

Without any further ado, Iris slid a third finger deep inside Rachel's quivering sex.

Rachel's eyes went wide, never leaving Felix. "*Thank you*!" Her breathing revved, her eyes streamed tears of joy. "Iris, I'm gonna come, gonna come, gonna…"

Iris had gently pushed the back of Rachel's head so that her mouth was filled with Felix's cock, and Rachel closed her mouth eagerly around him, sucking as if her life depended on it.

"Can't have you screaming aloud right now. We might scare people in the hall outside." Iris laughed quietly. "Make my boyfriend come in your mouth, princess. You know what to do with a cock in your mouth, don't you? Sure, you do."

Felix was already gritting his teeth, doing his level best not to roar with ecstasy. Iris had been keeping him just barely away from the point of no return for so long, but now Rachel was deep-throating him with wet abandon, her hands cupping his balls and squeezing the base of his length in tandem with each new slide into her skilled mouth. "Rachel, I'm so close for you, I'm almost there…"

He clapped a hand over his mouth to muffle his moans, and his overstimulated cock launched stream after stream of his seed down her welcoming throat, his climax nearly rendering him senseless.

Rachel's cries were muffled around his shaft, and she eagerly drank every drop of him.

Wordlessly, Iris dropped her shorts and bent over the registration table, spreading her legs and holding her ass high and inviting in the air, the lips of her own dripping sex flushed and swollen with need.

Rachel's mouth lifted from his lap.

Felix turned to Iris, and the sight of her silent offering sent a thunderbolt down his spine and into his loins, reinvigorating the erection that had been slowly fading a moment before. He stood, caressing Rachel's blushing cheek, and took a deep breath. Holding his throbbing length in his hand, Felix moved behind Iris, and lined himself up to her intoxicatingly beautiful womanhood.

"Your turn, beautiful." He slid inside her, her walls as smooth and sweet as the silk of Rachel's gifted panties, and he quickly built to a hard rhythm. Only moments later, Iris was already shaking, holding on to that table for dear life.

Rachel pulled herself to her feet using Felix's discarded chair, and walked unsteadily towards the them. Putting one hand around Felix's waist, she reached underneath Iris and found the woman's clitoris, wordlessly rubbing it as Felix continued thrusting. This was too much for Iris, and her orgasm shuddered through, her mouth clenched tight as bliss ripped through her.

Iris turned to drop to her knees in front of him. Rachel moved to join her, and the two women quietly licked his erection clean.

Felix lovingly ran his hands through the hair of his two lovers, unable to form a coherent thought beyond raw lust, adoration of both women, and amazement at everything that had happened.

Iris gasped for breath. She turned Rachel to face her, and the two women shared a long kiss.

CHAPTER THIRTY

RACHEL

A short while later, they had cleaned up as best they could, their clothes restored, their composure slowly returning.

Rachel breathed a sigh of relief. Her costume had somehow managed to avoid any stains. She flipped through her schedule planner on her phone. "Okay. I should meet up with Michelle and everyone soon. As much as I want to stay, I really shouldn't ditch them completely."

Iris had her arm around Rachel's shoulders. "Yeah, we'll have plenty of time together tonight. It's fine."

Felix looked up from the scattered forms. "Actually, I have an idea." He walked over to them, hands open. "Rachel, you want to spend time with us, but you also want to see Michelle, Raeshawn, Adelaide, and Edie. Michelle and the rest of the crew really want to meet Iris. I'd love to catch up with Michelle and Raeshawn. They've been coming to the con for five years in a row, and I feel like I should get to know Edie and Adelaide better. And Iris, you said you wanted to meet more people, anyway. Why don't we see if Michelle and company are up for just hanging out for a bit? Everyone wins."

Iris scratched her ear. "Sounds great to me, but later I'm going to need to get home and then back here. I didn't bring an overnight bag, but I sure as hell need one now." She turned to Rachel and grinned. "And that gives *me* an idea."

Rachel leaned away in half-joking fear. "Should I be worried about this?"

"You," Iris pointed at Rachel, "and you," now pointing at Felix, "should have a date tonight."

Felix rubbed his chin. "I need to meet with some other staffers over dinner tonight, some logistics have to be discussed, but after that, I have a completely open schedule for the rest of the night." He held out a hand to Rachel. "Care to accompany me around the con tonight?"

Rachel stood with a smile, taking Felix's hand and making a dainty little mock curtsey. "I'd be enchanted to do so, Mister Jackson." She turned to look at Iris. "Are you sure about this? I hate to think we're excluding you in anything going on tonight."

Iris stretched her arms up above her head. "You two are going to keep each other company, and maybe get a little warmed up while I'm running home to get some clothes for tomorrow. I'll be gone two hours, tops, and I'll text you when I'm back on site so we can all meet up." She put her arms around the other two. "I only have one request."

"What's that, beautiful?" Felix cupped one of Iris's buttocks through her shorts.

Before answering, Iris leaned in for a brief kiss. "Mmm. I only ask that you keep your cock in your pants until I get back. You need to rest up to get ready for tonight, and more to the point," she turned to look at Rachel, "I absolutely need to be there for your big moment, princess." Iris punctuated this by pulling Rachel into a long and lingering kiss.

Felix smiled. "I couldn't agree more."

Stepping back after the kiss ended, Rachel took a deep breath, fanning herself. "Goddamn, Iris, you're going to kill me with those kisses of yours." She smiled blissfully, taking another deep breath. "But this is going to work out great. While Felix is having his dinner meeting, I'll get changed into..." She blushed. "I actually get to use the line. Ahem." She struck a sultry pose, one hand gliding down her side as she tried to imitate what she thought of as Iris's bedroom voice. "I'm going slip into something more...comfortable."

Iris licked her lips. "Oh, ho! And what sort of naughty outfits did you bring, Miss Midnight?"

"Nothing too elaborate, but I do have some options." She turned to Felix. "I'll let you decide, lover. Would you rather see me in a pair of tight pants that hug the cheeks of my pert little ass like they've been painted on, or would you rather see me in a pleated schoolgirl skirt?"

While his eyes widened with interest at the first option, Felix seemed to know his answer immediately. "Definitely a skirt. Since you've given me these beautiful panties to keep," he gestured to his left pants pocket, "I like the idea of having easy access, in case you need a little warming up while we wait for Iris."

Iris bit her lip. "Oh, I like that. Don't you dare put on any new panties, princess. You're going to walk around the con with nothing under your skirt for the rest of the night."

Pulling Iris into a hug, Rachel nuzzled her shoulder. "You know, when other folks have called me a princess, they usually mean it with a sneer. But when you say it, Iris, it makes me feel amazing. Don't ever stop, okay?" She squeezed both of their hands. "And on that note, I need to run." Stealing one last kiss from Felix, she then backed toward the door, putting her wig back on in the process. "The Lazlo Akers panel that they're at ends in five minutes. But call me the instant that Prowl shows up and takes over for you here, and that way we can get everyone together, okay?"

As she unlocked the door, Rachel turned around. "And you're going to want to turn on that fan and leave this door open for a bit to air it out. The room still smells like someone had some absolutely amazing sex in here, although I can't imagine why." With a last wink and a wave, Rachel departed out into the hall.

Turning the Costume Contest sign back around to its Open side, Rachel walked her way through the convention crowd with a deliriously happy spring to her step. *I could never have imagined something like this happening to me, not in a million years, and I'm going to make damn sure I don't mess this up. Tonight has to be perfect.*

As she passed by one of the hotel's air conditioning vents, a small breeze drifted up her skirt and across her naked folds, sending a wonderful shiver up her spine and down the back of her legs. *I may have to go without panties like this again sometime.* There's just something about the little thrill of having a sexy secret going on. This must've been what Iris felt like when she was blowing Felix under the table. Oh, what a sight that was. She reached the panel room, but since the doors were still closed, she grabbed a nearby chair off to one side, and happily waited for her friends to emerge as she reminisced over the last several hours.

CHAPTER THIRTY-ONE

IRIS

As she watched Rachel leave, Iris happily settled down into one of the chairs while Felix turned on the fan. "You know, handsome, I've been in poly relationships here and there, but I've never actually been with more than one person at a time before. That was pretty amazing."

"One hundred percent agreement. I've never felt anything like that before." Felix crossed his arms on the table, resting his chin on them. "Not with any of the women I dated in college, not even close. This morning with just you, that was heavenly, no question, but all three of us together? That was indeed pretty amazing."

"What about high school flings? Those first fumbling moments of teen hormones gone berserk?" She smiled at some old memories. "Ah, those were the days."

"Not so much for me." He stuck out his tongue, rolling his eyes. "I was a mess in high school. No idea how to talk to girls, no concept of people's personal space, and I was not in a nerd-friendly situation. I didn't even get to second base with a girl until I got to college. Lydia Akers, who I eventually lost my virginity to, as well."

She had picked up one of the pens on the table, drawing doodles on some scratch paper, but she looked up. "Ooh, I want details."

"It's not exactly an epic tale." He sat down, watching her draw. "We had a couple of classes together our first semester, and got to talking over study sessions. We somehow ended up admitting to each other we were both still virgins, which led to us deciding we were both tired of that state, and we should help each other out. Over the next couple of weeks, we worked our way through various levels of intimacy, trying things we'd only read about. Not terribly romantic."

He smiled. "We were more than casual fuckbuddies, but we were never really a serious couple, and didn't really have any interests in common, beyond sex. Eight months later, we mutually broke up, but we've stayed friends since."

She paused her drawings. "Wait. Lydia Akers? That name sounds familiar."

He laughed. "One of our guests of honor this year is Lazlo Akers, the one Rachel mentioned a moment ago. He's a voice actor and director, who Michelle is rather infatuated with, and who is Lydia's big brother."

She let out a quick bark of a laugh. "Oh, my God! Does he know one of the con staffers here took his baby sister's precious maidenhead?"

"Yes. Yes, he does, and he's fine with that." He chuckled and picked up a pen, fiddling with the cap. "He's actually the reason she and I got to talking. She isn't into anime herself, but she knew her big brother worked in the field, so she mentioned the connection to me once, just to have something to talk about when we were first getting to know each other. She then brought me home for Thanksgiving while we were dating, so I got to meet Lazlo then. We stay in touch here and there, and I'm the one who got him to come to this con."

She returned to her drawing. "My first time was at a Jewish summer camp, between my junior and senior year of high school. I was a junior counselor, and I thought this other counselor named Josh was kinda cute, and I was horny as hell. So, one night, while his cabin and mine were having a group activity, I pulled him off to the side behind the arts and crafts building, took off my shirt and bra to let him know what I wanted, and he bent me over an old sofa." She waggled her hand. "It wasn't bad, but not great, either."

He sat upright and fiddled with the pile of pens. "Yeah. Lydia and I tried to make our first time a big moment, but since we didn't really have a lot of romantic chemistry, it ended up feeling like we'd just successfully completed a big science fair project. The experiment is successful. We're no longer virgins, hooray! Want to try some more sex? Why sure, that'd be nice." He laughed. "That's not an exact quote, thank God."

"The thing is," he continued, "that a person's first time should be special. Rachel deserves a perfect night, so if we can give her one, that would make me really happy."

"My feelings exactly. So, this leads me to a question, Felix."

"Okay."

"We're a couple? Like, officially."

A very emphatic nod from him. "The best moment of that amazing shower this morning was when you agreed I was your boyfriend. My heart damn near burst and melted at the same time."

She drew a little Pikachu and Snugglypuff, walking hand-in-hand. "I dunno, I think the best part was when you washed my hair with those wonderful warm hands of yours. I was putty in your arms all throughout that. You're so going to do that to me again, and soon. You should treat Rachel to that, too."

He reached over and drew a little con badge on Pikachu, and a rough version of Bronwyn's dragon helmet on Snugglypuff. "I would be glad to oblige, on all counts. But, yes. We are definitely a couple."

She smiled at his additions. "Good, but I have an idea." She drew a little war staff in Snugglypuff's free hand. "Would you be opposed to trying out something poly-ish?"

"Sure, but we should work out the *ish* part in more detail, naturally."

"Of course." She looked down at her sketch, tapping her pen against her lips. "Well, we're already inviting Rachel into our bed, so we're not exactly going the monogamy route."

He placed several kisses along her bare shoulder. "I think I know where this is going. You felt it, too, huh?"

"God, yes. That was the most intense sex I have ever had." She gave a content purr at the touch of his kisses. "I couldn't believe the words that were coming out of my mouth, and then Rachel just pouring her heart out, and the way the two of you barely even blinked, staring right into each other's eyes. That was something else. Then, at the end, it was like no words were even needed anymore. The three of us were just...in tune with each other."

"If only she lived closer." He craned his neck to look at the people passing by the office outside. "If she was local, and if tonight goes well, I'd find myself wondering if a three-person relationship is workable."

She started to draw a little fox-like Eevee creature next to the Pikachu and Snugglypuff, with a tiny *RWBY*-style scythe clenched in its fangs. "That might actually be an option. She was telling me that her family's pretty loaded, and that she already travels constantly, anyway, going to cons and meeting up with friends. Maybe she'll come to visit here pretty often now."

He smiled at the drawing as he looked over her shoulder. "Do we want to offer that to her? That she's officially part of this relationship?"

"If tonight goes like we think it will? Absolutely." She leaned back in her chair, her nipples suddenly visibly straining against her tank top. "Like you said to me, I don't want her to be a one-time fling, I don't want her to disappear." She reached up to pinch her nipples, but then put her hands back down. "Bad

Iris, no biscuit. I really shouldn't be revving myself up again just yet." She turned to smile at him. "But here's what I'm thinking. What else might happen this weekend? Or just in general? What sort of rules should we have about meeting people, flirting, and all that might come after?"

He looked up thoughtfully. "Well, my number one request would be this—at the end of the day, regardless of anyone or anything else, you and I are a couple. No one comes between us."

"Smart man." She grinned. "I'm thinking it's okay to flirt with whomever we want, whenever we want, but before anything physical happens, we'd have to check in with each other to make sure the other person's okay with it."

"Okay, and physical is anything beyond hugs and light kisses?"

She nodded. "Sounds fair to me."

"You know." He laughed. "Twenty-four hours ago, as Prowl and I were walking into this building, I was swearing up and down I was going to set my libido aside, and just focus on the convention this year. I just wasn't even going to think about trying to meet someone, and instead, I've not only met the woman of my dreams, but I seem to have found a second girlfriend in the process, and we're negotiating what happens if any more show up. *Oy gevalt.*"

"I hear you." She folded up the paper she'd been doodling on and put it into her shoulder bag. "This morning, I just wanted to hang out with my family, maybe buy a few trinkets, and enjoy the results of all the work I'd put into my cosplay. Finding a date, much less a new serious boyfriend, wasn't even on my radar." She suddenly looked up and spun around to face him again. "Wait. Did you just say '*oy gevalt*'?"

He nodded. "Yeah. I'm Jewish, and my Uncle Morrie used to say it all the time growing up, so I picked up the habit from him. Aren't you?"

Holding her sides with laughter, she grinned ear-to-ear. "And he's Jewish, too! You couldn't be any more perfect if you tried,

Felix! I swear, I'm going to do everything I can to make sure this works, because lightning like this sure as hell doesn't strike twice."

A voice came from the doorway.

"Hey there, Felix!" A huge man walked in through the door.

Iris was impressed. This guy was even bigger and stockier than her Uncle Marcus with a full beard a dwarf from the Tolkien movies would have envied. His outfit, on the other hand, definitely didn't come from those stories. A combination of a sailor-suit schoolgirl uniform and a glitter-encrusted ruffled prom dress in dazzling pinks, purples, lavenders, and even some shades of orange thrown in for good measure. He wore a gleaming golden tiara on his brow, and held a wooden baton painted bright pink.

Felix leaped out of his chair, grinning with joy. "Bubba, you made it!" He ran forward, and the huge bear of a cosplayer enveloped Felix in a hug. "Wouldn't miss it for the world, man! How you doing, my dude?"

Felix turned back to her. "Iris, I'm honored to introduce you to Magical Sparkle Princess Bubba, a dear old friend. I'm fantastic, Bubba. Never better. You?"

The gargantuan cross-dressing cosplayer smiled. "Life is good. You said her name is Iris? Nice to meet you, miss."

She shook his hand. "Likewise! I just moved here, so I'm still meeting everyone for the first time. Love the outfit!"

Bubba did a little twirl and posed, giving Iris a salute with his baton. "Why, thank you. Any friend of Felix's is a friend of mine."

Iris saluted back. "Amen to that. Are you part of the convention staff?"

"Yup! I'm with security. In fact, I gotta head over to ops to check in and get my radio, so I'm off. I'll see you both around!" With a wave and another playful twirl of his skirt, Bubba headed out.

"Felix, I'm so glad to meet more of your friends."

"Yeah, me, too! You'll get to meet even more soon."

"Well, I'm very glad to see that you two have hit it off so well!"
"Aunt Abby!" Iris turned to sweep her aunt into a hug.

CHAPTER THIRTY-TWO

RACHEL

As Rachel settled into one of the hotel's large, padded hallway chairs, a voice spoke from behind her. "I was starting to worry you didn't like me anymore."

She craned her neck to find Edie standing behind her. "Edie! What in the world gave you that idea?"

Vaulting over the back of the neighboring chair, the tall blonde then fell back into the thick padding with a loud *woomph*. "You ditched me. Twice. In one day." Crossing her arms in front of her, Edie's face twisted into a frustrated pout.

Rachel opened her mouth to respond, but paused. After a moment, she closed it again as she watched her friend carefully. *It doesn't matter that I walked out of panels where nothing was going on, or that I had something amazing happening that couldn't wait. All Edie knows is that she's hurting.* She started anew. "Yeah, I did. I could try and justify it five different ways, but it still made you feel left out, huh? I'm sorry about that."

"Thank you." Edie shifted position in her chair, crossing and uncrossing her legs a few times. "Look, I don't mean to be a bitch about it."

"You're not. I get it."

"Do you?" Edie ran her fingers through her hair in frustration. "I don't think you do, Rachel. Look, when we hang out online, I love roleplaying with you. You're a great storyteller, and you're really, really considerate of making sure everyone's having a good time in the game. When we talk on chatrooms or forums or wherever, I could talk to you for hours. None of the other girls in my school give a rat's ass about anything I care about, like anime, or boxing classes, or sculpture. They just want to shop and surf and go parading for boys like a pack of *putas*, and so the only real friends I have are online."

Rachel bit her lip, unsure what to say.

"You're my best friend in the world, Rachel." Edie leaned back in her chair. "You have been since we first met online a year and a half ago. It hurts that I'm not your best friend. I'm an afterthought, a sidekick. And the award for Best Supporting Fifth Wheel goes to...Edie Vasquez! Woohoo!"

"Oh, man." Rachel squeezed Edie's hand, who squeezed back gratefully. "I'm so, *so* sorry. You're awesome. You're not...an afterthought."

Edie frowned. "I'm not book smart like Adelaide. I'm not all cool and collected like Michelle. My best costumes look like cardboard trash next to stuff Raeshawn puts together in his sleep. You've known all of them longer than me, and because I can only afford to go to one major con a year that isn't right in San Simeon, I don't even get to see you in person as much as everyone else does. When I do get to see you—"

"I bailed. Shit."

"And you know what the worst part of it is?" Edie stood, pacing back and forth for a moment, then stopped in front of Rachel. "It's not even fair for me to be mad at you!"

"What?" Rachel was thoroughly lost.

"I mean, did you see yourself when you were walking down the hall just now? I did! You were almost skipping with a glowing smile! You were practically pulling a Snow White where little bunnies and kittens and bluebirds all start flocking to you because you're just so damn happy!"

Edie leaned forward, her arms on the armrests of Rachel's chair, looming over her. "You look exactly like what my big sister Esther looked like after she met Sunil, who went on to make her the happiest woman on the planet. You met someone today. Two someone's, judging by those kisses you gave out before, and what sort of bitch would I be if I tried to take that away from you?"

Rachel jumped to her feet and wrapped Edie in a tight hug, who immediately started bawling on her shoulder.

The other congoers milling around the hallway gave the pair a polite distance, mostly avoiding staring or walking too closely as Edie shook in Rachel's arms.

After a moment, an athletic woman with a red security cap and a U.S. Army t-shirt walked by. "Ah, pardon me, ladies. My name's Kalli. I'm with Convention Security, and we heard some raised voices over here. Is everything okay?"

Edie stood, wiping her eyes. "I'm sorry. I didn't mean to be that loud, I was...I'm okay, really."

Kalli nodded, and turned to face Rachel when she suddenly froze, staring in surprise at Rachel and her outfit.

"Um, is something wrong?" Rachel looked down at herself, but her Ruby Rose cosplay looked intact. Nothing was out of place.

The security guard looked to be wrestling with a difficult decision. "Do you...do you know Fe... No." The woman suddenly backed away, holding up a hand apologetically. "Sorry, never mind, and please forget I said anything. That was inappropriate of me." She turned and walked away, her back taut with obvious stress.

After a confused pause, Edie spoke up first. "What was that about?"

Rachel bit her lip. "I'm afraid to ask."

CHAPTER THIRTY-THREE

IRIS

"Aunt Abby!" Iris swept her aunt into a hug. "What are you doing here?"

As Marcus and their two daughters filed in after her, her aunt returned the hug in kind. "Well, we just came from a lovely panel about cosplaying on a limited budget, and we thought we'd see how you were doing."

Iris raised her eyebrows in surprise. "How'd you know I was here, though?"

Angelica lightly punched Iris in the hip. "Well, when *someone* didn't answer any of our texts, we figured that you might be with Felix."

Iris pulled her phone out of her pocket, and blanched at the multiple text notifications she'd missed. "Whoops."

Little Tracy had walked past Iris, and was giving Felix a grim stare as he sat behind the table. "I asked a security guard if they knew where Felix Jackson would be, and he pointed us here, saying that you'd probably be here with your new girlfriend." Tracy's eyes narrowed. "That *better* be my cousin they were talking about."

Eyeing the rest of the Weinberg family with a nervous smile, the towering Marcus in particular, Felix nodded agreement. "Word gets around fast, it seems."

Iris gently grabbed Tracy by the shoulders, steering her away from staring a hole through Felix's head. "Tracy, please don't threaten my new boyfriend with bodily harm, okay?"

Marcus stepped forward with an open hand.

Felix stood to meet his handshake.

"Nice to see that you two hit it off so nicely. Does this mean we should be having you over for dinner sometime soon?"

Obviously agog at being face-to-face with a favorite celebrity, Felix gave a stiff nod. "I'd be honored, sir."

Marcus studied Felix's face for a moment, and then turned to look at Iris. "Did you tell him, or is this disguise just not working?"

"I told Felix about how you helped me move here from New York, so it kinda came up." Iris put a hand on Felix's shoulder. "Please don't body slam my boyfriend."

Felix put his hands up in apology. "I swear, I haven't told anyone. You came to the con incognito, and I intend to respect that." He wiped sweat off his brow. "If I may, I'll just say I've been a fan ever since I first saw footage of your Hellbreaker Suplex a few years ago, and I'll leave it at that."

Marcus just laughed. "It's cool, Felix, don't sweat it. And thank you, it's always nice to meet a fan, especially a polite one."

"Did any of you want to register for the costume contest tomorrow night?" Felix held up a clipboard. "You've all done amazing work, honestly."

Angelica gently pushed the clipboard away, but with a regretful look on her face. "I totally would, but we won't be here that late tomorrow night." She gave her parents a frown. "Unfortunately."

Iris looked back and forth between Abby and Marcus. "What's the plan for tonight?"

Abby checked the calendar on her phone. "Well, Tracy wanted to attend the Learn How to Play Go and Shogi demonstrations, which start in half an hour, so Marcus was going to take her to that while Angelica and I meet some of her friends in the video game room. After that, we were going to get dinner in the hotel restaurant."

"If I might make a suggestion?" Felix picked up a pen. "While I love the folks who run this hotel, I have to admit that the restaurant here isn't really that good, especially for what they charge. Do you like Chinese food?"

Abby nodded. "Very much so."

Felix grabbed a spare sheet of paper and wrote down an address. "Type this into your phone for directions. It's on a back road and easy to miss, but it's within walking distance. The place is called Emperor's Delight. It looks like a shabby hole-in-the-wall, and the decor is pretty drab, but the food will knock you into next week." He handed Abby the paper. "I especially recommend anything with barbeque pork in it, and their soup dumplings are extremely tasty."

Abby folded the paper and slipped it into her purse. "I'm always on the lookout for new places to try, so thank you very much for the suggestion."

"*Oh*! That reminds me! Felix, can I grab one from the cooler?" Iris dashed over to the corner, lifting the lid. At Felix's affirmative nod, she pulled a chicken salad on honey wheat sandwich out of its bag, and handed a half of it to her aunt. "You need to try this right now."

Abby looked skeptical, but took a small nibble, and moments later, her eyes nearly popped out of her head. Swallowing carefully, Abby turned to face Felix. "Cold but spicy, nicely moist chicken meat, and absolutely perfect mayonnaise. Felix, did you make this?"

Angelica sniffed at the other half in the bag Iris still held. "Spicy? I'll pass."

"Sorry, not me." Felix grinned. "Prowl made that. It's his signature recipe, and before you ask, he guards that recipe very, very carefully."

"Prowl made this?" Angelica immediately reached into the bag and tore off a section, jamming it into her mouth. "I think I love spicy food now."

As Iris divided up the rest of the sandwich between Marcus and Tracy, Abby wrote down her phone number on another piece of scratch paper. "Felix, please ask Prowl to call me after the con. I have a pizza recipe that I'm quite proud of. If he might be interested in a trade, I'd very much look forward to that."

Felix smiled. "I'll see what I can do, Mrs. Weinberg."

"Aunt Abby, Uncle Marcus, I need to ask you a favor." Iris clasped her hands under her chin in supplication. "You're going back home after dinner, right? I was wondering, could I come back with you, put together an overnight bag, and then get a ride back?"

Tracy looked up, talking around a mouthful of chicken salad. "Ooh, are you having a slumber party? Can I come, too?"

"I'll handle this one." Angelica put a hand on top of Tracy's head. "Tracy, they're going to have a *grown up* slumber party. Where they talk about politics, taxes, elections, and stupid adult stuff. You'd be bored." She threw Iris a wink when Tracy wasn't looking.

"Oh, fine." Tracy folded her arms and pouted. "But Felix has to answer one important question, so I know he's okay." She looked at him, and adjusted the brim of her Jojo cap. "Answer carefully, mister. If the Mane Six were to have a throw-down fight to the death amongst themselves, who would be the Last Pony Standing, and why?"

Felix sat on the edge of the table, grinning. "A worthy question, Miss Weinberg." He seemed to think for a short moment. "Pinkie, definitely. Beneath that bubbly exterior, she's got a lot of pent-up anger and a painful past, and if things have gone so bad that they're fighting to the death, she'll fight without quarter or hesitation." Giving Iris a grin, who was rolling her eyes at this, he continued. "But the fact she can predict the future *and* warp reality to suit her needs is what really makes her dangerous. All the big attacks in the world don't mean a thing if every pony keeps missing."

Tracy nodded thoughtfully. "I still think that the Sonic Rainboom is the great equalizer in such fights, but you make a compelling argument." She turned to her cousin. "I approve of your boyfriend, Iris."

Iris pulled Tracy into a huge hug. "Thank you for your blessing, and I'll tell you what—sometime next week, real soon, we'll have a slumber party in my room, you, me, and Angie, and we can watch the DKD dub together. I know you've really wanted to watch that with me, and thanks to Felix helping me feel better about things, now we can."

Behind Iris, Abby and Marcus took particular note of this last statement, and looked at Felix with impressed interest.

Marcus stepped forward. "Iris, I'll be glad to drive you. While you're packing, I'll take a quick shower to get rid of this makeup, and then I'll drop you off back here. On that note, we should get going so that we're not late for those demonstrations. Felix, nice to see you again. We'll catch up more later."

After the Weinbergs had filed out, Felix sat in his chair. "I think I managed okay there. What do you think?"

Iris ran her fingers through Felix's hair, and kissed his forehead before she sat next to him. "They really like you, I can tell. But that does mean you're going to have to come over for dinner sometime soon for Round Two."

Felix laughed nervously, and switched to a game-show announcer voice. "Ah yes, the legendary lightning round, where the questions get pointed and the stakes grow ever higher! Big Money! Big Prizes! I Love It!"

Two young women walked in, both wearing costumes from *Sailor Moon*.

"Uh, is this where we register for the Costume Contest?"

Felix waved them over. "Absolutely, come on in! I've got some forms you'll need to fill out, and then we'll cover some of the basic details."

Iris cocked her head to one side, chuckling to herself as she recognized the Mercury cosplayer from earlier that morning.

"I'm Iris." She held out a hand. "What's your name?"

The young woman nearly did a double-take as she seemingly recognized Iris. "You're the girl in that beautiful green armor at the registration desk!" She blushed as she shook Iris's hand. "Um, Mercy. Mercy Norelli. H-hi."

"Hi." Iris flashed her a wide grin. "Just so you know, I did notice you this morning. And I have to say, you look fantastic in blue."

CHAPTER THIRTY-FOUR

RACHEL

"And while we're on the subject on different kinds of fun at a convention, it's time to address the elephant in the room." Michelle stood against the back wall of an empty panel room, speaking directly to her camera, which Edie was operating. "Convention romance. There's no need to get into salacious detail here, but let's be honest. It happens. Sometimes, you just meet someone who knocks you off your feet, and before you know it, you're sharing a tender kiss in the back row of a video room."

Michelle gestured to an empty space on the wall next to her. "No matter what, *this* is still the first rule. No means no. If you're with someone who doesn't listen when you say no, get out of there immediately. If someone says no to you, pay attention and stop.

"On the other hand." Michelle broke into a wide grin. "If everyone's happy and things are going in certain directions, then it's time to talk about safe sex. Guys, it's never a bad idea to have a package of condoms in your suitcase. Ladies, that's a good idea for you, as well. If you're on the pill, make sure to take it with you to the con, and take those pills on time.

"On the *other*-other hand, or the gripping hand as some old-school SF fans like to say, who says sex has to enter into it at all? Maybe you just want to kiss a bit. Maybe you just want someone to hold you. Intimacy can mean a lot of different things, and the only person who gets to decide what's right for you, is you." Michelle held up her hands in a wide shrug, still smiling for the camera. "And maybe what's right for you is not to bother with romance at a con at all, and just enjoy the anime, the good times with friends, the guest panels, and the vast array of fun to be had at a con."

Michelle made a show of pointing at her wrist, despite not wearing a watch. "Well, that's all we've got time for right now. Before we sign off, I'd like to give a big shout-out to the super-friendly staff here at Anime Horde, and in particular to Felix Jackson, the master of ceremonies for this con. If you get a chance to attend any of the costume contests he hosts, you should absolutely go for it, because he makes it a fantastic experience not just for the audience, but for the cosplayers taking part, like myself and my friends.

"Now, if you'd like to see a future episode that talks more about convention romance, or any of the other side topics we've discussed today, leave a comment below and say so!" She pointed down. "If you're enjoying the show, don't forget to hit Like and Subscribe. I have to tell you, I'm so thrilled and flattered we hit fifty thousand subscribers this week! This is Michelle Liang, heading out from the west coast and into a convention near you, for another Journey From the West—and this is day one of Anime Horde. Have a great time with whatever you're doing, and be excellent to each other!"

After a brief pause, Edie put the camera down. "Awesome take, Michelle. Adelaide finished the No Means No graphic already, so I'll insert that next to your right hand for that bit before we post this tonight."

Michelle unwrapped a lozenge and popped it into her mouth. "Sounds great! I had an idea for a thing for tomorrow morning, so I want your opinions on this."

As Michelle and Edie brainstormed, Adelaide, Raeshawn, and Rachel were sitting off to one side, watching. Raeshawn stood, stretched, and walked over towards Michelle. "Hold up, let me get in on this pow-wow. I've got some ideas, too."

Adelaide watched Raeshawn walk away, and then looked at Rachel, sitting on her left.

Taking off her glasses to clean them with a small cloth from her pocket, Adelaide leaned in Rachel's direction to give a quiet whisper. "So, how's it feel to lose your virginity?"

Rachel licked her lips and smiled. "Oh, that's not happening until tonight, and I can't wa—" She suddenly blinked and sat up. "*Oh, God*. I mean. Um. Heh."

"Is that so?" Adelaide donned her glasses again and gave a quiet laugh. "Wow, you're something else. I didn't think you'd actually answer that."

Rachel looked down and tried to busy her hands by smoothing out her skirt. "I, ah, zoned out there, I guess."

"Looks like I owe Michelle and Raeshawn five bucks each." Adelaide turned in her chair to face Rachel. "When we left you behind in Felix's office, I was convinced you were about to drop your panties for that man, but they disagreed."

Rachel squirmed in her seat, forcibly reminded of her silk underwear now residing in Felix's pocket, and not under her skirt. "I'll just say we shared a moment, and leave it at that."

"A moment that led to your planning your own deflowering tonight, eh?"

"I can't believe I said that out loud. *Do not* repeat that, please." Rachel's cheeks were flaming hot.

"No worries, Midnight." Adelaide pulled out her phone to check her schedule. "You know, now that I think about it, you could probably take him back to your room tonight. Michelle and Raeshawn were talking about hitting the dance tonight while Edie and I go to the board game tournaments. We were all going to work on the latest Journey video in our room afterwards, so Michelle won't be back to your and her room for hours, easy. Plenty of time."

Rachel thought it over. "That's...that's a really good idea. Felix is probably rooming with Prowl, so his room is out, and we hadn't worked out where yet."

"Glad to help." Adelaide patted Rachel's shoulder. "How on earth did you manage to steal him away from that curly-haired white girl, though?"

"Um." Rachel grinned nervously. "I didn't. She's going to be there, too."

"My goodness. The last virgin of our little troupe, and she's gonna go out with one hell of a bang." Adelaide licked her lips. "Can I tell you a secret?"

Rachel nodded.

"You're in for a treat. Threesomes are goddamn amazing."

Rachel's jaw hit the floor. "You?"

Adelaide nodded with a huge smile.

"Who? When?"

"When was last Halloween after the party in my dorm, but I'm not going to tell you who. Well, my sweetheart Harris was one of 'em, obviously, but you don't know the other guy, and he's kinda shy. I will say if you get a chance to have two people kissing you all over at the same time, slipping into you at the same time, *go for it*. Best night of my life, a *very* Happy Halloween indeed." Adelaide hugged herself. "You'll have to let me know how this turns out."

Rachel could only shake her head and laugh. "Everything I thought I knew was wrong. Wow."

"*Oy*, Rachel!"

Rachel looked and Michelle held up her phone. "Your sweetheart just texted. He wants us to come meet him and this Iris lady at the mezzanine lounge in twenty. You up for it?"

CHAPTER THIRTY-FIVE

BIANCA

As Bianca entered the Costume Contest office, she paused only long enough to wave to Felix and Iris before heading straight to the blue cooler in the corner. "Prowl, why didn't you tell me you'd made a batch? I would've left room for 'em if I'd known!"

Iris laughed from where she sat at the table. "Ah, a fellow worshipper at the Altar of the Prowl Sandwich, I see. Don't worry, there's plenty more chicken salad left."

"To hell with that!" Bianca went digging in the cooler. "Where's my...aha!" Pulling forth and holding aloft one bag with a triumphant flourish, Bianca stood back up. "Canadian bacon with Ezekiel bread, toasted. My freaking kryptonite." She opened the bag, and inhaled deeply. "Oh, and you're still using that onion spread on it. Prowl, I love you."

Prowl smiled as he walked in. "I knew you only loved me for my kitchen."

"That's not true!" Bianca mock-pouted, blinking coquettishly. "It's all the little secret goodies in your basement deep-freeze that truly hold my heart." She walked back over to where he was standing, and gave him a gentle kiss on the lips, which he returned with a happy murmur.

"I can't tell you how happy the sight of you two makes me, seriously." Felix grinned from ear-to-ear. "Eight long years of bad timing, and now this. You two are far too cute together."

Iris raised an eyebrow. "Eight years?"

Bianca nodded. "Long story, but yeah. We three all met at college, and were damn near inseparable from freshman orientation to graduation. Folks called us the Three Musketeers, even, but as much as Prowl and I desperately wanted each other, it never worked out. First, I was dating someone else, then he was, then I was again. Back and forth for years." She put her arms around Prowl, and kissed the tip of his nose. "Nothing in our way anymore, thank God."

"If you three were all so close, did you and Felix here ever date?" Iris leaned her head on Felix's shoulder, who rolled his eyes at her question, albeit with a smile. "What? I want to hear all the best stories of your wild college days."

Prowl chuckled. "I wouldn't call it dating."

Iris sat up. "Ooh, I smell a *good* story now. C'mon, someone tell me!"

Felix shrugged. "Bianca, if you're cool with recounting the Night of Infamy, I don't mind."

"Oh, so it's *my* job to spill your sordid history, now?" Bianca grabbed an empty chair next to Iris. "Actually, it'll be fun to tell this. It was such a goofy night, but it's not really a tale for polite company."

Prowl retrieved a sandwich for himself, and sat down on another chair nearby. "That's one way to put it. The aftermath was the only time Felix and I damn near came to blows, but in a weird way, we became better friends for it. Go figure."

Iris sat forward, elbows on the table. "Oh man, I can't wait to hear this now. Does this mean I get to be D'Artagnen to your musketeers once I've heard the tale?"

Bianca pulled off her t-shirt to once again reveal her swimsuit costume, and fanned herself with a stack of contest forms.

"Well, first a little set-up. Every time Valentine's Day would come around on campus, a bunch of us who were single would get together and have a Night of Debauchery, or Anti-Valentine party."

Felix chimed in. "Basically, we'd rent some deliberately cheesy porn videos from the local video store, buy a pile of junk food, and spend the evening giving the porn the *Mystery Science Theater* treatment, to take our mind off of being single."

"Hey, I said I was going to tell this!" Bianca threw her shirt at Felix's face, whose laugh was muffled by the impact. "But that's about right. Our sophomore year, we actually had like fifteen folks all crammed into the dorm TV lounge for one of these parties, but this particular tale was in our junior year."

"This sweetheart was dating a certain horrific bitch at the time." She pointed to Prowl. "Who wound up cheating on him two months later, and then getting her ass kicked by me, which is another story for later, so he was ineligible for the Anti-Valentine party." She pointed to Felix next. "He'd just been dumped by Anissa, since she was about to graduate and didn't want to do the long-distance thing, so he was super-maudlin and kinda weepy still."

"Guilty." Felix leaned back in his chair. "The poetry I wrote in my grief back then was just inexcusably stupid. Words like 'My Ebon-Skinned Angel' or 'Her eyes like coals, they lit upon my soul', and other ridiculous tripe. Oh, it was pathetic."

Iris covered her mouth with her hand, barely holding back a howl of laughter. "*Please* tell me you still have these poems. I have to see these."

"You know, I might..."

Bianca cut in. "But we digress! As for myself, I'd been single for something like six months, trying to get my grades up, and was so damn horny, I had nearly worked up the nerve to buy my first vibrator, and then the party happened."

Prowl swallowed a bite of his sandwich. "Not really a party, honestly. It was just the two of you."

"Not for lack of trying." Bianca leaned back in her seat now, staring at the ceiling in memory. "Everyone was getting lucky that year. Jody and Karl had finally both come out and admitted they wanted to bang each other into oblivion. Toby had hit it off with that cute freshman chick, whose name escapes me…"

"Chloe Lagana." Felix snapped his fingers as the memory hit him. "They bonded over his *G.I. Joe* collection, remember?"

"Right, right." Bianca nodded and stretched in her chair.

"Anyway, everyone else in our group was actually dating someone for once, so that left just Felix and me to celebrate Anti-Valentine's together, and since we'd both finally turned twenty-one, we decided to booze it up for good measure."

"I think I can see where this is going, but don't stop, this is great!" Iris turned around and gave Felix another kiss. "Thank you for sharing this with me, handsome."

Bianca grinned as she watched the kiss. "So, there we were, in Felix's dorm room, watching bad porn, eating bad food, and drinking bad booze. No one else around, even his roommate Freddie had bailed, spending the night at his boyfriend's apartment." She sat back up, smiling. "We're commiserating over being single, we're just laughing it up, we're all relaxed from being friends for a couple of years already, and we're drunk. Suddenly, I blurt out how I hadn't had anyone lick my pussy in months, since we're watching an oral scene in the movie, and Felix oh-so-politely volunteers."

"In my foggy mental state, it seemed like the gentlemanly thing to do, to help out a friend. No, I'm serious!"

"Well, regardless of his motives, I took him up on it, and now he's under my skirt, and we're just drunkenly throwing ourselves at each other." Bianca cupped her hands underneath her breasts. "He'd spent the last two and a half years trying not to stare too much at my tits, and I'd whipped off my top and bra. He was as happy as a lotto winner." She paused, noting Iris's gaze watching her chest, and smirked. "Now, on my end, if he thought he was just being polite, I was trying to tell myself I was helping him out by taking his mind off Anissa—even though, really, I just wanted to get laid."

"Nothing wrong with that," Felix quipped. "At this point, we were just wasted enough we got this idea it'd be fun to re-enact the porn on the TV. If they're doing missionary, we'd do missionary. If they did reverse cowgirl, so would we. That sort of thing, and it was fun."

Bianca looked right into Iris's eyes. "As I'm sure you've found out, D'Artagnen, Felix does have some nice skills in bed. His first girl, Lydia, trained him pretty well."

"Point of order. We trained each other." Felix smiled. "She was just as much a virgin as I was at the time."

Bianca nodded, never taking her eyes off Iris, her fingertips idly tracing along the curve of her breast. "And that's when the girl on the screen bent over her couch and took the dude's ten-inch ramrod right up her ass. And drunk idiots that we were, monkey-see, monkey-do, we try that ourselves."

Prowl laughed. "This still cracks me up. You'd have thought that at least one of you would've known you needed lube for that."

Felix smiled. "I was so drunk, I'm frankly amazed I remembered my own name at the time."

"And I had never tried anal before, so I had no clue." Bianca licked her lips. "I bent over, and Felix shoved it right in like I asked him to, and that sobered us both right up. Ow."

"Maybe not sobered, but certainly a wake-up call." Felix winced. "It sort of shook us out of the moment. After she yelped loud enough to wake the dead, I pulled out, and I remember mumbling about *let's do other stuff instead*, and we fooled around for a little bit more before falling asleep in bed together."

Bianca let her gaze glide across Iris's figure, especially the scoop neckline of her tank top. "The next morning, it was kinda awkward. I mean, it was a fun one night stand, except for the butt part, but now that we'd sobered up and fucked our respective craziness out of our heads, we both just looked at each other and agreed that we liked being friends a lot more than sex partners."

Felix traced his fingers down Iris's back, who shivered in response. "I was so hung over and freaked out by the whole thing that I had to tell someone, so I knocked on Prowl's door and told him. I distinctly remember what I said when he first opened the door. 'Prowl, I just had buttsex with Bianca, and it was weird.' Oh man, the look on his face. He damn near clocked me right then and there."

"But I didn't!" Prowl said. "I mean, sure, I was upset you'd slept with her when I'd been wanting her for two plus years, but just as quickly, I was like, why am I pissed, I have a girl-friend already. I called up Bianca, and the three of us huddled in my room, talking about the whole thing while I whipped up hangover cures for these two. Since then, we've been able to talk about absolutely anything, just about, so it worked out really well."

"Aside from my not being able to walk straight for the whole damn weekend, that is." Bianca straightened. "But, thus endeth the story."

"Thank you for that!" Iris adjusted the strap of her tank top. "I've got some good ones to tell myself, but I think I'll save some of those for the next party we all have down the road. Don't want to dish all the best stuff right away, right?"

Prowl stood and threw his empty sandwich bag in the trash. "Are you two sticking around, or are you gonna walk the con for a bit?"

Felix stood as well, pulling out his phone. "Stretching my legs with a walk would be nice, actually, and Michelle said she wanted to meet Iris and hang out for a bit today. I should text her to let her know we're free. How's that sound for you, Iris?"

A big stretch, and Iris laughed. "I'm all for it, especially if Rachel's there."

Tapping a message into his phone, Felix nodded. "The mez-zanine lounge should work for that...and sent."

"Isn't that where we got cranberry juice spilled on each other?"

Bianca and Prowl exchanged looks of raised eyebrows, and Prowl spoke up first. "Is that a euphemism, Felix?"

"Nope, literal truth." Felix grabbed his suit jacket. "I'll tell you both about it later. Iris, let's run to my room real quick so I can change clothes, then we'll head back down to the lounge. I told them we'd be about twenty minutes, so that should be enough time to change." He turned and waved to his best friends. "Catch you two later!"

"Thanks again for the great story, Bianca." Iris waved as well, as she slipped an arm around Felix's waist. "Just an F.Y.I., Prowl, my aunt really wants to trade recipes with you, just so you know."

After Felix and Iris had left, Prowl sat down in one of the chairs behind the registration desk and tidied up some of the papers laid out there. "Think they were doin' it in here before we showed up?"

Bianca put her t-shirt back on. "Uh-huh. I've never seen Felix look so relaxed. I have to admit, the more I talk to Iris, the more I like her."

"Uh-huh, I saw those looks you two were giving each other." His shoulders shook with a laugh. "Should I be worried she's gonna steal you away before you and I even get started?"

"I wouldn't go that far, but if I was going to try kissing a girl for the first time, I wouldn't mind it being her." She looked sidelong at him to watch his reaction, and wasn't disappointed.

He set down the stack of papers he was fixing, and loudly exhaled. "Now that is one hell of a hot mental image. Hoo, boy."

Bianca licked her lips, and smiled.

CHAPTER THIRTY-SIX

IRIS

"So, where do you know all these folks from?" Iris had changed back into her Bronwyn armor after fixing the minor damage from earlier. The elevators seemed to be taking forever to show up.

"Well, let's see." Felix had changed into some khaki docker pants and a black polo with the Anime Horde logo on the left breast, and a pair of black shoes. "Michelle and Raeshawn are from San Francisco. They've been coming to the con every year for something like five years now, entering the costume contest each time. We got to talking backstage after their second show. Raeshawn makes the best costumes I've ever seen, and he's won a lot of awards here."

The elevator finally arrived, and Iris playfully tapped the Mezzanine button with her war staff. "While I was under the table, I heard Michelle say something about making a show?"

"Heh, yeah. A little over two years ago, Michelle created a YouTube show called *Journey From the West*, where she travels to different cons all over the US and Canada, and talks about all the ins and outs of life at a con, or fandom in general." As the glass elevator descended, Felix looked out into the open-air atrium. "It's doing pretty well, I hear."

"And the other two girls?"

Felix craned his neck as if looking to spot his friends. "Edie's from somewhere up the California coast. She became part of Michelle's crew last year, which is when I met her. She's nice, but we haven't talked as much. Adelaide's a couple years older than the others. She's already in college, also in the Bay Area, and she's been doing the graphic design for Michelle's show since last year." He laughed nervously. "I tried to flirt with Adelaide a bit last year, but she shut me down gently. She's got a very serious boyfriend named Harris."

As the elevator door opened, the noise from the hotel poured in.

"Why didn't Harris come to the con, then?" Iris looked around, trying to get her bearings. "Is he not into anime?"

Felix pointed left, towards the restaurant lounge area. "Oh no, he loves it, but Adelaide said he's terrified of flying. I've talked with him online a little. He and Adelaide are really cute together." He turned and looked to Iris as convention-goers drifted around them on the open air floor. "I guess Rachel told you about how I helped her out a couple years ago?"

"She sure did. We covered a lot of ground in just one hour." As they approached the lounge, she reached out and clasped Felix's hand with her left and her war staff with her right. "Okay, let's do this."

"Don't worry, beautiful." Felix squeezed her hand. "This isn't an audition." He pulled Iris as he headed towards the group's table.

Rachel jogged towards Felix and Iris. As she reached them, she slowed down, and took both of them by the hand. "Good to see you again," she whispered with a shy smile. "I know it's only been a little while, but I was missing you already."

"Same here, princess," Iris whispered back. "So, how much do your friends know?"

Rachel bit her lip. "Let's not advertise tonight's plans just yet. I mean, I don't think they'll care, but..." She squeezed their hands. "Tonight is about us, not them."

Felix squeezed back. "Tonight is about you, Rachel. It's your call. We'll follow your lead."

Rachel turned around, and led Felix and Iris the rest of the way back to the large table Michelle had commandeered. "Everyone, you know Felix already, of course, but let me introduce you to Iris Weinberg. Who not only makes awesome cosplay armor, but is herself, awesome. Iris, meet the *Journey From the West* crew."

CHAPTER THIRTY-SEVEN

FELIX

Leaning back against the padded restaurant bench, Felix gave a happy sigh of contentment. To his right, Iris was deep in conversation with Raeshawn and Michelle about the mechanics of costume construction, holding out her helmet and talking about what she'd done to make it. On his left, Rachel was leaning against him as they chatted with Edie and Adelaide.

"As far as I'm concerned, this third season of *RWBY* is basically the *Empire Strikes Back* part of the story." Edie leaned forward, counting off talking points on her fingers. "You're seeing characters disillusioned, the institutions are breaking down, the villains are getting what they want, heroes are getting maimed and killed, the stakes have risen, but despite that downer ending, I think the next season is going to be a big turnaround. They had to bring things down in order to make the inevitable victory all the more meaningful and sweet."

Felix raised his glass. "Agreed on all points, but speaking of downers, here's to Monty Oum. Rest in peace."

The three women nodded solemnly, raising their own drinks. Adelaide pulled off her glasses and rubbed her eyes. "Still tears me up a bit to think about it, even though it's been over a year since he passed. The thought of dying so young and so suddenly, when you still have a lot left to give? I had nightmares about that for a week afterwards." She put her glasses back on with a sigh. "At least his friends had enough notes and such to keep *RWBY* going, and they've been doing pretty well so far. Here's hoping his legacy continues at that pace."

The quartet sipped at their drinks, and were silent for a moment.

Rachel broke the silence first. "Okay, on happier notes—Edie, you said you joined a new boxing gym in San Simeon, right? Let's hear more about that!"

As the tall blonde eagerly dove into her description of said gym, Felix glanced around the mezzanine, and his eyes lit up as he spotted someone in particular. "Hey, I'll be right back. Adelaide, I need you to do something for me. Keep Michelle distracted for a minute until I get back. Don't let her see where I'm going."

Adelaide looked to where Felix's gaze fell, and smiled. "Can do. Go, go, go!" While Edie and Rachel continued their conversation, she got up and walked over towards Michelle as if to listen in on her discussion of hair treatments, conveniently blocking Michelle's line of sight in Felix's direction.

Felix quietly stood up, and quickly walked to where two people were ambling through the mezzanine. One was a short man in his late thirties with glasses, a light brown beard and mustache, and carrying an oversized water bottle in his left hand. The other was a willowy short-haired redheaded woman in her late twenties, a head taller than her husband. Both were dressed casually, taking in the sights as they walked through the crowds.

As Felix approached, he circled around to face them from the front. "Lazlo, Christy! How's the con so far?"

Lazlo Akers's mouth spread into a huge smile, and he walked forward to embrace Felix in a big hug. "Felix! Oh, it's been great. Your staff has been phenomenal. I was worried we wouldn't get to catch up this weekend!"

Christy joined in the hug, giving Felix a quick kiss on the cheek. "Lydia sends her love. She expressly asked me to give you that kiss when I saw you."

"Aww, I miss her, too. May I send a reply?" Christy grinned and offered her cheek, which Felix gave a friendly smooch. "How's she doing at med school?"

"Exhausting but amazing is her exact answer to that whenever anyone asks. She's really in her element." Lazlo patted Felix on the shoulder. "As are you! Look at you, all smooth and smiling. Let me guess—did you meet someone?"

Felix couldn't help but bark a quick laugh. "Is it that obvious? Yeah, it just happened this morning. I'm still figuring it out. Hey, I actually had a question for you. Are you two heading anywhere in particular right now?"

As Lazlo took a sip from his bottle, Christy checked a paper schedule she retrieved from her pocket. "We've got a couple of hours before Lazlo's first autograph session, so we were just wandering around for a bit. What's on your mind?"

"Well, aside from catching up with you two in general, there's someone who I'd like to introduce you to."

"Your new girlfriend?" Lazlo chuckled. "Lydia will want to hear all about this woman, you realize."

"Well, her, as well, yeah." He gestured towards where his friends were sitting in the lounge. "But one of our con regulars, who's also a friend of mine, is probably your biggest fan. It would make her entire year if you came over to say hi."

Lazlo looked over to where Felix was pointing. "I think I saw some of those costumes at the panel, yeah. Which one in particular?"

"The one with the white hair. Her name's Michelle Liang."

"Oh, from *Journey From the West*!" Lazlo snapped his fingers. "I thought she looked familiar. I couldn't recognize her with the cosplay hair thing going on."

Felix's jaw fell in surprise. "You know about her show?"

"Oh, yeah! We're big fans. She's doing great stuff." Lazlo took another sip from his bottle. "So, you going to introduce us?"

Christy nodded. "Heck, we want *her* autograph!"

"Okay, I take it back." Felix grinned as he started to lead the pair towards the restaurant. "You're not going to make her year, you're going to make her decade."

As Felix drew closer, approaching Michelle from behind as she was talking to Iris, Raeshawn spotted him, and then who was walking behind him. His eyes went wide, flickering to Michelle, his lips clamped shut. Rachel and Edie were both staring in surprise, recognizing full well the pair in tow behind Felix.

"Hey, Michelle?" Felix tapped her on the shoulder. "Sorry to interrupt, but I wanted to introduce you to an old friend of mine."

Michelle turned around with a smile...

"Hi! Michelle, my name's Lazlo, and I'm so pleased to meet the hostess of *Journey From the West*. Mind if we join you guys for a few?"

The table was completely silent, everyone watching Michelle's reaction.

Her mouth opened and closed a few times, as if unable to form words. She held up one finger, turned away, and gulped down a mouthful of her ginger ale before turning back. "You're Lazlo Akers."

"Yup!"

She looked behind him to his wife standing there. "And you're Christy Akers."

Christy waved, clearly enjoying the moment. "We're huge fans."

Michelle's eyes crossed for a moment, as if someone had just poked her in the forehead. "My favorite voice actor and director.

And my favorite webcomic artist. Are fans? Of *me*." Her eyes uncrossed, and she grabbed the armrest of her chair for support. "Oh. My. *God*!" She gestured to the row of tables, chairs, and the large, padded bench. "By all means, join us, please!"

As Lazlo and Christy gratefully took a seat, Michelle reached out and grabbed Felix by the forearm. "What do you mean, old friend?"

"Well," Felix said with a sheepish smile, "I used to date his little sister back in college."

Michelle stared hard into his eyes, and let go of his arm, but pointed right at him with one long-nailed finger. "I'm going to have a word with you later."

Felix watched happily as Michelle and the rest of her crew fell into conversation with Lazlo shortly afterwards, and then settled down between Iris and Rachel to watch.

Rachel snuggled in on Felix's left. "I don't think you realize just how big this is. This is going to be something Michelle remembers for the rest of her life, and did he mean it when he said he was a fan of hers?"

Christy chose that moment to sit across from Felix. "He sure did. We especially loved the episode she did last fall on bullying. Smart stuff." She held out a hand to both Rachel and Iris. "Christy Akers, pleased to meet 'cha." As both women shook the offered hands, she continued. "So, which one of you is the mysterious new girlfriend we heard about?"

Rachel blushed, but Iris answered with a huge smile, reaching out to squeeze Rachel's hand. "Oh, that's both of us. We're sharing him." As Rachel's blush reddened further and she hesitated to respond, Iris continued. "That's Rachel, and I'm..."

"Melanie Manson, right? I wasn't sure at first, but the Bronwyn armor was a big clue."

Iris went pale. "Um, how do you know that name? I'm pretty sure we've never met."

Rachel's blush faded, replaced by a look of confusion.

Felix turned to watch Iris's expression, concerned.

Christy blinked. "Oh. Shit. I put my foot in it like always, didn't I?" With a grimace, she gestured with an open hand. "A couple of months ago, we were at a con in Boston, and there was this guy in the green room from Downtown Dub-Media, a real asshole named William Worchester." Christy ran a hand through her hair. "He made a point of showing everyone his war chest photos on his phone, this collection of girls he'd met. Before we told him to buzz off, he showed us one of you, and mentioned you were the voice of Bronwyn in his DKD dub."

Iris was shaking. "He was showing photos of me? Like a trophy?"

Christy waved her hands frantically. "They weren't like nudes or anything! It was a picture of you and him sitting in his office, that's all. Oh, gosh, I am so sorry I brought this up."

Iris rubbed her gloved hands over her face for a moment. "No, that's okay. And thanks for clarifying that." She held out one hand for a new handshake. "Hi. I'm Iris Weinberg. I've done a little voice acting, yeah, but I don't use the Melanie name anymore. Worchester can die in a fire for all I care."

While this was going on, Rachel tapped Felix on the wrist, silently mouthing the words, "Iris was a voice actress?" to which Felix nodded affirmatively.

Christy nodded. "For what it's worth, Lazlo and I don't know of anyone outside of Worchester's little circle of yes-men who actually likes him. He's a pig, everyone knows it." She leaned forward, forcing a smile. "So, changing the subject. Felix, can you imagine the giggles I'm going to get from Lydia when I tell her you suddenly have not one gorgeous girlfriend, but two?"

Rachel waved her hands frantically. "That's not...I mean...I'm just...um. Friends. We're friends." She looked away.

Christy slapped a hand across her forehead. "I'm just batting a thousand tonight. First, I make Iris uncomfortable, now you, too. I am so sorry."

While Iris rose to sit on Rachel's other side and take hold of her fidgeting hands, Felix put an arm around Rachel's shoulder.

"Christy, let's just say that this is still new, and we're still figuring things out about how to frame everything. I can tell you that the three of us all have some pretty strong feelings for each other."

Rachel smiled at Felix's words, snuggling against his side again while squeezing Iris's hands in appreciation. "I worry that I'm getting in the way, like a third wheel. I mean, you two are about the same age, but I'm five years younger."

Christy held up a palm. "Okay, let me say something about that. Lazlo and I met at a con. It was a pretty whirlwind weekend for both of us, but it worked out in the end." She turned her hand around to show her wedding and engagement rings. "And as for the age thing, I'm twelve years younger than him. That age gap has never, ever been a real problem for us."

"Twelve? Seriously?" Rachel craned her neck to look over at where Lazlo was talking to Michelle and the others. "Suddenly, my worries seem, ah, not so bad. Thanks."

"Least I could do after putting my foot in my mouth and then swallowing it." Christy grinned. "I will say the three of you look really cute together."

Rachel beamed at that, but then looked away. "The thing is, I live on the west coast. They both live right here. So, I'm certainly enjoying the moment, but conventions have to end eventually, y'know?"

Iris and Felix exchanged a nod, and Iris leaned over to kiss Rachel's forehead. "Hey, no frowning now. This weekend is just getting started. We're going to make this the best con ever."

Rachel pulled Iris into a brief kiss. "I know we will. Thanks, Iris."

"And with that, you've officially graduated from cute together to smoking hot." Christy rested her chin on her upraised palm. "Two beautiful women and one handsome guy all falling for each other at once? Lydia's going to flip a table, wishing she'd been here to see it." She looked over to the other group. "Actually, we should break this up and join in the other conversation or something if you want to keep things stealthy. You three are getting pretty cuddly over here." She grinned.

Iris stood with a smile. "I think I'm making up for lost time. Back at my high school, people would actually get a detention for public displays of affection, including such scandalous activities as holding hands in the hallway. Assistant Principal Hoffsteder was a real bitch." With a chuckle, the four decamped, and moved over to join the rest of the group.

CHAPTER THIRTY-EIGHT

MICHELLE

"Wait. Say that last part again." Michelle set down her glass, and took a deep breath. "I couldn't possibly have heard that right." The last hour had gone by too fast. It wasn't every day she got to hang out and have fun conversation with one of her idols.

Lazlo shrugged, glancing at his schedule. "Well, I've got a lot of free time on Sunday morning, so I'd really, really like to use that time to film a segment with you for your show."

Michelle shot Felix a look. "Did you put him up to this, Felix?"

"Not me." Felix sat off to one side in one of the restaurant chairs, and he held up both hands. "I'm glad I could introduce you, but that's all I did. Lazlo's just a classy guy. Aren't you, Lazlo?"

Lazlo snorted. "Yeah, that's me. Classy and savoir faire as all hell. Michelle, I'm serious. It doesn't have to be anything complicated, maybe an interview or something. What would help out the show?"

She frowned, working through some ideas flitting through her head. "Doing just a general interview about your work wouldn't really fit. If we wanted to make it about convention life in particular, though... Hmm." She closed her eyes in thought, leaning back in her chair. "Let's interview both you and Christy together, and we'll talk about what conventions are like from a guest's perspective, what goes into getting invited, what guests like to see in the con staff they work with, that sort of thing." She opened her eyes. "For all some people know, the guests' green room is some sort of palatial affair with servant boys feeding you grapes, so this would paint a more realistic picture for your average congoer."

Lazlo clapped his hands together once. "I like it! Let's do this." He pulled out his phone. "Now, Christy and I should get back to my room for a bit before this autograph thing, but let's trade numbers, and we'll meet up here for Sunday breakfast at eight. Sound good?"

Five minutes later, Michelle was looking at her phone, and the new contact entry titled: Lazlo Akers. As she watched Lazlo and Christy walk away, she tapped the icon to add him to her Favorites list, and stood up.

Edie looked up from the conversation she had just started with Rachel. "Michelle, you doing okay?"

Michelle started pacing back and forth. "This is a day I'm going to remember for the rest of my life. I mean, not only did I get to meet one of my favorite directors, who is also one of my favorite voice actors, and his awesome artist spouse, but they told me they're fans of *my* work." She paused, and gestured to her four west coast friends. "*Our* work! I couldn't make the show without all of your help! I mean, I'm kind of freaking out here! Why am I the only one freaking out?"

"I think," Felix chuckled, "you're having a big enough freak-out that you're covering their quota, Michelle."

"And *you*!" Michelle whirled on Felix, looming over him as he sat. "We've known each other for how many years? And you not only knew Lazlo, who you knew I had a thing for, but you dated his sister *and* have had Thanksgiving dinner with him? And you're the reason he's at this con to begin with?" She spun away from him, her hands opening and closing as she continued pacing, her mind whirling.

"I mean, everything I've done with this show for these last couple of years, everything I've been worried about, is paying off!" She put a hand to her forehead, checking herself for a fever. "Our subscriber count is growing like crazy, we're starting to get some actual money from this—not much, but that's okay, and the man whose professional decisions I respect more than anyone just spent an hour at my table talking about being a fan and helping to make the show even greater!" Another spin as she paced back and forth, the laced edge of her white mini skirt twirling with each lap. "And do you know what the worst part of this is?"

Raeshawn snorted. "Worst? I dunno, this all sounds pretty good to me, so far."

Michelle ignored him. "The *worst* part is that I am so keyed up, so excited, so happy, so goddamned high on life right now, and I can't even do anything about it! I certainly can't kiss Lazlo to thank him, because he's married, and his wife is awesome, and that would be rude!"

Edie leaned over to whisper sidelong to Rachel. "Holy *deja vu*, Batman. Is that what I looked when I was ranting before?"

Rachel covered her mouth to stifle a giggle. "Maybe just a little, old chum."

Another quiet chuckle escaped Felix's lips, and Michelle was suddenly looming over him again, having shot over to his chair like a bullet. "And *you*! I told you I was going to have a word with you when this was over!"

Felix opened his arms and was about to speak, but Michelle's mouth was suddenly upon him, her tongue hungrily dancing with his. She'd practically leapt into his lap, her bare thighs wrapping around his waist, her hands on the back of his head.

A surprised gasp went up around the table.

All the boiling emotions building within Michelle over the last hour were bursting through her now, through her lips, and through the thin lacy underwear that was rubbing against Felix's lap. A moment later, he hardened against her, and it only spurred her on further, grinding against his erection, thinking of nothing but pure emotional and physical need.

A moment later, their lips parted, both of them taking deep breaths. As they looked into each other's eyes, they both smiled with happy surprise, and the recognition of shared arousal.

"Okay, I lied. Two words. Thank you." She slowly untangled herself from their embrace and stood, smoothing her skirt. "I didn't know I was going to do that."

Noticing she'd drawn a few amused smiles from some of the other congoers and restaurant staff at nearby tables, Michelle abruptly grabbed an empty chair next to Felix and sat down, her hands folded primly on her lap, right across from Iris and Rachel.

"I am so sorry."

Rachel could barely contain her mirth. "Oh, like I'm one to judge! Michelle, that was the hottest kiss I've ever seen, damn! Right, Iris?"

Iris's shoulders were shaking from quiet laughter. "Michelle, do you see me complaining? Trust me, I enjoyed every second of that. Although, not as much as Felix did, I bet. How you doing over there, handsome?"

Turning around to face the table, Felix shifted in his chair a bit. He turned to look at Michelle with a flushed smile. "And you're welcome." He turned to look at Iris. "To quote myself from earlier today—if you're good, I'm good. Wow."

Raeshawn stood behind Felix, patting him on the shoulder. "Felix, all I gotta say is this: *damn*. And I thought I had game." He squeezed Michelle's shoulder. "You got that little manic moment out of your system now?" Michelle crossed and uncrossed her legs. *Not hardly. I may need to borrow that dildo from Rachel that she thinks I didn't notice in her suitcase.* "Yeah, I'm good. Sorry about that." She turned to look at Felix again. "Are we cool?"

Felix nodded, looking at his glass, making a show of taking a sip. "One hundred percent."

Smiling at his reaction, Michelle allowed herself another quick glance at the slight tent in Felix's pants before noticing Edie and Adelaide were holding their sides with laughter. "What's so funny?"

Edie wiped a tear from her eye. "I'm sorry, but it's kinda gratifying to know the normally unflappable Michelle Liang, the Zen lady, the cool collected one, is able to have moments of weirdness like the rest of us."

Adelaide nodded. "I dub thee, Lady Flappable!" The pair dissolved into giggles again, Adelaide even going so far as to pound her fist against the restaurant table.

Rolling her eyes, Michelle rose. "Thank you, Duchess Adelaide, Princess of Gigglesnorts." She made a little curtsy. "And on that note, I think it's time to bail. I need to get ready for the dance tonight, and I need to hang up this costume to air out until tomorrow."

Rachel got up as well. "Yeah, I need to get some grub from our supplies. I'm actually getting kinda hungry. Iris, Felix, drop me a line after dinner?"

With that, things broke up, with Raeshawn, Adelaide, and Edie going back to their room, and Rachel and Michelle going to theirs.

The instant Michelle closed her room's door, she immediately turned to Rachel. "Okay, tell me straight. I still can't believe I did that, so if you're upset about it, please tell me. God, I feel like I should have *poor impulse control* tattooed on my forehead or something, like the villain from *Snow Crash*."

Rachel was already unzipping herself out of her Ruby Rose skirt. "Like I said downstairs, it's totally fine. I kinda did the same thing this morning, so it's not like I have room to talk, but I'm not jealous in the slightest." As she unwrapped the tight bindings around her chest, she gave a small laugh. "And I think Iris was just as turned on as I was, really." She looked up, one eyebrow raised. "Why, do you want to kiss him again or something?"

Michelle shrugged. "I'm not exactly planning on it, but the last thing I want to do is hurt people's feelings if I happen to stand too close to him later on." She glanced over to her friend again as Rachel removed her black ruffled skirt. "Rachel, what happened to your panties?"

Rachel pulled off her wig and set it down on a foam mannequin head, now standing completely nude in front of their hotel room's desk. "I gave them to Felix while you were at the Lazlo Akers panel." She waggled her eyebrows at Michelle. "For all I know, he's working off that stiffy you gave him by wrapping my little silk underwear around his rod right now."

Michelle paused in the act of unzipping her own costume, her eyes wide at the thought. "Now that was just mean."

Rachel laughed, walking past Michelle and towards the bathroom. "Consider it payback for your teasing me this morning. I'm gonna grab a shower."

Hanging up her white dress in the closet, Michelle returned to the room's king-sized bed, and fell backwards onto it with a loud *woomph*, lying there in her matching underwear, staring at the ceiling.

"Damn, Michelle. Just...damn." She breathed in and out, and reached for the nightstand to get her phone, taking a moment to check her emails.

A few seconds later, she looked down at herself. She didn't have the toned abs that Edie did, but she liked how her body looked. She idly ran the palm of her hand across her stomach, just enjoying the feel of her own smooth skin. She looked at her panties—really, not much more than a thong. A slender little string of a waistband, holding up a panel of white flower lace, her patch of dark hair visible through the sheer fabric. She closed her eyes, and remembered the feeling of grinding that lace against Felix's covered crotch.

She opened her eyes again, and looked at her phone. *To hell with it. Do it. You know you want to.* She clicked on Felix's name in her contact menu, and typed a text.

Michelle: *Sorry about assaulting you back there.*

A few moments later, he responded.

Felix: *Nothing to apologize for. Iris even asked me just now to thank you for 'warming me up' for her for later. ;) Hope that's not TMI. You're an amazing kisser and absolutely gorgeous. I feel very privileged.*

Michelle: *Maybe next time you should kiss me back a bit. Why should Iris and Rachel have all the fun?*

Michelle ran a finger along the edge of her thong, contemplating it for a moment. She bit her lip, and typed again.

Michelle: *I want to show you something. I can trust you, right?*

Felix: *Iris is here. She's seeing this, too, just FYI. We promise, you can trust us, and we're alone in my room. What's on your mind?*

Michelle pondered grabbing the high-quality camera, but decided to just use the phone's camera instead. She angled it carefully to take a picture of her own belly and waist, naked save for the lacy thong. She took a moment to admire her body in the picture.

"Not a bad shot, if I do say so myself."

Michelle: *I know you could feel me grinding you back there. I figured you should at least get to see what you were rubbing against.*

Felix: *We both want you to know how incredibly turned on we are right now. You're a beautiful sight. But if you want to play a little, I'll show you mine if you show me yours, I suspect you wouldn't be interested in the sight of my boring boxer-briefs.*

Michelle paused. Rachel was still in the shower, singing to herself, which meant she'd probably be in there for a while yet. She unhooked her bra, set it aside, and lightly caressed her nipples to hardness before responding.

Michelle: *You want me to say it? I'll say it. Show it to me.*

A long moment later, her phone chimed again, and her thighs shivered as she tapped on her screen.

Felix: *Gladly.*

It was a close-up of his waist, similar to her picture. His pants and underwear had been pulled off entirely, and his naked erection was on full open display, standing straight up against his stomach so that she was looking at the underside of his length, resting against a nest of dark brown curls. He was circumcised, with a nice pair hanging underneath.

She squeezed her breast, remembering her last boyfriend's reaction when she gently took his balls in her mouth. "Would you moan for me like that, Felix?" she whispered to herself.

Her phone suddenly chimed once more.

Felix: *Iris wants to give you a two-for-one deal.*

Michelle gasped. This photo showed the tip of his rod being suckled by a pair of very full lips. Iris had been careful to not show anything else of her face, and the sight sent a new tide of warmth and wetness through Michelle's womanhood. Again, her phone chimed.

Felix: *Iris here. A pity we're all about to be busy right now and can't play too much longer. I know you want to feel him get hard for you again before this weekend is out.*

Michelle groaned, and reached between her legs, her thighs spreading eagerly.

Michelle: *Iris, I want you and I to lick that nice looking rod together sometime very, very soon—and then maybe we can find some other ways to play. One last picture—it's not fair for you to send two when I've only sent one, after all.*

Michelle took a picture between her spread thighs, the lace panel pulled aside to reveal a patch of straight black hair, and a beautiful array of blushing pink folds, clearly glistening with aroused moisture. She had slipped one finger inside herself.

Michelle: *I'm in room 1207. I wish you could come up here right now, and bury yourself balls-deep inside me, just in time for Rachel to walk naked out of her shower and watch us fuck. Maybe*

Iris could lick her until she screams while you bend me over and grab my hips from behind. Goddamnit, I was not planning on this. I have to go now and make myself come before she finishes her shower. I can't blame you two for not finishing me off, because I started this, but I regret absolutely nothing. I desperately need a one-night-stand now. Gotta go.

Michelle was indeed bringing herself to a climax, bent over on her knees on the bed, her ass lifted into the air as she reached underneath to push two fingers in and out.

He'd walk into the room, his zipper open and his cock already out and hard, Iris stroking him all the while. Without a word, he'd see me all exposed, get behind me on the bed, and just plunge it in while Iris plays with my clit. I want them to touch me all over.

She turned her head towards the sound of Rachel still singing in the shower, and envisioned her future roommate's naked body, glistening with droplets of steaming hot water. *Or Rachel would suddenly walk out here, and see me desperately getting myself off. She'd reach into her suitcase and slide her dildo inside me, gently fucking me with it as I buck and grind against her. "I know what you need," she'd say. "Just relax, let me help you."*

Gonna come, gonna come hard…

With one last pinch along the hood of her clit, her entire body quivered like a violin string, and just collapsed onto the bed in a heap, letting the aftershocks work their way through her belly and limbs.

Sitting up slowly a few moments later, Michelle took a deep breath. "Ha. I'm not interested in seeing anyone right now, I said. I'll just take things as they come, I said. What a liar I turned out to be."

She looked at the clock. *Well, maybe there'll be someone at the dance up for a fling tonight who might help.* Time to get dressed.

CHAPTER THIRTY-NINE

FELIX

"Barry, this is my girlfriend, Iris Weinberg." Felix gestured to the tall, dark-skinned man behind the array of food platters. "Iris, this is Barry Drake, head of A.H. Staff Food Services. Barry, is it cool if she grabs dinner here tonight?"

Barry gave Iris a warm smile and an appraising look, one finger smoothing out his close-trimmed mustache. "I would eagerly serve a woman this beautiful, regardless of who she came in with."

Iris raised both eyebrows, and tucked one finger under the man's chin. "If you're going to *serve* me, then maybe you should kneel in my presence, hmm?"

Barry's eyes went wide. "Oh, damn. Oh, *hell* yes." His head reared in a good deep laugh. "Oh, Felix, my man, you gotta hold on to this lady." He flashed a wide grin. "Iris, welcome to my impromptu kitchen, and help yourself. I just know we're going to get along just fine." He held out a plate containing a dozen small, breaded spheres, still steaming. "Care for a cheese and rice fried croquette? They're still hot and fresh."

"Just like their chef, I'm sure." She eagerly plucked three onto her plate. "If these are even half as good as Prowl's chicken salad, I'm going to be a very happy woman."

Barry put down the plate with a pout. "Goddamnit, Felix. Why does everyone have to discover that mother-bleeping chicken salad first? How the hell am I supposed to compete with that?"

Felix held his sides with barely restrained laughter. "Let's be honest, Barry. Iron Chef Sakai couldn't compete with that chicken salad, you know that. Iris, you should know Barry and Prowl are constantly waging food wars, much to all of our benefit. However, by mutual agreement, that aforementioned chicken salad recipe has been banned from competition."

Barry rolled his eyes. "Damn right. It's not fucking fair, like bringing a nuclear bomb to a nice, civilized knife-fight. And while he may be the master of the cold sandwich, I am the undisputed Lord and Emperor of all things fried." He gestured to the croquettes on her plate. "Iris, indulge me if you would, and give one of those a try. Everyone else here has had these lots of times already, and they're just jaded now. I want to see a new reaction."

She picked up one of them. "Oh, I'll indulge you anytime, big man." She brought the sphere to her mouth, and made an exaggerated show of sensuously wrapping her lips around it before cracking up into a fit of laughter. "Sorry, I'm being bad."

Felix shook his head. "Oh no, you're being *very* good, indeed. Don't mind us."

Barry punched Felix lightly on the shoulder. "You should be glad I like you, or I would snatch this woman away from you so fast, you'd think we'd just jumped to lightspeed. You lucky, lucky son of a bitch."

"Okay, seriously now." Iris took a careful bite into the croquette, and immediately tilted her head back with a rapturous expression. "Oh, that's good. That's *so* good. What kind of cheese is that?"

"Gouda from a little farm I know that makes the best cheese on the planet." Barry smiled. "Store gouda's good enough, but I break out the real stuff for special occasions."

She put a hand on Felix's shoulder. "Please, tell me that you know how to cook, too?"

"I know half a dozen recipes that turn out pretty well, but that's about it." Felix shrugged. "I keep meaning to learn, though."

She leaned in to whisper privately in his ear, her husky growl sending shivers down Felix's spine. "You need to learn right away. Because if you can get to cooking even a third as good as Barry or Prowl, you have no idea just how much piping hot thank-you-for-the-food sex and blowjobs I'm going to give you, right there in the kitchen." She stepped back and licked her lips. "Consider it incentive to learn."

Felix leaned in to give her a warm kiss. "Maybe we should take a cooking class together, then."

"Okay, y'all need to stop." Barry made a fanning motion with his hand. "Getting so steamy in here, next thing you know, you're going to set off the smoke alarm, seriously." He gestured to the rest of the food trays laid out. "I'm so very glad you liked the croquettes, Iris. Grab anything you want from the rest of the table, and you have a lovely dinner."

As Felix and Iris headed towards the dining tables with full plates, Bianca suddenly popped up between them.

"Felix, since Iris is going to be bored out of her mind while you, Prowl, and the rest talk show logistics for tomorrow, I'm going to kidnap her for some more girl-talk, okay?"

"She's right, this meeting is going to be pretty dull." He gestured towards the far corner with a nod of his head. "We'll just be right over here."

"I'll happily allow myself to be taken away, then." Iris offered her elbow to Bianca. "Lead on, Miss Torres."

While Felix, Prowl, and half a dozen other staffers all sat down to eat and meet, Bianca and Iris gleefully chowed down a few tables away.

Bianca gestured with a celery stick. "So, you're local, right?"

"I am now. Just moved here last January, but I have zero intention of moving back to New York." Iris took a bite from another croquette. "Oh God, these things are going to be the death of me. I may need to get half a dozen more."

Bianca smiled. "Well, I figured since we're probably going to be seeing a lot of each other in the near future, it might be nice to meet properly. Actually talk, hang out, just you and me. Nothing to do with who we date, just us."

"Hence the girl-talk kidnapping."

"Yes, indeed." Bianca pointed the celery stick. "Tell me about yourself. You mentioned New York. Is that where you grew up?"

"Yup. Right in Manhattan, your classic Jewish-American princess. Although, I'd like to think I got over being an insufferable spoiled brat."

"Let me guess, you're an only child?" When Iris nodded, Bianca leaned back and sighed. "I was the last of six kids in my family, so I was the baby, and I got spoiled rotten because of it. Funny how that happens, so many ways for us to turn into little monsters."

Iris took a sip from her cup. "You seem like you're doing okay now. I wouldn't have pegged you as spoiled, at all. What was your wake-up call?"

"Well, when I was between my sophomore and junior years of high school, my parents sent me on this Teen Tour thing, basically a summer camp by way of tour buses, up and down the west coast." Bianca scratched the tip of her nose. "We were pampered, staying in nice hotels the entire way, going into all these cool touristy places and fancy restaurants. But, then we went to Tijuana for a day, and that's when shit got real."

"I've never been that far west, so I have no idea what Tijuana's like." Iris studied a meatball on the end of her fork. "What happened?"

"First, some context." Bianca picked up a couple of assorted vegetable sticks, and took a bite. "Before I was born, my family struggled a bit. Five kids are a lot of mouths to feed, after all. Then Papa had his big break, got made a partner at his firm, and by the time I was born, we were sitting pretty. Not super one-percenter rich, but doing pretty damn well. I knew growing up not everyone was as well off as we were, and that our family hadn't always been rich. I'd never seen it, experienced it."

Bianca took another bite of her veggie sticks. "Mmm. So, we're walking through Tijuana, and it's just awful. Squalor doesn't even begin to cover it. I had no idea people lived like that, and it just broke me. I was crying for days about it, especially every time I thought about that little girl with a food cart, trying to sell this block of fudge or something to anyone who'd pass by, but it was all covered in shiny green flies. And she didn't even notice or care, that's just how life always was for her. Covered in vermin."

Iris swallowed her mouthful. "What did you do?"

"Got my mind right, first of all." Bianca speared her fork through one of Iris's meatballs. "Started volunteering at soup kitchens, reading about how charity non-profits worked, and really throwing myself headlong into my church." She solemnly signed the cross over her chest. "Too many folks just ignore everything the Lord said about charity, about giving to others, because it's inconvenient. And that really upsets me. As soon as I get everything settled, now that I'm back home, I want to open a charitable foundation, make that my life's work. Put that business administration degree to work."

"Wow." Iris blew a long breath out between pursed lips. "See, for me, I'm still coming up for air. Ever since I was a kid, I felt like I had to protect myself by being in control of everything." She grabbed a strip of red bell pepper off Bianca's plate. "Being a selfish terror of a woman worked for me—until it didn't." She took a bite. "Last January, my wake-up call came in the form of my world crashing down around me, and me starting over here."

"Do you want to talk about it?"

"Another time, absolutely. If I focus too much on it now, I'm going to be a mess for days, and now is not the moment for that." She looked into Bianca's eyes. "The important thing is what came afterwards. I learned so much from my Aunt Abby these last few months. She is the most amazing, kind, and generous person on the planet, and it's completely sincere. I saw how she acted with people, how she loved her husband, her daughters, her friends, and me, and never asked or expected anything in return, not even as any sort of passive-aggressive guilt trip thing. To her, kindness really is its own reward." She made a bitter laugh. "When I was younger, I thought she was an idiot, a stupid hippie. Thanks to her example, this year, I've been letting go of a lot of crap in my head, and it's not done yet. Damn if I'm not glad for the chance to be a better person."

Bianca raised her plastic cup. "Here's to being the best selves we can."

"Amen." Iris clinked her cup against Bianca's, and did her best Bogart impression. "'Louis, I think this is the beginning of a beautiful friendship.'"

"Who says anime nerds can't appreciate the classics?" Bianca pushed a lock of hair out of her face with a smile, and then looked up with an impish grin. "Is that why you and Felix like that Ruby Rose girl? Because she looks a little like Ingrid Bergman?"

Iris sat up, thoroughly enjoying the mental image of Felix and Rachel dressed as Bogart and Bergman in *Casablanca*. "Her name's Rachel, and she does, doesn't she! Good eye, Bianca."

"May I join you?"

Iris looked up at the worried expression of a young Hispanic woman in a sleeveless t-shirt.

"Uh, sure." She paused for a moment, squinting in concentration, one hand to her forehead. "Hold on, I can do this. Kalli, right? The security guard who helped with the little *Pokemon* girl?"

Kalli managed a smile. "We did find her mom pretty quickly, by the way, thanks to Felix's suggestion."

Iris held out a hand. "Well, don't be a stranger. Please, sit! Felix said you were an old friend of his, and I want to meet as many of his friends as I can." She flashed a wide smile. "I'm Iris Weinberg, pleased to meet you."

"Yeah, I know." Kalli set down her plate, and shook the offered hand. "I asked around."

Bianca watched Kalli, and a moment later, moved to stand up. "You know, maybe I should leave you two to talk for a bit."

Kalli held up her other hand. "Actually, could you stay, Bianca? I was hoping to talk to both of you. You've known Felix longer than anyone, after all."

"Um, what's this about?" Iris pulled her gaze away from the two partially missing fingers on Kalli's raised hand, and looked over to where her boyfriend was still deep in conversation with his colleagues on the other side of the room. "Is everything okay?"

"If you insist, Kalli, sure." Bianca sat back down and leaned forward in her chair. "Looks like I missed more than I realized by not being here last year."

Kalli sat, looking over her plate of hot food before her, but made no move to eat any of it. "Okay, I shouldn't beat around the bush with this." She looked into Iris's eyes. "Are Felix and you dating? Or are you just his Snugglypuff for the weekend, a convention fling? I really need to know."

"Oh, no." Iris bit her lip as she took in Kalli's expression. "He doesn't know how you feel, does he?"

"Answer the question." Kalli looked away. "Sorry, that came out badly. I just, I really need to know where things stand, so I don't make a fool of myself. Please."

"Okay." Iris took a deep breath. "While we only met this morning, things between Felix and I have been pretty wonderful already, and we've already agreed to try dating after the con is over. I'm so, so sorry."

Bianca silently watched Kalli's reaction.

"Damn." The ex-military policewoman drummed her fingers on the table for a moment. "Missed my chance, then. Twice.

Three times, maybe. And there's no way I can compete in this race." She looked to Bianca. "I mean, let's be honest here. Bianca, if we asked any man out there to pick between me and someone stacked like *that*," she said, gesturing towards Iris, "I'm always going to come up short."

Bianca opened her mouth to say something, but Iris spoke first.

"No. He's not that shallow." She frowned, fidgeting with her napkin. "I may have only known him for one day, but I know that much."

Kalli looked at her plate again, and bit into a croquette, silently chewing for a few moments. "You're absolutely right. I was out of line. I want you to understand just how lucky you are, Iris." She glanced toward where Felix and Prowl were sharing a laugh together. "Last year, he made a pass at me, badly. I pushed him away because I wasn't in a good place in my own head, and I was pissed at him over that. Over the next few months at the staff meetings, I got to see better sides of him, and I saw him really trying to be a better man."

She took another bite, seemingly pausing to think as she ate. "He was helping people out, he was being super careful not to repeat his mistakes from before, and eventually, I saw him for who I think he really is. A good man with a lot of love to give, who deserves someone special to hold him. He sure as hell doesn't deserve to be so lonely." She looked back to Bianca. "Tell me I'm wrong."

"I can't, because you're right." Bianca glanced at Felix, as well. "All through college, he was like that. He wanted to be friends with everyone, not just Prowl and me and the rest of our little gaming group. And he'd been so miserable in high school." She ran one hand through her hair. "During that first term, he was so glad to have Prowl and me as friends, but we were the notable exception. Everyone else just ignored him. I remember walking into his room one Saturday night, and he was standing at his window, singing along to *Somebody to Love* by Queen on his stereo. He was crying his eyes out, pounding on the wall in time to the beat, and he hadn't heard me walk in."

Iris closed her eyes to imagine it. "He didn't understand what was going wrong, did he?"

"Yeah. He had no idea how to talk to girls, and the only reason he was able to talk to me is because he knew I was already firmly taken, and we could gab about all the hobby stuff together." Bianca frowned. "But when it came to anyone else, he was all thumbs, and no one wanted to see the good heart he had to offer. So, he stood there alone in his room, freaking out. I came up behind him and gave him a huge hug, and he just fell apart in my arms. That was when I knew that he and I would always be close."

Bianca managed a smile. "Things got better after that. I started giving him some pointers on how to talk to women, how to be calmer, how to handle conversations better. And he improved a lot, and had a few girlfriends in college, most of whom treated him pretty well." Her smile suddenly vanished. "Until that fucking bitch Tia came along his senior year, and ripped him apart inside. Just murdered his self-esteem, and I may well murder her if I ever see her again. He's been alone since then, until today."

"That almost changed last night." Kalli took a drink from her cup. "I'd made up my mind two months ago, I was going to ask him out at the con. Megan and a few others told me I should've done it at one of the staff meetings beforehand, but I wasn't ready." She pointed to Bianca. "You know that balcony thing he does before every con?"

"Where he watches the lobby from above on Thursday night? Of course."

"Well, I started chatting him up there last night. He'd just made up with Amanda a few minutes before, whom he'd thought he'd pissed off badly last year, and it reminded me how he'd really turned a corner. We're talking, and then out of the blue, he goes and helps out this poor guy in the lobby who was having a rough time of it. Never even thought twice. He just saw an opportunity to help someone in pain, and did it. May have even changed that guy's life." Kalli took a deep breath. "I know it sounds corny, but in that moment, I witnessed a beautiful soul in him. We were talking, really talking, and it was going so well, and then I got called away to help out with a stupid drunk asshole causing trouble. By the time that was over with, he'd already gone to bed."

Kalli scratched the stumps of her missing fingers. "Last night got weird after that. Did you know a full-on, real-life orgy broke out around the hotel swimming pool?"

They shook their heads, eyes wide in surprise.

"Well, it's the truth. It was something like two in the morning, and I'm around the swim deck, just doing my security rounds, while a couple dozen folks were hanging out and relaxing under the moonlight. All of a sudden, people were pulling off costumes and pulling on condoms."

Bianca chuckled. "Did you get invited to join them?"

"Someone did invite me, actually."

"Whoa, I was kidding!"

Kalli exhaled, blowing a lock of hair out of her eyes. "He sure wasn't. Rock-hard abs like nothing I'd ever seen before, a face movie stars would kill for, and a thickness hanging hard, halfway to his knees, and he oh so politely asked if I'd like to give him a lick while his pretty little girlfriend watched."

"That could be either super hot," Iris said with a shiver, "or super creepy."

"I won't lie, I nearly did it. He was something to behold, and there was definitely something in the air. When I hesitated, his girl just dropped to her knees and started going down on him right in front of me, and watching nearly made me pull off my clothes, but I walked away."

Kalli laughed. "So, I wake up this morning, horny as all get out, and determined more than ever to get Felix's attention. And I figured, hey, I've got the perfect sexy icebreaker for when I see him next, to tell him about the crazy poolside orgy." She paused. "Minus the I almost sucked off a complete stranger that was hotter than Captain Jack part." She sighed. "I had to go on duty immediately, but *then* I ran into Felix anyway because of the lost girl this morning. I told him afterwards I wanted him to buy me a drink later. By then, it was too late. He'd already met you."

Kalli clenched one fist, her knuckles popping loudly, but then just as quickly relaxed it, and leaned back against her chair. "Let me say this, Iris. Understand how lucky you are he wasn't already taken when you met him, because I had plenty of chances I should've taken. And understand how lucky you are to have him in particular over nearly any other man here, including certain swimming pool sex gods with eleven inch packages. Because if I know Felix as half as well as I think I do, he's going to move heaven and earth to make sure he is the best lover, friend, and companion you could ever hope for."

"Just so you know, Kalli," Bianca said as she swallowed another meatball, "I already told Iris if she did anything to break Felix's heart, I'd look on that very, very poorly."

Kalli held out her hand to Iris again. "Count me in on that. I'd like to think that I'm mature enough to be friends with you despite my jealousy issues, but I will definitely make you hurt if you hurt that good man."

Iris accepted the handshake solemnly. "I understand completely, and God as my witness, if I screw up that badly where I've hurt Felix Jackson in any way, then I want you to punish me for it. I've already seen how sweet and kind he is, and I'm not going to take that for granted for a second."

With her costume packed and ready to go in a bag over her shoulder, Iris walked with Felix towards room 1207. "You let Prowl know you'll be out late?"

Felix smiled. "It's just as well, actually. Prowl and Bianca definitely need some serious alone time. I'm glad I have somewhere to go to give them some space."

"You've got some good friends here, Felix."

He nodded. "Better than I deserve." He looked down the hall. "Pretty quiet here tonight. The room parties haven't started up yet, I guess."

"Why would you say that? That you don't deserve good friends?"

He shrugged. "I dunno. I mean, I try to do right by folks, but it seems to me like I fuck it up more often than not, but then I've got people like Prowl and Bianca who would walk over broken glass for me if I needed it, and that freaks me out a bit. I don't feel like I've done anything to warrant that level of love."

"Did something happen during that staff meeting?" She cocked her head as if to look at him from a new angle. "Where'd this morose stuff come from? Are you okay, handsome?"

Looking at his feet as he walked, he sighed. "Pre-date jitters, I guess. I spaced out for a bit during the meeting, and found myself going down memory lane to the last date I went on before tonight, a little over four years ago. A date that truly earned the phrase FUBAR. Fucked Up Beyond All Recognition, indeed. I really don't want to mess this up for Rachel."

She grabbed his hand and gave it a tender squeeze. "Trust me, the only way you could mess this up is if you pulled off your face to reveal you're actually one of those Gorn lizard-guys from *Star Trek*—and even then, she might not think that's so bad." She pulled his hand upward to give a kiss to inside of his wrist. "If anything, I'll bet money she's just as terrified as you. If not more so, of messing this up for you. You'll be fine, and I'll be back in two hours. Maybe less."

He kissed her hand in return. "I need to get out of my own head. I wasn't this nervous or neurotic with you this morning, even before we really broke the ice. Why am I freaking out now?"

"Because it's a date with a big scary D, I'm guessing." She thought back to Bianca's words earlier today. *What in the world did this Tia woman do to my sweet man back then?* "You said it yourself, your last date was rough, so anything that feels similar to it is bound to feel a little unsettling."

"I know I shouldn't let it scare me like this, but I have no idea what I'm doing." He threw up one hand in exasperation as he gripped Iris's with the other. "I'm wearing khaki docker pants and a convention polo shirt. Not exactly suave fashion. I have no idea where to take her, what to talk about, what I should say when we get to her room..."

As he spoke, she watched him, and it seemed to her he was shaking in near panic. She suddenly dropped her bag off her shoulder, spun Felix around, and pinned him against the wall. Her mouth enveloped his, her chest pressed against him, and her hands grabbed him by his shoulders.

After a long moment, she pulled back, and looked inward as his breathing slow to normal. *A year ago, I would've dumped him right here and now, because I would've thought he was acting weak. Now, all I want to do is help him because I know he's worth it. I like this new me so much more.*

Felix's eyes were happily dazed and calmer now.

She kissed the tip of his nose. "Better?"

"Yeah. Sorry about that. I kinda wigged out there."

"It's okay. I know what that feels like." She kissed him one more time, a quick peck on the lips. "If it helps, try this. From the moment we shared our first drink together at the restaurant this morning, you knew exactly what to say, what to do, and you never doubted yourself for a second. Sexy as hell, I might add." She pulled him away from the wall, grabbing her discarded bag, and they continued their walk towards Rachel's room. "Try thinking back to how you felt then, and what was on your mind when we were hanging out, so if you get nervous, copy and paste that good feeling with me onto the moments you're sharing with Rachel. Trust me, you'll be fine."

He looked down at himself. "I'm not used to being called sexy as hell. I could grow to like that."

"You'll be hearing it a lot from me, and from Rachel. Something to look forward to, handsome." They were in front of room 1207. "And here we are."

Before he fully reached the door to give it a knock, it suddenly opened, and Michelle stepped out. She wore a pair of black yoga pants that were so tight against her skin, they looked painted on, along with a bright red t-shirt sporting the golden symbol for the Principality of Zeon from *Mobile Suit Gundam*.

She closed the door behind her, turned, and jumped in surprise as she noticed Felix and Iris for the first time. "Dear God! Speak the devil's name, and he really does appear." She hesitated for only a moment, and then quickly stepped right up to both Felix and Iris, hooking a finger into the waist of each of their outfits. "I came to this con with zero impure intentions, and you two wrecked that little plan in no time flat."

He leaned in and gave a gentle nibble on the side of Michelle's ear, eliciting a surprised gasp from her. "Did you manage to climax before Rachel finished her shower?"

He gave a low quiet laugh, and Iris marveled at watching Michelle go weak in the knees at the sound of his rich, deep voice. *And he's back. I knew you wouldn't be gone long, handsome.*

On a whim, Iris leaned in, and gave Michelle's other ear a little kiss.

Michelle nodded, biting her lip. "Not as hard as I would've if you two were there with me." She shivered at the touch of Iris's lips on her right ear, and took a step back, but not letting go of her hold on them. "God, listen to me. There is something about the two of you together. I swear, you set me off like nothing else." She gave a grin, and pointed at her room with an upraised thumb. "And clearly, I'm not the only one. Are you here to collect my roommate? She let it slip you had some sort of date tonight, and she can't wait to see you."

"Indeed, I am. Iris needs to head home to collect some things, and Rachel and I are going to have a quiet evening getting reacquainted until she gets back."

"I wondered what was going to happen after Rachel kissed you like that. Nice to know everyone present is so cool about it." Releasing her fingerhold on Felix, she ran a hand through her white hair, now released from its cosplay hairstyle and hanging down to the middle of her back. "I'd love to tag along, but I know she really wants that alone time with you. Instead, I'm going to the dance to see if I can work off some of this extra tension I've suddenly got going, thanks to you two." She suddenly pulled Iris close, her lips almost brushing Iris's cheek. "But I'm not leaving this con without licking the taste of you off your boyfriend's cock. You understand me?"

Iris flashed in delight at that mental image. "Only if Rachel gets to watch."

Michelle gave Iris's neck a quick kiss before darting back out of her grasp. "You have yourself a deal. If Rachel doesn't mind my joining in this little fling, then it's going to be one hell of a party. I'm off to go find some random cute man to take the edge off tonight, but tomorrow, we're going to find some time for this." She adjusted the strap of her purse and headed toward the elevators.

As Felix watched her leave, he called out, "Hey, Michelle?"

She looked over her shoulder. "Hmm?"

"You look fantastic. Go show the world what you're made of."

Michelle grinned, and made a show of running her hand along her thigh and up the curves of her firm backside. "Thank you, Felix, and I will."

She resumed walking, and Iris couldn't help but admire the extra sway she put into her hips, knowing full well she was being watched.

After Michelle had turned the corner, Felix let out a low whistle. "Today just keeps on getting... I don't even know how to describe it anymore. Surreal doesn't quite cover it."

Iris closed her eyes, remembering the feel of Michelle's cool lips on her neck. "The word delicious comes to mind." She opened her eyes. "Or maybe crazy. We've got not one, but two absolutely gorgeous women practically begging to jump into bed with us. But who's complaining? Not I."

Felix stepped up to the door. "Likewise. Time to get things started." He knocked on the door, and a few seconds later, it opened a few inches to reveal Rachel's face.

"Felix! I thought I heard you talking to Michelle. Did Iris leave already?"

Iris leaned into her field of vision. "I've still got a few minutes. I thought I'd drop him off for you."

"Oh, good! I'm glad you're here. I wanted you to see this, too." Rachel bit her lower lip. "Neither of you have ever seen me just wearing clothes instead of a costume, so I hope you like what you see." With that, she opened the door all the way, posing in the doorway to reveal the results of her wardrobe choices.

Both Felix and Iris's jaws dropped, and they whispered in unison, "Oh, wow."

Gone was the youthful cosplayer, replaced with a woman in full ownership of who she was and what she wanted. Her dark blonde hair was pulled back into a loose French braid that ended at the back of her neck. Her blouse, left untucked at the waist, was a snugly fitting white button-down, the top two black buttons undone, and with each short sleeve ornamented by a row of three similar buttons. Below that was a pleated skirt that fell to mid-thigh in bright jewel-tone green, the color coordinating perfectly with her small emerald earrings. She wore black leather boots that stopped just below the knee. As she posed, she leaned back a little to show the curve of her neck, now accentuated with a black ribbon choker ornamented with a small silver buckle.

"What do you think, sirs?"

Felix found his voice first. "Dear God in heaven, Rachel. Smoking hot doesn't do you justice. Wow."

Iris stepped in, putting her arm around Rachel's waist. "You weren't kidding when you said you were binding your chest with that other outfit. These girls look ready to come out and play tonight. Are you even wearing a bra?"

The playful blonde grabbed Iris's hand and pulled it under the back of her skirt. "I'm not wearing any underwear tonight. As ordered, ma'am. Care to inspect me?"

"Did you just call me ma'am? You're going to get it for that."

Iris pulled Rachel into a long kiss, her fingertips gliding along the naked valley below the back of Rachel's skirt. When she came up for air, Iris smiled.

"It's going to be torture to be away from you two for a couple hours."

Felix picked up Iris's garment bag, glancing down the hallway at the sound of other people approaching. "Ah, we should probably move this inside for the moment."

They nodded, and scurried back into Rachel's suite with Felix following.

Iris sat on the edge of the king-sized bed. "I do need to get going, princess, but before I do, you should know something."

"Do tell?" Rachel walked up to Felix and greeted him with a tender kiss, her arms wrapped around his waist. "Missed you."

"Mmm, good to see you, too." Felix gave Rachel a squeeze around her waist. "First, just to check—did it bother you at all when Michelle kissed me right in front of you?"

"Not at all. What I said before still stands. That kiss was hot as hell. Why?"

"Because," Iris chimed, "we seem to have gotten Michelle's motor running on overdrive. She really, really, *really* wants to get into our pants before the weekend is out." She grinned. "How would you feel about that?"

Rachel blushed. "That's...um. Wow." She sat on the bed next to Iris. "Does that include me?"

Felix leaned against a nearby wall. "It could. Michelle hinted she'd be into that, but I didn't want to speak for you. I mean, you two are roommates, and if you're not comfortable with us fooling around with her, then we won't."

"Wait, seriously?" Rachel turned to look at Felix. "If I told you I was jealous, you wouldn't do it?"

He responded immediately. "Of course."

"Your feelings absolutely matter, Rachel." Iris's fingers toyed with the end of Rachel's braid.

Rachel turned and gently pulled Iris close for another kiss. "First of all, I'm not jealous of Michelle in the slightest. I've been wondering what it might be like to kiss her for a while now, even if I couldn't admit it to myself until today." She stole another quick kiss from Iris, and then jumped up to do the same to Felix. "Second of all, I don't know what I did to deserve two amazing people like you, but I am so very thankful right now. You just don't know."

Iris stood up, checking the time on her phone. "I really do need to go. I told my family I'd meet them downstairs in ten minutes. Before I do, a couple things." She moved to put an arm around both Felix and Rachel. "Feel free to get warmed up, but don't get too frisky until I get back, okay? I don't want to miss the really good parts."

"I promise to keep it in my pants, beautiful," Felix replied with a chuckle.

"Beyond that, I want you two to just relax and have some nice, quiet time together." Iris hugged them both. "Walk the con, find a movie to watch, or just hang out by the fountain or something, but know I'm thinking about you both, and I'll be back as fast as I can. Keep your phone ringers on."

"We should all head downstairs, then." Rachel grabbed her purse. "If Felix and I stay alone in here, I'll be too tempted to jump the gun." She gave Iris's backside a squeeze. "Hurry back, lover girl."

Fifteen minutes later, Iris sat in the backseat of the Weinberg family van. Marcus was driving, with Angelica riding shotgun, and Abby was sitting next to Iris, a half-asleep Tracy resting her head on Abby's shoulder.

"Iris, I want you to know how happy I am you met someone so nice today. I do hope I'll get the full details later?"

Angelica called back over her shoulder. "Aww, why can't we get the story now? Felix seemed pretty cool. I wanna hear all about him. Did he say if Prowl had a girlfriend or not?"

"I hate to be the bearer of bad news, Angie, but Prowl is almost certainly off the market." Iris gave Abby a grin as she rolled her eyes in Angelica's direction. "Even if you were old enough, there's a six foot tall Filipina named Bianca who's got dibs on him, and the body of a supermodel, to boot. She'd crush you like a grape."

"I may be small, but I'm fierce." The teenager sniffed disdainfully. "The instant I turn eighteen, I'll grab him up so fast, he won't even remember that woman's name anymore." With a laugh, Angelica made her voice sound old and raspy. "I have foreseen it." She switched back to her normal voice, a whine creeping in. "*C'mon*, Iris. You gotta tell me something!"

"Well, I can tell you this, Angie. I think this thing between Felix and I is going to be serious, and he's a very, very good kisser. That's all you're getting out of me right now."

As Abby laughed quietly, Angelica turned back around with a huff. "Fine, I can take a hint. But later on, I want to hear at least a little more than that, okay?"

Marcus just shook his head, concentrating on the road. "Whatever happened to the little Angelica who just wanted to go on roller coasters all the time?"

"Dad, I hate to break it to you, but there's this thing called puberty. Maybe you've heard of it?"

As Iris joined her aunt in a new round of giggling in the backseat, she rested her head on her aunt's shoulders.

After a moment, she turned her head and whispered, "Abby?"

"Yes?"

"Thank you again. For everything. I really don't say that out loud enough, and I really want you to know how much everyone here means to me."

Abby squeezed her hand warmly. "And you mean the world to us, Iris. After the con is over on Monday, you and I will crack open a nice bottle of wine, and you can tell me everything."

"Everything?" Iris raised an eyebrow.

"Everything you're willing to share. I'm just so happy for you."

Iris sighed happily. "Yeah. Me, too."

CHAPTER FORTY

FELIX

"I love this place. 'I'm Commander Shepherd, and this is my favorite spot in the citadel.'" Felix turned to give Rachel a warm smile. "And I'd like to share it with you."

Rachel offered a raised eyebrow in return. "No-no-no. I'm Commander Shepherd, and you're my Garrus Vakarian. FemShep/Garrus O-T-P." She looked around at the crowds below, and at the people walking back and forth behind them. "It is a nice view of the hotel lobby, sure, but what's so special about a mezzanine balcony?"

He leaned into the railing, watching the thick crowds shifting and moving. "Exactly—because it has a nice view of the lobby. Although, I'll grant that the view on a Friday night is very different from a Thursday night."

"Less crowded, for one." Rachel leaned against Felix and put an arm around his waist. "You like watching the people walk by, is that it?"

"It's more like I like watching people living their lives." He draped his arm over her shoulder, his fingers brushing across the back of her neck as they reached around her. "Back in high school, I had zero instinct for how other people thought. I couldn't understand why anyone did anything at all. One day, I sat down in the middle of a food court at one of the local malls, and just watched people go by, or sit down and eat, or talk on their phones, or what have you. I watched what they did, and tried to piece together their story."

"Obviously, it helped." She snuggled. "Honestly, you usually seem like you've got everything together, generally doing the right thing at the right time."

"I hate to disappoint you, but I definitely have my bad moments." He turned and inhaled deeply, savoring the scent of her subtle perfume. "On my way up to get you, I damn near had a panic attack, worrying about making sure you had a good night tonight." He gestured at the milling crowds below. "It's weird. When I'm on stage, staring out at a crowd of three thousand people hanging on my every word and gesture, I know exactly what to do, and I don't even need to think about it. But if I'm talking to just one person right in front of me, I'm terrified I've already said something wrong. I'm just glad you didn't see me at last year's Horde, when I literally did do everything wrong."

"Actually, I did. Up close and personal."

He tensed. "I wish I could just erase last year's con somehow. You saw me at my worst."

"No, I saw you when you were hurting." She squeezed him again, harder this time. "Think back to when we first met, two years ago. Five words in, and I had a nervous breakdown. I was freaking out, screaming, crying, and you didn't care. You saw me at my lowest point. You just wanted to help." She breathed in and out slowly, remembering that awful moment with perfect clarity, and then set it aside. "Last year, when you were hitting on Adelaide, I was the girl in the full face and body *Spider-Gwen* costume next to her. I saw the whole thing."

"Huh." He ran a hand through his hair. "I remember that outfit. You looked really good."

"I still have it at home. I'll bring it for the next con we go to together." She purred, imagining Felix peeling her out of that skintight bodysuit. "My point is, I could tell in that moment you were hurting just as bad as I was the year before. You didn't know what to do, you just knew that you hurt, and you sort of...flailed. I knew all too well what that was like, so I never thought ill of you. I just wish I'd been brave enough to try and help in that moment."

Before he could answer, she put a finger to his lips. "But here's the thing. What happened afterwards made me fall for you even more than the crush I'd had from the year before. Because right after Addie turned you down, your friend Prowl found you, and I overheard what happened."

"He'd just walked in on his girlfriend cheating on him." He frowned. "I didn't do anything special there."

She shook her head. "I'm a little ashamed to admit it, but I actually tailed you and Prowl for a few minutes. I saw you pull yourself out of your tailspin to be there for your best friend when he'd needed it the most. You took him to the bar, bought him a drink, and helped him talk it out. Like you helped me, and that's special."

"That's not special." He rubbed his eyes. "That's just the right thing to do. You see someone hurting, you help. It's that simple."

"Felix, I hate to break it to you, but a lot of people out there don't do that." She turned to face him, one arm resting on the balcony railing. "They don't want to get involved. They say it's somebody else's problem. They gripe it's too much trouble. They sneer because there's nothing in it for them." She stroked his cheek. "To you, kindness is instinct, and when someone's in real pain, you immediately reach out and help." She leaned forward and pulled his chin to face her, giving him a brief kiss. "That kindness is why I've fallen for you."

He opened his mouth, but no words came out. After a moment's hesitation, he straightened and pulled her close for another kiss, this one much longer.

She melted in his arms, more safe and content than she ever had been before in her life. She never wanted the kiss to end.

"Ahem."

Her eyes flew open, and she whirled towards the voice.

There was a tall and slender man in a suit standing there, his pale features pinched in apparent disapproval. Behind him, the hotel's continuous stream of foot traffic continued, some of the other congoers shooting her and Felix amused looks as they stood in each other's embrace.

"Mr. Jackson," the man intoned, "I wish to share a concern with you."

Felix's eyebrows lowered in obvious annoyance. "I was giving my date a kiss, Brian. There's nothing in the convention bylaws that says I can't have a tender moment with someone I care about, and don't start with that conduct unbecoming line again. I'm really not in the mood for that right now."

Brian held up one hand, palm out. "My apologies, Mr. Jackson. Allow me to rephrase the situation." He put that hand to his mouth, covering it as he cleared his throat. "You may not be aware of this, but your intimate moment a few moments ago was drawing a fair amount of attention from others present in the lobby. I spied one person taking digital pictures of you, undoubtedly without your knowledge, and I politely but firmly had them delete those pictures, upon pain of badge forfeiture." He reached behind his head, and tightened the tie around his ponytail. "I can certainly understand becoming lost in the moment, but my concern is for your safety and privacy."

She looked back and forth between the two men, watching Felix's face as he digested this. "Um, Felix? Who is this?"

The taller man inclined his head. "My apologies, miss. My name is Brian McHenry, and I am the Convention Chair for this year's Anime Horde. I would normally avoid interrupting such pleasant encounters, but the behavior of your onlookers necessitated an intervention."

"Uh, thanks, I think? Rachel Midnight, pleased to meet you." Unsure of what else to do, she held out a hand. "You run a great con."

Brian accepted the handshake with a thin but warm smile. "I am exceptionally glad to hear you feel that way. As an attendee, your enjoyment is entirely the point of this endeavor."

"Sorry I snapped at you, Brian. And thank you." Felix scratched the back of his head. "We'll try to be less obtrusive."

"Romance is not objectionable, Mr. Jackson. The two of you are just a little exposed here. No harm has been done, but before you leave, I do need to speak with you."

"Is now really the time for this, boss?"

"I promise the interruption will be brief, Mr. Jackson." Brian put his hands behind his back, and lifted his chin slightly. "You and I had some personal friction this morning, not for the first time, and I have spent some time since contemplating the reasons for this ongoing antipathy between us. I would value your analysis."

Seeing Felix's mouth pinch shut, Rachel spoke up. "I can hazard a guess."

"Yes, Miss Midnight." Brian swiveled to face her again, leaning forward just the smallest amount. "Your opinion, if you please?"

"Well, I think it's an oil-and-water thing." She hooked her arm in the crook of Felix's elbow. "Felix is a pretty spur-of-the-moment guy, doing what seems right in the moment. You seem more the type to like things precise and laid out beforehand. Am I right? Some personalities just clash, that's part of being human."

"Just so." Brian nodded. "I value Felix's skill as a crowd entertainer, being able to read the mood of a collected room and to keep them happy, an ability that does not come easily to me, but he does not seem to appreciate the value of controlled agendas, or a well-organized plan."

"It's not that I don't appreciate them, boss. That approach just doesn't work for me, personally. I feel constrained by it. I like having flexibility, being able to look around and adapt as things change." Felix shook his head. "If I seem annoyed, it's because I worry you get so bogged down in minutiae that you miss the big picture. I'll always grant it's important to have someone who can handle the little details."

Brian's eyes widened, and he stood silently for a few moments before responding. "This has been enlightening, Mr. Jackson. Miss Midnight's insight and your elaboration have given me much to consider, and I would value speaking with you on this subject again on Sunday, after the convention is over."

"Sure, I can do that. Thanks for what you said." Felix held out a hand.

Brian took the offered handshake, and then shook Rachel's hand. "I will bother you no further tonight. Miss Midnight, I hope you do not mind my saying that your choice of fashion aesthetics is excellent, and I'm glad one of my staffers has made you happy. Good evening to you." And with that, he walked away, touching one finger to his earpiece as he whispered something into its receiver.

"Well, he's a little stiff, but he seems nice." She looked at Felix. "You okay?"

"Yeah." Felix's shoulders dropped an inch, releasing some tension. "He's been a pain in the ass over the last year, but he's generally steered the con right." He looked down at her, smiling again. "Having an outside perspective suddenly made that really clear as to why he got my hackles up. Thanks for that."

She started walking, towing him along with her. "Well, let's find somewhere to sit for a bit, and you can thank me all you like."

CHAPTER FORTY-ONE

FELIX

Felix looked at the video room's sign. "You want to watch this in particular?"

Rachel nodded enthusiastically. "I heard it's really good, been meaning to take a look for a while now. We can just sit and relax for a bit."

He raised an eyebrow. "Well, *Kimagure Orange Road*—um, Rachel, I hate to bring this up, but this show is about a messy love triangle between one guy and two women. Are you sure you want to watch this?"

"Well, if they can't figure out how to make that work, that's their problem, not ours." She flashed him a smile. "C'mon, it's about to start. Let's grab a seat."

"Sure thing. Hey, Debbie." Felix waved to the staffer who was checking for badges at the door. "Busy night?"

Debbie was a middle-aged Caucasian woman with long and graying black hair, busily working on what looked to be a crochet project as she sat watch. "Not hardly, Felix. Everyone's at the dance or one of the room parties, and there's nothing new and flashy on tonight's video room schedule, so we're enjoying the quiet for now." She looked at Rachel. "I suspect your night's all spoken for, though."

Rachel's cheeks reddened a bit, but Felix just grinned. "Something like that. Hey, how is Jen doing?"

Debbie smiled. "Oh, I'm finally getting used to using her new name and pronouns. I kept using the old ones by mistake. I'll tell her you asked, she'll be so happy to hear from you."

As Rachel walked in, Debbie gently caught Felix by the wrist, and cast her voice low. "Felix, I'm very happy to see you smiling again. I know last year's con was difficult for you."

He smiled, and leaned down to kiss Debbie's forehead, as they had done for each other so many times over the many years he'd known her. "Thank you, Convention Mom. And yeah, it is nice to see a smile in the mirror again." They shared a grin, she pulled him down to kiss his forehead in return, and he followed Rachel into the video room.

This was one of the convention's smaller makeshift theatres, a meeting room set up to seat perhaps forty people at most, with a large projection screen set up at the far end, the room's only source of light. As his eyes adjusted to the low illumination, he realized there was absolutely no one else in this room other than Rachel.

A creak came from behind him, and he turned to find Debbie closing the room's door, flashing him one more smile before the outside world was shut out.

He turned to look for Rachel. She had already taken residence in the back row and far corner, and beckoned him over with a single curling finger. He walked over, and she patted the seat next to her, the one closest to the wall.

She giggled, looking past him and towards the door. "Did your friend just close the room behind you?"

"She did." He took his seat, leaning half against the chair and half against the wall, and Rachel immediately leaned back into him, her head resting on his chest and shoulder. "Debbie's a sweetheart. She's sort of a surrogate mom to us younger staffers. I think she's giving us some privacy."

She murmured happily, and made a show of undoing the third button on her blouse. "Hooray for privacy." She kissed his cheek. "Your friends here really care about you. It's sweet."

He put his arm around her shoulders, squeezing gently. "So are you, gorgeous."

The next few minutes passed in silence as they watched the show's two leads meet for the first time, a teenaged boy and girl bonding over a nearly lost hat and the number of steps on a local landmark stairway, falling into easy conversation almost immediately.

"I like this show already," she whispered. "It's adorable."

"Yeah, I like it, too." He looked at her, and as if sensing his gaze, she turned her face to look at him in return. "Here's a question for you. What got you into anime to start?"

"Why do you ask?"

"Well, I want to get to know you better." He chuckled at a sight gag on the screen involving the hero's cat. "I mean, we talked a lot about what was going on with you when we first met, with your dad and that jerk-ass boyfriend you had at the time, stuff like that. I want to know more. I want to know what makes you tick, what drives you, what brought you to this moment. Stuff like that." He caressed her cheek. "You're more than just a beautiful woman in my arms. You're already a close friend, and I want to be closer still."

"Well, since our shared love of this stuff helped us meet, makes perfect sense to me." She glanced at the screen, watching the action for a moment. "When I was eight, my parents took me with them to visit a friend of theirs who worked on a college campus. We passed through the student union, and the campus anime club had a poster up for a series called *Gankutsuou* they were going to show."

He smiled. "Oh, that's a good one. *The Count of Monte Cristo* for a new age."

"I know, right?" She shifted in her chair a little. "All I knew at the time was that the colors and the designs were just so beautiful, so I begged my mom to take a picture of it so I could look it up later." She smiled in the darkness, and he marveled at how beautiful she was in that moment, the light from the screen making her eyes sparkle. "And I did. I devoured everything about it, even though my mom wasn't sure if it was age appropriate for me. I went looking for other stuff made by that studio, and it just snowballed from there." She sat straighter, and turned to look at him. "Your turn, sexy."

"Well, I've got a brother who's about ten years older than me, and he's even more into Japanese stuff than I am. His name's Donald." He toyed with the end of her braid, savoring the feel of her soft hair tickling his fingertips. "From a real young age, I saw a lot of anime stuff in his room, but I had no idea what it was. When I was six, he and I both came down with a really bad flu at the same time, and had to stay home for a few days. I was bored out of my mind, so he put on some giant robot videotapes that he had to take our mind off things. *Gundam*, *Macross*, the old *Voltron* dubs from before I was born, stuff like that."

He gave her hand a squeeze. "The one that really jumped out at me was *Mobile Police Patlabor*, because I was really into the idea of being a policeman at the time. These were police with giant robots, so I was already hooked. Then my brother told me about how the main heroine, Izumi Noa, liked to call her robot Alphonse, and how she also called a lot of other stuff in her life by that name, like her dog." He chuckled to himself. "For the next year, I went through an Alphonse phase. When I got a new stuffed animal, I named it Alphonse. When we got a cat, I named it Alphonse, and so on. I collected any robot toys that looked even remotely like the ones from *Patlabor*. Like you said, it just snowballed from there, aided and abetted by my big brother."

She smiled. "Sounds like your brother's a nice guy. Where's he at these days?"

"Boston, working for this small engineering firm." He leaned back, glancing at the ceiling. "Now that I think about it, I haven't talked to him since March. I need to give him a call."

"I've got a little brother," she said. "He's a good kid, about to start high school." She put a finger to his lips. "But right now, instead of talking about him, I want to just sit quietly in your arms and enjoy the show for a bit." She drew her knees up onto the row of chairs, and leaned against his shoulder.

He kissed the top of her head, and silently put his arm around her shoulders, settling in to watch the screen.

CHAPER
FORTY-TWO

IRIS

At the carriage house behind the Weinberg's home, Iris stared at her dresser drawer as if it might contain the answer to world peace, if only she could decipher the clues.

Abby was sitting on the bed nearby, having traded in her Mon Mothma gown for a pair of sweatpants and a button-down pajama top. "Iris, stop trying to figure out the perfect outfit. From the way Felix was looking at you, you could probably walk in wearing a literal potato sack and a bowl of spaghetti in your hair, and he'd still want to kiss you."

"I want him to do a lot more than kiss me, Aunt Abby." Iris pulled open another drawer, stared at its contents, and then slammed it closed again. "And you didn't see the hot number Rachel put on just before I left."

"Oh, ho!" Abby stood and walked over to Iris's closet, sifting through the various items hung there. "You've already got some competition for your man's affections, eh?"

Iris opened another drawer, and pulled out two pairs of underwear. One was black, with a sleek and satin-like texture, while the other was ocean blue cotton with white stripes. "Actually, no. All three of us have, well, kinda fallen for each other. Felix and I have already talked about seeing if we might try a three-person polycule sort of thing." With a frown at the two pieces of fabric, she put both panties back in the drawer, and rummaged around for more options.

Abby turned around, holding up a hanger that bore a long summer dress in a soft beige color. "Well, well. If you're looking for tips on how to manage poly relationships, you're in the right household for that, but you knew that already. How about this one?"

Iris looked and shook her head. "A dress might work, but not that one. It's too drab. I need something spicier." She pulled out a matching bra and panty set in a rich green color, with little patches of black peek-a-boo lace scattered around each piece. She remembered the mini-skirt Rachel wore in a similar shade of green, and with a grin, tossed them onto the bed. "Those will work. Actually, Abby, this isn't going to be my first trip down Poly Lane. I dabbled in college."

"Fair enough, but I'm still here should anything come up." Abby held up another blouse, a loose black top with a scoop neckline, long airy sleeves, and part of the upper arm and shoulders cut out to give a little artful exposure. "I like this one. Very flirty."

When Iris nodded agreement, Abby carried it over to the bed. "Tell me about this Rachel."

"Well, she's both utterly adorable and incredibly sexy at the same time, which is one hell of a one-two punch." Iris shivered happily as she remembered reaching under Rachel's skirt during that kiss in the hotel hallway. "She's known Felix for a couple of years, and been crushing on him for that entire time, but didn't really act on it until now. She and I got talking about him, and before we knew it, we were seriously hitting it off ourselves." As Iris reached the bottom of her underwear drawer, she found a contoured rod covered in a silvery chrome finish, with a small dial on the base. After twisting that dial for a moment to test the motor, she tossed the vibrator onto the bed as well. "If only she didn't live in California."

Abby laid out a pair of form-fitting blue jeans on the bed. "This should go with that top, and I think your sandals should round out that outfit." She looked at the vibrator with a smirk. "It's nice that you don't feel like you have to compete with her."

"That's the best part. I could care less about competing with her, because I want her just as much as I want Felix. Almost. We're all in this together, and it's surprising how natural it feels." Iris threw a few more miscellaneous pieces of clothing on the bed pile, and walked over to the closet. "Everyone has fun, everyone feels beloved, everyone is turned on beyond words. Everyone wins. So much more fun that way." Her fingers rested on a zipped garment bag with a label that read Miranda Lawson. "Ooh, yes. If this still fits, it'll be perfect for tomorrow. I'll have both of them drooling like a waterfall."

She immediately began disrobing, and a couple of minutes later, she had squeezed herself into the costume. It was a white bodysuit with black sleeves and accents, and it clung to her hourglass figure like a tight glove. She ran her hands across the suit's hexagon-grid texture, and marveled at herself in the mirror. "Goddamn. That's pretty freaking hot, if I do say so myself. Felix and Rachel are going to have a stroke when they see me in this."

Abby clapped appreciatively. "I remember when you wore that to Worldcon several years ago. You had to fend off boggling admirers with a stick, and I'd wager good money that history will repeat itself tomorrow." She laughed. "Ah, to be twenty-six again."

Iris just grinned, peeled herself out of the costume, stowed it back into its bag, and added it to the pile. "I should finish packing everything. Don't want to keep Uncle Marcus waiting too long."

"Better yet, I'll finish packing for you. Go and take a quick shower." Abby grabbed her lightly by the shoulders, and steered her towards her bathroom. "Marcus is probably still cleaning up, so you've got plenty of time." She turned and grabbed her aunt into a huge hug. "You're the best family ever, Abby."

Abby returned the hug in kind, kissing her cheek in the process. "I love you, too, Iris. Now, go wash up."

CHAPTER FORTY-THREE

FELIX

As the second episode of *Kimagure Orange Road* ended, the closing credits rolled, showing various images of Ayukawa Madoka, the show's long-haired heroine, set to beautiful music.

Felix smiled at a memory, and spoke up for the first time in nearly half an hour. "My brother told me an interesting story about this show. Back in the late 80s and 90s, this character, Ayukawa Madoka, was considered the epitome of beauty by American anime fans. When this show's creator attended an American con in 1994, fans showed up in droves, all begging for sketches of Madoka. Donald was there. He said it was an amazing weekend." He gestured to the empty room. "But within just a few years, when *Pokémon* kicked off the big anime boom in the USA, *Kimagure Orange Road*, and Madoka by extension, were all but forgotten. Kind of a shame, that."

Rachel lifted her head from where it had been resting on Felix's right shoulder. "Every old-school anime fanboy's fantasy girlfriend, eh?"

He gave a slightly guilty nod. "When I was a kid, I thought she was pretty damn hot, yeah, but I'd rather think about a real woman in my arms."

Her eyes going wide with mischief, she moved quickly, and was now sitting sideways on his lap. She threw her arms around his neck and pulled herself close, the side of her firm chest pressing against him. "One flesh and blood woman in your arms, coming right up."

Felix squeezed her bare thigh, and put his other arm around her waist. "You really are a dream come true, you know that? Too beautiful for words."

"Stop stealing my lines, Felix. Now, make another one of my dreams come true, and kiss me again."

The third episode's opening credits began unheeded, and he bent to meet her lips once more. He reveled in the taste and especially the sound of her kisses, sweet and punctuated with breathy little gasps. As her naked thighs shifted on his lap, his hand slid upwards, coming to rest on the curve of her backside under her skirt.

As he gently squeezed and caressed her soft skin, her kisses grew more forceful. As she slid her tongue deeply into his mouth, he opened one eye to discover she was unbuttoning the rest of her blouse, confirming she had, indeed, gone without a bra. He wordlessly accepted her invitation, slipping one hand inside to touch her naked breasts for the first time.

As his hand closed around her, she gasped aloud again, and broke the kiss. "Don't ever stop," she whispered, kissing and licking along his neck.

Her nipple stiffened when the pad of his thumb brushed across it, and he was certain that she could feel him hardening as she writhed against him. Her mouth sent delicious tingles through him where she kissed along his neck, and soon he was moaning aloud.

He released her breast, and took her nipple between thumb and forefinger, gently pulling and pinching it as Iris had asked him to do to her that morning. Rachel's reaction was immediate, her hand darting beneath her skirt, followed shortly by the wet sound of her folds opening to accept her fingers.

"Push it deep for me, Rachel," he murmured in her ear.

"You're touching my breasts. Felix Jackson is touching me." As she fingered herself in his lap, her eyes seemed unfocused as if she couldn't believe this was really happening. She blinked and looked at him. "You're really going to make love to me tonight?"

He took hold of the hand she'd been pleasuring herself with. He locked eyes with her as he pulled her hand upwards and licked her fingers clean, and then reached below her skirt himself.

"You and Iris and I are all going to make love to each other tonight. But we're going to take special care of you." His fingers stroked along the sensitive skin of her inner thighs, then moved higher. He loved experiencing the texture of a woman's inner folds, the soft lips slick with arousal, the slow yield to an entering finger or manhood, and Rachel's body was exquisite to the touch. As two of his fingers slowly entered her, her body clenched and pulsed around him, as if trying to pull him in deeper, and he eagerly obliged.

She leaned against the wall next to his chair, and lifted one leather-clad ankle to rest on the back of the row of chairs in front of them, opening wider still.

"Deeper, Felix. Please, please."

When he carefully slipped a third finger into her, and started stroking along the hood of her clit with his thumb, she cried out in ecstatic surprise.

"Fuck, that's good. Don't stop, Felix. Ever." With shaking hands, she reached up to caress his cheek. "The only reason, and I mean the *only reason* I'm not demanding you take my virginity right here, right now, is because I promised Iris I'd wait until she got back." She leaned forward to kiss him again, and did so with a hungry fervor. "But damn, if you're not making that a hard promise to keep."

He pushed his fingers in as deep as possible, relishing the fresh moan she released as a result. "Do you want me to stop?"

She shook her head. "Just...just ease up a little. Leave my clit alone for a bit, and just use one finger for now. No need to ah, race to the finish, let's just cruise along for a while." She clenched once more, giving his fingers a brief, wet squeeze.

He slowly exited her, and then smeared his wet fingers across her mouth. He leaned in to kiss her, and gently slipped the one requested finger back inside her.

"You taste wonderful," he whispered after the kiss ended, licking her arousal from his lips. "I can only hope I'm living up to your fantasies about me."

She pulled her unbuttoned blouse open, caressing and squeezing her breasts as he continued his gentle motion below. "Lived up to and exceeded, lover. That is absolutely the last thing you need to worry about, believe me. Mmm." She cupped one of her breasts, lifting it slightly toward him.

He bent his head to take her nipple into his mouth. For a few moments, no words were shared, just her soft gasps of bliss against the sound of the forgotten anime on the screen before them.

She caressed his hair as he nibbled her breasts, then she spoke again. "Felix, do you...*uhn*. Do you have any fantasies?" Despite him slowing down between her legs, she was still having trouble finishing her sentences.

He sat up, trying to give the question real thought, despite the distraction of the nubile near-naked beauty purring in his arms. He wondered if Debbie or anyone else in the hall could hear the sounds Rachel was making. For all he knew, there was a small crowd of listeners outside, hanging on her every last gasp of joy. The idea sent a little extra jolt down his spine, and his erection stiffened even further.

"Well, there's one that comes to mind, but this might sound silly."

Easing her boot off the back of the other chairs, she sat up in his lap, making sure he could still push into her at will. She rested the side of her head against his shoulder, leaning against him.

"I promise not to judge." She bit her lower lip. "Two fingers, now, but really slow. Just like that, yeah."

"Well, I really got off on Iris blowing me under the table while you all sat around filling out your forms."

On the projection screen, one of the heroine's little sisters suddenly shrieked out an admonition, and he looked up in surprise, having almost forgotten they'd been watching anything to begin with.

"When you walked in, that little secret made me harder than I had ever been in my entire life."

Nuzzling his shoulder, she murmured agreement. "Iris has a real knack for turning people on, God bless her. Mmm. Go on."

"I was thinking just now how hot it would be if someone could overhear me when I'm making love to someone, to you." He paused, savoring the sensation of his fingers buried inside her to the last knuckle, and then slowly resumed his gentle motions. "They couldn't walk in, they couldn't stop us or anything. They'd just hear us, and how turned on we were. And maybe it would turn them on, too. Then they'd start, and we could hear their noises, and it would just be this harmony of gasping and moaning."

She shivered. "Last fall, Michelle and I went to a con in New York, and she brought her then-boyfriend Randy along. In the middle of the night, I got up to go to the bathroom, and just as I reached the door, I heard them fucking in the bathroom. It was hot. I could just imagine her, bent over and grabbing the counter for dear life as he opened her up from behind. They were both grunting and moaning so hard, I couldn't help but rub my clit as I stood outside the door. I came two minutes later, and I'm pretty sure Michelle heard it." She paused as his fingers pushed all the way in again, resuming as he slowly pulled back. "To this day, I wish I'd been brave enough to open the door, so I could've watched." She looked into his eyes. "How about a fantasy I could make happen directly? Or that Iris could help me with for you?"

"Wow, where to start?" He chuckled. "I mean, I'm going to be sharing a bed with two women at once, that's already pretty fantastic." He kissed her forehead. "I don't think there's a straight man alive who hasn't dreamed of taking one lover from behind while she's licking the other woman."

"I want to feel that so badly." She kissed his neck. "I want to be the one in the middle, and then I want to watch while you take Iris that way, while she licks me. Merciful heavens, a thousand times yes to that."

"Okay, I've got one." He suddenly got nervous. "Please don't laugh."

She shook her head. "I would never laugh at you, Felix. Ever. It's okay, you can tell me. I want to know because I want to make it happen for you."

"Well, it's...dull. Boring." He paused in his movements. "I know I'm really, really vanilla, and I hate it."

"Felix, I promise you, if it's something that turns you on, then there's nothing dull about it." She reached down, and gently prodded his fingers to start moving again. "Now, come on, it's fine. Talk to me." Another gasp, and she spoke up again. "Think about this way, Felix. Your vanilla-ness is so damn hot, you've got two women sleeping with you tonight at the same time, and a third waiting in the wings who wants to take you for a joyride first chance she gets. None of us would ever accuse you of being dull. Ever."

He nodded. "Sorry, had another bad moment there. I'm not used to..." He suddenly stopped. "I was just about to say, I'm not used to being happy." His throat suddenly closed tight, his eyes filling with tears. "Oh, God." His hands fell bonelessly to his sides, and he took several deep breaths.

She sat up abruptly, turning to face him, her thighs straddling his lap. She put her hands on his face. "Felix? What happened? What's wrong?"

He looked up and blinked to clear away the tears, rubbing his eyes with the back of his wrist. "I'm...I'm okay. Sorry." He gulped a lungful of air. "That's just it. I really am okay. I just didn't want to believe it." He met her concerned gaze, and put his arms around her. "I just figured something out. Something important."

Dabbing at the remnants of his tears, she cocked her head to one side. "I hope it's a good thing?"

"It really is, and I have you to thank for it. Iris, too." He pulled her in close. "I realized I haven't been happy. For years. Since my senior year of college, maybe more. But right now, right here, in your arms, I am happy. I was happy with Iris this morning. I'd forgotten what that even felt like. For years, I've just been getting by, at best. I haven't been genuinely happy, but now I am. Thanks to you."

She kissed his cheeks. "I don't know what I did, but I'm glad it worked. Your happiness is, well, it's pretty damn important to me, I'll tell you that."

"I want you to know this, Rachel. The reason why I'm here with you right now, the reason why I want to be with you and with Iris, is because the two of you make me happy." He sniffed and wiped away the last of the tears. "Not just because of everything physical going on between us, amazing as that is, but because you really accept me for what I am. What I do. You help me remember I've done good things."

"Like saving my life, for one." She put her hands behind his head, and kissed him with a firm intensity. "Let's not forget that. Kinda important."

"Exactly! I didn't know it at the time, but I wanted to help you. I did help you." He kissed her again. "It felt really, really good to help you, but somewhere in the back of my head, a little lying voice would say things like, *well, that doesn't count*, or *anyone would've done that, don't think that makes you a good person*, or even something like, *you don't deserve to feel good about that, because you're pathetic*. Such lying bullshit, but I listened to it. I would throw away things I deserved to feel good about because, somehow, I had convinced myself I didn't deserve to be happy."

She rested her forehead against his, a tear running down her cheek. "To hell with that lying voice. To hell and begone with it, and good goddamn riddance. Are you happy right now?"

"Yes, and you helped me this time. I can never thank you enough for that. This is why I want to be with you, why I want to make love to you. Because you and Iris showed me I'm worth more than that lying voice inside my head would ever let me believe. I do believe it, now." He squeezed her tight, hugging her close.

She squeezed back just as hard. "I never thought I'd be able to help you the way you did for me two years ago," she whispered in his ear. "I'm so glad I could, Felix. You beautiful, kind, sweet man."

They just sat for a few minutes, saying nothing, not letting go of their close embrace. Eventually, the mutual hug relaxed, and she sought his lips for an equally long kiss, tender and silent.

When their lips parted, he gave her a very relaxed smile. "I'm ready to tell you my fantasy now."

The blonde beauty straightened in his lap, reaching her arms upward for a long stretch. As she lowered them, her hands caressed across her own face, along the curve of her long neck and the choker she wore, and then came to rest under the pert globes of her breasts, lifting them towards him.

"Give these a kiss, and then tell me all about it."

With a deep-voiced laugh, he eagerly did so, lavishing attention on each nipple for a few moments with his tongue before sitting up. "My fantasy is to watch a woman pleasure herself. I want to sit with you on a bed with covers thrown back and the lights on, and watch you slide your favorite toy into yourself." He reached under her skirt again, his fingers toying with her outer folds, teasing the edges of her clit. "I want to see this beautiful body. I want to see what it looks like up close when you take that toy inside you. I want to see the look on your face when you come from thinking about me. I want to see you making love to yourself. That's what I want, Rachel. That would turn me on more than anything else." His fingers slipped inside her.

She nodded, her hips rocking on his hand. "Not even a little dull, lover boy. I nearly came just hearing you describe it. Not only will I do that for you, but I'll make sure Iris does, too. Think how hot that would be to watch both of us touching ourselves for you at the same time."

"That is going to be perfect." He laughed and caressed one of her nipples with his free hand, her cooing approval in response.

Moments later, both of their phones chimed an incoming text.

They paused, and then gave each other a broad grin. "Iris," they said in unison, and with an eager laugh, Rachel climbed off his lap, straightening her skirt and buttoning her blouse.

He stood and reached into his pocket, and there was indeed a new text from their mutual lover.

Iris: *Hey, lovebirds! I'm ten minutes from the hotel, so you need to wrap up whatever (or whomever) you're doing, and let me know where you're at. I can't wait to see you. I brought a couple toys, and I have a special surprise for tomorrow morning! ;) I missed you two so much!*

Rachel looked at the group-text on her phone. "Tomorrow morning?"

"Well, we'll see what she has in mind when she arrives, I guess. I'm sure it'll be awesome." He checked his clothes for anything looking out of place, and sent a return text.

Felix: *We really missed you, too, beautiful. All promises have been faithfully kept, and I've got some really good news to share when you arrive. We're at Video Room C, over by the Devonshire ballroom, through the right hand hallway off the lobby when you walk in the front door.*

Rachel: *Also, Felix has confided a totally hot fantasy to me that you're absolutely going to help me make happen tonight.*

He looked up, and she blew him a kiss as she typed on her phone. "Not that she needs something to look forward to, with everything we've already got planned, but every little bit helps," she said with a giggle.

Rachel: *Our man has warmed me up and then some. I am going to come SO HARD when you two are done with me.*

Iris: *You two better be ready to go as soon as I get there, because I am going to rip your clothes off the instant we get back to... Um, where are we doing this? Felix's room?*

Rachel: *Nope! Mine, room 1207. Michelle's going to be at the dance all night, so we'll have it all to ourselves, and I've got the big deluxe king-sized bed, perfect for a private orgy. Tell your aunt and uncle to start running red lights, we want you here now.*

CHAPTER FORTY-FOUR

MICHELLE

Back in room 1207, Michelle was not at the dance, but was instead standing under a hot shower spray, the last of her white hair color spray washing out and circling the tub's drain.

"Stupid, negging asshole," she muttered to herself. "If you'd just kept your mouth shut and not freaked out about a girl taking the initiative, I'd have given you a one night stand so mind-blowing, you'd still be telling folks about it when you're ninety goddamn years old."

With a frustrated snarl, she wrenched the shower faucet to its off position, and stepped onto the bathroom's tile.

She looked at the mirror, and on impulse, struck a pose and used her broadcaster voice. "Hey, everyone! Michelle Liang here for a special late-night update for *Journey From the West*! Live from Anime Horde, it's Friday night!" She spun around in a circle, humming the opening bars to her show's theme music, and then faced the mirror again.

"First of all, I'd like to give a big thank-you shout-out to Anime Horde security. If you're ever about to be groped by some pick-up artist asswipe who won't take no for an answer, the almighty redcaps of this con have got you covered! And who would've thought—did you know that misogynist assholes make the most adorable sounds of despair when tiny Latina women with combat training fold a jerk's wandering hands up behind their back like a human origami paper? I didn't, but I learned something new today, gosh golly!"

"Speaking of learning something new, I also found out the other security guard, a screamingly choice blond guy named River, is both transgender *and* only into guys!" She put her hands to her cheeks in an exaggerated gesture of surprise. "Now, I've dated trans folks before, so that's not even a thing for me, but if he's only into guys, then I'm just out of luck. Now, how do I know all this? Because, dear audience, I made a fool of myself by hitting on River as some sort of twisted thanks for the assist with Mister Negging Fuckwit of Not Gettin' None, Mississippi, and the lovely River shot me down oh so politely, and with the cool determination and professionalism I've come to expect from the staff of Anime Horde. Mister River, we salute you on your journey through your transition, and we hope you find the dude of your dreams in the near future."

She stood straight, and mimed a serious face as she snapped off a salute.

"But where does that leave me, the charming hostess of this show?" She grinned vapidly at the mirror for a moment, and then dropped the pose, her shoulders slumping. She looked at the sink counter, and picked up a hairbrush, running it through her shining black hair, still slightly damp even after being toweled off. "Leaves me high and dry," she said in her normal voice. "Up a creek without a paddle. With a massive itch that just isn't getting scratched tonight. Dagnabbit."

She looked at herself and addressed her reflection again. "Hey, it's not all bad. Rachel's no doubt going to lose her virginity tonight in the most epic way possible, getting double-teamed by the man of her dreams, and a woman who redefines the words living, breathing, sex goddess. I mean, goddamn, Iris."

Michelle mimed pouring herself a glass of wine, and raised her imaginary glass. "So, here's to you, Rachel Galadriel Midnight, wherever you are tonight. May your orgasms be multiple, may your partners be kind and gentle, and may someone be going down on you as soon as is humanly possible."

She lifted her hand as if to pretend to drink, when the hotel room door suddenly opened.

Iris's distinct voice, already purring with high-octane arousal, filled the room. "Rachel, you get right over on that bed and lift up that skirt. I need to be going down on you as soon as is humanly possible."

Michelle froze, both Rachel and Felix happily laughing as they walked quickly past the bathroom door.

She looked down at herself, completely naked, with no way of collecting any clothes or her room key before sneaking out.

Oh, shit.

CHAPTER FORTY-FIVE

RACHEL

The elevator ride to the twelfth floor seemed to take forever. Rachel clung to Felix's arm, her knees shaking, her body being deliciously invaded by one of Iris's fingers reaching under her skirt from behind.

"Iris, what if someone else gets on?"

Iris continued working her middle finger in and out of Rachel's warmth, but otherwise stood placidly next to her, giving no indication of her actions unless someone looked behind Rachel's back. "Then you can experience for yourself how turned-on Felix was when I was sucking him off under the table in front of all your unknowing friends."

Felix smiled. "Very, very turned on, indeed." He squeezed Rachel's hand. "Do you want her to stop?"

Rachel shook her head vigorously. That finger felt so good, especially when Iris would slip it out and rub a little circle around her clit, before pushing back into her quivering folds. "Wh-where did you learn to be such an exhibitionist?"

Iris shrugged, making a show of looking at the elevator's display screen. "Dunno. I've never done anything like this in my life, but damn if I'm not having fun with it."

The elevator chimed, and the doors opened on the twelfth floor. "Aw, what a pity. No one joined us for the ride." She shot Felix a wink. "We could just ride the elevator all the way back down again, see if anyone gets on this time, so that they can fail to notice Rachel getting off."

"No, that's okay!" Rachel shot forward, and hit the Open button before the elevator could start moving. "C'mon, I want to get you two alone in private. Don't be a tease."

Adjusting her fully-stuffed duffel bag and garment bag as they hung from her shoulder, Iris laughed, and Felix and her followed Rachel into the hallway.

"I am not a tease, I'll have you know. I'm simply doing my part to get you warmed up, although I'm quite sure Felix did a wonderful job while I was away."

"He most certainly did! Such wonderful hands." As she walked ahead, Rachel did a few playful twirls, before realizing she was potentially giving anyone who walked by a very intimate show. Although, the hallway seemed deserted for the moment. She pushed her skirt back down, her cheeks glowing with a kaleidoscope of emotion. "Whoops."

Licking her lips, Iris turned to Felix. "Tell me, what sexy little sounds did she make when you went down on her?"

He gave an obviously exaggerated sigh. "Actually, we never got that far. She was sitting in my lap for most of the time." He looked around, and a wicked smile spread across his face. "Rachel, come here for a second."

She stepped into his arms. "I have no idea where this is going, but my room is right over there," she said, holding up her room keycard.

Without another word, he suddenly dropped to one knee, lifted up the front of Rachel's emerald-green skirt, and helped himself to a taste from between her thighs.

Rachel immediately reached out with one hand to steady herself against the nearby wall. "What are you...!"

She slapped a hand against her mouth, muffling the scream of pleasure his warm tongue had just inspired. His hot breath was against her clit, and it was nothing like she had ever experienced before. She reached down to run her fingers through his hair, and then just as abruptly, he stood up. She had to grab the wall again to steady herself, the change of pace was so abrupt.

He ran a fingertip across his lips, and offered it to Iris, who eagerly licked it clean.

"A delicious flavor, if I do say so myself, Iris. Robust, clean, and eager." He chuckled, and reached for Rachel's hand. "Sorry, I couldn't resist. I hope you'll forgive me?"

Rachel pretended to look angry for a moment. "You better make it up to me in my bed, Mister Jackson." She pulled him in for another kiss, hooking one leg around his thigh.

Iris smacked her lips, apparently still savoring her brief taste. She abruptly snatched the keycard out of Rachel's hand, crossed the last few steps to room 1207, and unlocked the door. "God, that tasted good. C'mon, you two. Get over here." As she stepped inside, she beckoned them over. "Rachel, you get right over on that bed and lift up that skirt. I need to be going down on you as soon as humanly possible."

Rachel and Felix shared a laugh and a smile as they followed Iris inside, who disappeared into the room's huge closet space to stow her bags. They passed the closed bathroom door, holding hands as they reached the suite's interior.

Looking around the room, Rachel smiled. *It was worth spending extra for the deluxe suite,* she thought to herself. The oversized room had walls painted a rich forest green, with wood panel accents and metallic gold trim, plus a thick brown carpet that was absolutely decadent against her bare feet. Just past the bathroom area was a set of lush recliners in matching green and brown, a nice bit of open floor space, and then the bed. Overall, the room's color gave her the feeling of a verdant forest, which she found quite relaxing.

Letting go of Felix's hand, she walked right up to the giant king-sized bed that dominated the back part of the room, decked out in a thoroughly soft green and gold comforter, and sat on the edge, crossing one thigh over the other. "Could someone perhaps help me with my boots?"

"Why, milady," Felix said with an exaggerated British accent, "please allow your humble servant to assist you." Kneeling next to her leg, he reached out and slowly undid the buckles running down the side of her sleek black leather footwear, looking into her eyes as he did so.

Iris had returned from the closet, chuckling at Felix's playful voice, and immediately knelt next to Rachel's right leg, affecting a thick Cockney accent. "Oi, Mister Jackson, you be watchin' those hands, guv'nor!"

As Rachel and Felix laughed at this, Iris pulled gently at Rachel's leg so her knees were spread wide. She ran her fingers along Rachel's smooth inner thigh, then down the length of her leg to start unbuckling the other boot. "Yer can't trust a man not to take a liberty or five, not wit' such a fine lass as ye'self!"

As the boots slid off her feet, Rachel braced her hands behind her and leaned back a little, looking at the pair of eager smiles kneeling before her. "Why, Miss Iris, I do declare," she said in a breathy Southern Belle voice. "You'll protect me from the scheming depredations of this charming rogue, won't you? My innocence, it's the only thing I have left in this cruel, cruel world!" She punctuated this by reaching up and undoing the top-most button of her blouse.

Felix touched her bare thigh, his fingertips leaving warm trails across her skin, and barely brushing against the edges of the damp folds beneath her skirt. "If you must know, madam," he said, giving Iris a haughty look down the length of his nose, "I am not taking a liberty. I am merely, ah, inspecting this beautiful maiden for any signs of malady or distress."

Rachel shivered at his ginger touch, and spread her legs wider still, lifting up the edge of her skirt and forgetting her affected accent. "Iris, whatever happened to your promise to lick this pussy as soon as humanly possible?"

She looked at Iris and took in the other woman's elegant beauty. The black blouse Iris wore managed the amazing trick of both hanging loosely from her body, and yet still emphasizing her voluptuous breasts, especially with the scoop neckline giving everyone a tantalizing glimpse of those curves. The shoulders being cut out of the upper sleeves only added to the enticing effect, and Rachel's cheeks warmed as a new thought came to her.

Iris had started to lean closer, but Rachel held up a hand. "Before you start, I have one request. Leave your blouse on so I can take it off you later myself. Please."

"Absolutely, princess." Iris kissed one of her fingertips, pressed it against Rachel's smiling mouth, and then let that finger trail its way down the line of Rachel's chin, along her neck, and then across the covered curves of her firm breasts "I've been wanting to lick you ever since you put my hand under your skirt this morning, you brazen little thing. I'm not going to wait any longer."

Bracing herself, Rachel tensed in anticipation as Iris bent to put her mouth over the juncture of her thighs, and the instant her tongue slid along her opening in earnest, she very nearly collapsed backwards onto the bed. Her entire body went from tension to unclenched release, and at the second pass of Iris's warm tongue, Rachel moaned uncontrollably with raw pleasure. A third lick, this time just above the hood of her clitoris, and she did fall backwards—into Felix's arms.

"If that feels as half as good as it looks," he said in her ear, "you must be in heaven right now."

Rachel nodded. "Seventh heaven, cloud nine, something like that. Oh, my God, this is good." She unbuttoned another black disk on the front of her blouse, and turned her head to look at the man cradling her. "You're gonna take a turn down there, too, right?"

"If Iris ever lets me, absolutely." He stroked her still-clothed stomach, watching Iris hungrily devour her newest treat.

Iris looked up, her lips already damp with Rachel's abundant arousal. "I may be here for a good long while, you two. Get comfortable, because I'm enjoying myself far too much to stop anytime soon." She lowered her head for another lick, but then looked up sharply. "Rachel, that's okay, right? Do you want me to stop?"

Gently but firmly taking a handful of Iris's curls in hand, Rachel pulled the woman's face back down to her open thighs. "Less talk, more pussy. Lots more pussy."

Iris's tongue eagerly obeyed, and Rachel happily slumped against Felix's chest. The initial shock of this new pleasure had tapered off, and Rachel spread her legs as wide as she could to give Iris every possible access. She slid her own hands along her bare thighs, and settled in to enjoy every new touch, every new sensation. Felix's brief tease in the hallway aside, this was Rachel's first time on the receiving end of oral sex, and it was clear Iris was working hard to make it exquisitely memorable.

As she watched Iris's every move and savored what came from each touch, her already strong feelings for this woman grew with each passing moment. *Iris doesn't care that I'm rich, or who my dad is. She's not doing this to me just to get a rise out of Felix. She's making love to me with her mouth because she wants me. Because I turn her on. Because she missed me while she was gone. Because she thinks I'm beautiful.*

That last thought sent a tremor down her legs, her toes curling and uncurling as Iris continued.

Closing her eyes, Rachel breathed deep, and let the room's landscape wash over her. The musk of her own damp arousal seemed to cover the surroundings like a warm blanket, but she could still taste Iris's own desire in the air. She snuggled closer into the warm arms holding her, and savored Felix's well-remembered scent.

She'd touched herself many times over the last two years while thinking about him, remembering his exact redolence as she screamed his name to her empty bedroom. Now, it was around her for real, no longer a fantasy, and a single tear ran down her cheek, unnoticed by her lovers. *He's real. He's right behind me. He's holding me in his arms. He listened to me. He held my heart when I nearly gave up on everything. And I held his heart in return tonight, at least a little. He said that we made him happy. I made him happy.* Her back arched in ecstasy as his mouth gently closed around the edge of her ear, nibbling and licking along the sensitive skin. The pleasure from two mouths kissing her, licking her, adoring her—the sensations blended together, blurring her senses until she could feel kisses on every inch of her soft skin.

Moments later, her mewling gasps were replaced by a sudden cry of delight as all of her senses focused on the feeling of Iris sliding two fingers deep into her eager wetness. Her body clenched around those fingers and then released, a tiny echo of an orgasm sizzling from her abdomen, up through her chest, and out through her fingertips.

Felix's hands had moved to her breasts, slowly squeezing and caressing them through her blouse.

Rachel looked down at his hands and smiled. "Dreams do come true. I've had so many dreams about you touching me like this, exactly like this. Could you unbutton me next?"

His hands moved to the vertical row of black buttons on her blouse, undoing them from top to bottom. "Of course, Rachel. Of course." As the last button came undone, he pulled her blouse open, and her nipples stiffened in the cool air.

Iris looked up from her happy task, and was clearly quite excited at her first glimpse of Rachel's naked breasts, judging by her broad smile. "Rachel, you're a knockout. Felix, come here for a second and let her lie back, I want to try something. Rachel, get in the middle of the bed, if you would."

As Felix stood up, Iris walked over to him and pulled him into her arms for what looked to be an intense kiss, her lips still covered with the copious moisture from between Rachel's thighs.

She sat up and pulled off her blouse as she watched them, tossing it to the floor and leaving her wearing nothing but her pleated green miniskirt and the black ribbon around her neck. She shimmied to the large bed's center as directed, watching as Iris ended the kiss and whispered in Felix's ear, who nodded agreement with a smile.

"I could watch you two kiss all night," Rachel said with a grin. "You were made for each other."

Iris shook her head, and climbed into the bed to Rachel's right. "I beg to differ, princess. *We* were made for each other. All three of us."

Kicking off his shoes first, Felix joined them, lying on his side to Rachel's left. "Absolutely. This is exactly where we should be, all three of us, here and now." He looked like he was about to say more, but paused and looked at them, then towards the door.

Iris asked, "Felix, did you hear something?"

He hesitated before answering. "No. Probably just a room service cart going by or something." He broke into a wide grin as he turned back to Rachel, lying on her back between him and Iris. "But let's get back to the matter at hand, shall we?" He bent his head to take her nipple into his mouth, gently licking around and suckling at the hardened tip.

Running her fingers through his hair, Rachel was already lost in ecstasy when Iris moved to follow suit, taking Rachel's right nipple into her mouth.

"You two are more than I could ever deserve. What are you...?"

As she spoke, Iris and Felix had reached down in unison, and while Felix was pushing two fingers deep inside her, Iris used her nimble fingers to pull back the hood of Rachel's clit and gently massage the soft flesh beneath. Rachel's hand fell limply from Felix's hair, and all she could do was stare at the ceiling while her body vibrated like a tuning fork. This exquisite play continued for several long minutes, with Rachel lifting and spreading her thighs to give them as much access as possible.

She looked at herself, her legs high in the air, and remembered another treasured fantasy, of Felix kneeling between her raised thighs, her ankles on his shoulders. As the real Felix filled her with his thrusting fingers, she imagined what his face might look like above her when he was pushing his cock inside instead.

I'm going to find out soon. Very soon. Oh, hell yes!

She managed eventually to touch both of her lovers on their shoulders. "This is amazing, but you're going to wear me out early at this rate, and we're just getting started." She bit her lip, savoring the last few touches and thrusts before they stopped. "Iris, stand up. I want to peel you out of those clothes. Felix, I'm gonna do the same to you, so don't take anything off yet."

Iris licked her fingers clean as she stood. "Ready and eager, Rachel. Undress me. I want to be naked for you."

Rachel slid the skirt off her hips, and let it drop to the floor as she climbed out of the bed. "Look at you, Iris. You're just, well, so damn hot!" She ran her hands across the soft fabric covering Iris's stomach. "And a snazzy dresser as well." Looking up into Iris's eyes, she gave an awkward smile. "This might seem like an odd moment to ask, but before I leave town, you and I need to go shopping together. I want you to dress me, to deck me out in something that has you desperate to rip off the outfit and take me hard in the dressing room. Can you do that for me?"

"You don't need my help for that, Miss Miniskirt. I damn near ravished you on principle when you opened the door before your date." Iris ran a finger along the line of Rachel's neck. "And leave on that choker tonight. But yeah, we'll make for some shopping playtime, absolutely."

Sliding her hands underneath the hem of Iris's blouse, Rachel indulged herself for a moment, savoring the feel of her lover's smooth skin around her waist. "I'm ready to play, alright." She lifted the soft black blouse upwards, and helped Iris to pull it off entirely.

Iris squared her shoulders as her choice of lingerie was revealed—a beautiful and perfectly fitted bra in rich emerald green, with patches of black lace over her nipples. "Like what you see?"

Felix moved closer. "Very, very much. That is gorgeous on you, Iris."

"It'll look even better off of her." Rachel leaned forward and kissed the upper curve of Iris's breasts, and reached around to smoothly release the bra's hooks.

As Rachel pulled the bra away to reveal Iris's rich curves, Iris held them up as an offering. "Each of you give one of these a kiss," she said. "I want to feel what we just did for Rachel."

They needed no further prompting, and soon Iris was happily moaning as Rachel nibbled on one nipple, while Felix suckled gently on the other.

Before long, Rachel dropped slowly to her knees, and unbuttoned the tight jeans that Iris wore. "Felix, won't you help me peel her out of these?"

"Gladly." He moved to kneel behind Iris, and as Rachel undid the zipper on the jeans, Felix gently pulled them off of Iris's hourglass hips. Rachel could hear Felix softly kissing somewhere along their mutual lover's back, or perhaps along the cheeks of her backside. Iris wore the most contented smile Rachel had ever seen.

Iris stepped out of the jeans with a little help from Felix, and ran a finger across the front of her last remaining piece of underwear. It was green with black lace, a matched set with her discarded bra. "Rachel," she whispered, "give me a kiss. Right here." Iris pointed right at the front of her panties.

Rachel bit her lower lip, and suddenly burst into laughter as she put a hand on Iris's hip.

Felix stood again behind Iris, cupping one of those beautiful breasts and using his fingertips to tease her nipple. He craned his neck to look around at Rachel. "Everything okay down there?"

Stifling her laugh with the back of her hand, Rachel nodded, and reached out to stroke along the edges of the lace before her. "Couldn't be better. It's just, well. I'm about to go down on a woman for the very first time, and part of me wondered earlier tonight if I was maybe going to hesitate, or be all *am I really doing this* when this moment came." She looked into Iris's eyes, her own lust echoed in the other woman's eyes. "But instead, as soon as I was told it was time, all I could think was *finally*" Rachel leaned in and kissed the soft green fabric that lay between her and soft naked flesh. "You smell so good, Iris. So good." She mouthed her way over that front panel, and she could taste a hint of the other woman's wetness through one of the mesh panels.

Sliding a finger underneath the edge of those panties, Rachel pulled the fabric aside and dove in without pause, her tongue searching for the clitoris nestled within the revealed womanhood. Iris grunted in approval, and a strong hand grasped Rachel's hair, urging her to continue. Instead, she pulled back for a moment, and slid the underwear down and away entirely before returning to the curls between Iris's thighs.

"How's she doing down there, Iris?"

Rachel loved that deep purr which crept into Felix's voice when he was turned on, and she licked a long trail from top to bottom of Iris's opening.

"She's a natural, handsome." The hand in Rachel's hair spasmed and clenched slightly when Rachel pulled back the clitoral hood with her fingers. "A little more practice, and she's going to give your hot tongue a run for your money."

Rachel chuckled to herself, and nudged Iris's legs open a little so that she could slip a finger inside those wet folds.

"Mmm, just like that, Rachel. If you want me to come, keep that up."

Instead, Rachel withdrew her questing finger, and gave one last lick before she stood up. "Not just yet. Call me greedy, but I want you two to make me come first." She leaned to one side, and gave Felix a smile as he stood behind Iris with his hands on her hips. "And you're criminally overdressed. It's time we fixed that."

Playfully pushing Felix onto his back on the large bed, Rachel and Iris stripped him, starting from his socks and working upwards to his shirt, until he lay there wearing nothing but a pair of black boxer-briefs.

"I have to say," he said with a grin as he propped himself up on his elbows, "the experience of being undressed by two eager naked women is one that I never thought I'd have. I definitely feel blessed right now."

Iris responded by climbing into the bed, practically ripping his underwear, and taking his erect sex into her mouth.

His eyes rolled back, and he wasn't shy about moaning aloud his approval. "Damn, Iris. Goddamn."

Rachel climbed in as well, and reached between Felix's legs, gently caressing his balls while Iris slowly bobbed up and down on his length. "Felix, I'm going to let Iris work a little more magic on you, but I'm ready. I want you inside me, more than I've ever wanted anything." She threw one leg over his head, straddling his face. "I want you to do a little more of what you teased me with in the hallway."

She spread her knees and lowered herself, bracing for the first touch of his tongue. When he licked her again, his hands caressing her thighs, she leaned forward with a pleased squeal. Placing a hand on Iris's shoulder, Rachel braced herself as she watched Iris bring Felix to full hardness.

Moments later, Iris sat up, licking her lips. "He's definitely ready. I gave him just enough to keep him nice and stiff, without setting him off early." She gave Rachel a kiss. "Rachel, thank you so much for letting me be here for this. I'm being really good and not taking him for a quick ride while he's occupied with you."

Rachel shook her head. "No, do it." She held Felix's member upright. "I want to watch it slide into you for a minute. Just neither of you come yet, that's all I ask."

"Anything you want, princess." Iris moved forward, still facing Rachel, and sat gingerly on the tip of Felix's cock.

Rachel was spellbound as she watched the lips between Iris's thighs spread open to accept Felix's length inside her. His tongue was going crazy along her inner lips, and his cries of pleasure would no doubt have filled the room had his mouth not been muffled and occupied. Iris wasn't silent, either, taking deep and loud breaths as she raised and lowered herself with her knees.

"Lean back, Iris," Rachel said, stumbling over her words as Felix's mouth closed over her clit.

Iris complied, and Rachel bent down. Her tongue traced a trail from the root of Felix's rod, to where he was pushing into Iris, and then along that delicious wet slit to seek out Iris's clit once more.

Iris erupted into loud cries of pleasure, and a few moments later, she pulled herself off of Felix's lap. "Too close. I was three seconds from coming. We're definitely doing that again later. That was intense."

Rachel had already lowered her mouth over Felix's length, but going very, very slowly so she didn't set him off just yet. *My first sixty-nine, she thought. So many delicious firsts tonight. Life is good.*

Reluctantly, she climbed off the warm man below her, and pulled Iris into an embrace as they kneeled on the bed. "The next time Felix and I sixty-nine like that, I want you to fill my pussy with my vibrator." She purred as Iris nuzzled her neck and cupped one of her pert breasts. "Can you do that for me?"

"I can do that and more." Iris was all over her ear, licking and kissing as she murmured a happy response. "I brought my own favorite toy, as well. Maybe I'll lube that one and slide it into your perfect little ass. Would you like that?"

At that moment, Felix moved behind Rachel, kissing the back of her neck. "Now that would be one hell of a sight, Rachel. Up to you, of course." He embraced her from behind, his firm erection pressed between their bodies as his kisses trailed down one shoulder.

"You're both so warm." Rachel held onto Iris's shoulders, happy beyond words to be pressed between her two lovers. "I'm ready. I'm really ready. I want this."

As they untangled, Felix lifted a finger under Rachel's chin, his eyes alight with desire as their gazes met. "How do you want me?"

Rachel lay down on her back, and spread her legs wide. "I want you on top of me. I want to feel your warm body on mine." She reached down, and slipped a finger inside herself. "Start slow." She reached for Iris. "Lay here next to me. Just be with me for now. I know I'm being greedy."

Iris shook her head, watching as Felix moved to kneel between Rachel's spread thighs. "Tonight is all for you, princess. Anything you want. Anything."

"If you need me to stop, just say so." Felix slowly stroked his length, looking hungrily down at her body.

"That's not going to happen." Rachel's eyes misted over with a few drops of joyful tears, and she squeezed Iris's hand tight. "You two have made me the happiest woman on the planet tonight. Everything has been perfect. This wouldn't have been right without both of you here." She spread her thighs as wide as she could. "Make love to me, Felix. I want to feel you deep inside me. Please."

Taking his length in hand, Felix moved in closer, rubbing up and down across her opening. Her right hand squeezed Iris tight, and she reached up with her left to grasp Felix. Their fingers intertwined, and as she locked eyes with him, pressure built and stretched when he entered her to the hilt. Minor tingles of pain, and then gone.

Felix bore down on her, his hips slowing grinding as he covered her with his body, kissing along her neck.

Rachel looked to her side, watching Iris happily play with herself with her free hand.

As those warm thrusts continued, Rachel hooked one leg around Felix's waist, enjoying every moment, every touch, every kiss that he lavished upon her. "It had to be you, Felix," she whispered between the gasps that escaped from her lips with each new deep slide inside her. "Thank you, thank you. I needed you so much." She turned to look at Iris again. "Help me come,

Iris. Touch me. Kiss me. I need you here, too. I want. I want to scream your names. I want my pussy to squeeze Felix when I come. I want him to come deep inside me."

Felix eased into a kneeling position, lifting one of her ankles onto his shoulder, with Iris stroking Rachel's belly. "And then I want you to lick it all out of me while he takes you from behind, pretty lady."

"I love the way you think, princess." Iris ran her fingers through the little patch of blonde hair remaining between Rachel's thighs, and then moved a little lower to stroke some very warm places that made Rachel's toes curl.

Rachel arched her back, savoring the feel of skilled hands on the outside, a firm rod inside, and cooed happily. "Fuck me, fuck me..."

"And I really love the way you move with Felix inside you." Iris leaned down to kiss the curve of Rachel's breast, continuing her hand's wonderful work down between her thighs. "I only hope you'll enjoy the show as much when it's my turn."

"Never had to think about pacing myself like this before." Felix smiled as he spoke, and turned to kiss the ankle resting against his shoulder. He had settled into a slow and steady rhythm, pulling nearly all the way out before slipping back inside her, and Rachel was loving every second of it.

"Felix, are you okay?" Rachel watched his face, pleased beyond words that he seemed to actually be enjoying himself, and wasn't just doing this out of some sort of sense of obligation. *Shut up, brain,* she thought to herself. He clearly wants to be here.

"Just making sure I don't wear out too soon, Rachel. I want to give both of you everything I can." He caressed her stomach as he slipped deep inside her again.

Rachel bit her lower lip, and looked towards Iris before returning her gaze to the handsome man above her. "Is...is my pussy nice and tight, Felix?" She clenched as best she could as she said this, hoping it was something he could feel.

Iris didn't give Felix a chance to answer Rachel's question. She rose to her knees, and turned Felix's chin towards her, so that she could pull him into a long kiss without interrupting his rhythm. "Felix, I think Rachel wants to hear you talk dirty to her. She wants to know how her pretty little slit feels around your cock."

Rachel nodded, pinching her own nipples as she listened to that rich voice, a husky purr from the lips of this curvaceous siren that had somehow agreed to make love to her tonight. "Please, Felix. Tell me. Fuck me. Fuck me harder."

Felix obeyed, grabbing hold of both of Rachel's thighs, and pushing deep with each shift of his hips. "Your pussy feels so good, Rachel. I love how wet you get for us, and I love it when you squeeze me." He turned to Iris, and flicked his eyes downwards, and she reached down to start vigorously rubbing Rachel's clit once more. "It's time to make you come for us, Rachel. Time to feel your pretty little blonde pussy gush and squeeze me." He sped up, breathing harder, sweat beading on his brow. "Talk to me, princess. Tell me what you need. Tell me how you feel."

Her senses revving to the point of no return, Rachel could barely speak. Iris's fingers knew exactly where to touch her, and the sound of their voices sent shivers down her spine. Felix felt so good inside her, and... and...

"*Felix*! *Iris*! *More*! *Harder*!" She gasped, and with a whisper, barely managed a small "please" before it became impossible for her to speak.

Her lovers obliged her request, and with one last tender flick across her hood exactly in time with a wet thrust from Felix, Rachel's insides clamped tight around the firm erection inside her. A vibration rippled outwards from her belly, sending a spasm down all of her limbs, and a rush of pure ecstasy shot up her back to explode behind her eyes.

Felix's face echoed the pleasure she was feeling. His eyes were alight with desire for her, staring right through her, and although his mouth was open, no sound came forth. His hands clenched her thighs, and there was a pulse between her legs as he filled her.

A moment later, and he carefully withdrew.

Her body ached, half of her wanting nothing more than to feel him take her again this instant, the other half screaming with overstimulated senses and demanding at least a few minutes to recover.

"That was perfect. Thank you. Thank you both." She slumped against the pillows as Felix laid beside her, flat on his back and breathing deeply.

Iris stood, stretching her arms for a moment as she smiled down at them. "You two rest up for a minute. I'll be right back with some warm wet washcloths."

As Iris walked toward the bathroom, Rachel looked at Felix, and discovered he was already looking at her. They shared a silent smile, her hand grasping his.

I know I shouldn't, but saying I Love You feels like the most natural thing right now. Hold that in, Rachel. You've been greedy enough tonight.

Instead, she rolled and placed a tender kiss on his lips before resting her head on his shoulder, curled up in the crook of his arm.

CHAPTER FORTY-SIX

IRIS

Iris grinned from ear-to-ear as she stepped away from the oversized bed, already pondering what might happen next once her two lovers were given a chance to recover. She paused mid-step in front of the large wall mirror, admiring her own curves.

As she reached for the bathroom doorknob, she paused. The door was just slightly ajar.

I'm positive this was closed when we walked in.

She stepped inside, and was face-to-face with a completely naked Michelle Liang. The Chinese woman frantically held a finger to her lips, and motioned for Iris to come in. She then mouthed, "Shut the door," and Iris did so, an eyebrow raised.

Iris didn't attempt to hide her admiring once-over of Michelle's figure. "Good to see you again, in all respects. You look even better with your natural hair color." She smiled. "What are you doing here?"

"Jesus, Mary, and Buddha, Iris. It has been the weirdest night possible." Michelle's eyes did a bit of wandering, as well, and her returned whisper was full of frustration. "Long story short, I nearly got assaulted at the dance when I told a guy off for being too pushy, then got shot down by a hot security guard who turned out not to be into lady-parts, and just generally had the wind ripped out of my sails, so I came back here." She ran her hands through her still lightly damp hair. "I swear, I had no idea you three were coming back *here*. I assumed you were going to Felix's room or something!"

"Well, we thought you'd be gone all night. Sorry you had such a rough night, though." Iris shook her head with amazement. "You were in the bathroom when we came in?"

"Yeah. My clothes and key are on the far side of the bed, so there was no way I could sneak out."

Iris covered her mouth with her hand to muffle a quiet laugh. "I can only imagine how frustrating that must've been."

"It has been a very long night, striking out in every way possible," Michelle said, a small blush creeping onto her cheeks. "And watching you and Felix beautifully fucking Rachel's brains out has been nothing short of pure torture."

Her grin growing wider, Iris put one hand on her hip. "Did you enjoy the show?"

"I saw you riding our favorite con-staffer while Rachel licked you and got licked in return." Michelle's dark nipples stiffened slightly as she spoke, but she looked away with a slight frown on her lips. "I would've given my entire college fund to be in the middle of that."

"Hmm." Iris traced a fingertip across the line of Michelle's jaw. "Maybe you can, and free of charge, to boot."

Michelle looked up in surprise. "Wait, what?"

"Consider this an official invitation to an orgy." Iris leaned in and kissed Michelle's neck, just the way Michelle had to her hours before. "Seeing your pretty little pussy on Felix's phone wasn't nearly enough for me."

A small "Yes" escaped Michelle's lips, and she put an arm around Iris's shoulders. "You're sure it's okay?"

"It'll be fine," Iris murmured against her neck, pulling Michelle close and rubbing her full chest against Michelle's perfect proportions. "Didn't you say you desperately needed a one night stand tonight?" She smiled as Michelle's hand cupped her ass.

"I might need more than that." Michelle pulled away so she could look Iris in the eye. "Could I get an upgrade to friend-with-benefits, maybe?"

"I swear, this is the craziest weekend." Iris grinned, her fingertips now tracing the contours of Michelle's firm breasts. "In one Friday, I've met the man of my dreams, a woman I really didn't expect to fall for so hard, and an amazingly hot Youtuber who's going to put her tight little ass in the air so I can watch my boyfriend fuck her hard from behind." She reached out and slid a finger between Michelle's thighs, and summoned her best I Want You Now bedroom purr. "You're going to do that for me, aren't you?"

Michelle's eyes went wide at Iris's gentle touch, then wider still at the sound of her voice.

She attacked Iris's lips with a hungry kiss. When it ended a moment later, she was already breathing heavily. "Right before you three walked in here, I used the words living, breathing, sex goddess when thinking about you, and I mean that even more right now. I will eagerly do anything you want."

Iris smirked, and after a moment's thought, she gently pressed down on Michelle's shoulders. "Believe it or not, I did come in here to get something, so why don't you have your first taste of me while I take care of that, hmm?"

She needed no further prompting, dropping to her knees and eagerly lapping at the thick auburn curls between Iris's legs. With a happy sigh, Iris widened her stance just a little to give Michelle better access, and then grabbed a washcloth.

"Wow, these are soft."

Michelle looked up, her mouth already wet with the fruits of her labor. "We bring our own from home. Hotel towels are like sandpaper." She dove back in without any further ado.

Iris nodded and ran the cloth under a stream of warm water from the sink. As she squeezed out the excess, she looked down. "Having fun down there? It's almost showtime."

Michelle stood up, her eyes wide and smiling, her arms going around Iris's waist. "How do you do it? You look hot, you sound hotter, you smell fantastic, you feel so good, and you even taste amazing. You're a feast for the senses."

Iris licked Michelle's mouth, cleaning away the last drops of her own arousal that had smeared on Michelle's chin. "And so are you. This is going to be fun." She gave the washcloth one last squeeze. "I'll bet you when we walk out there, Rachel is on her knees giving Felix a beautiful blowjob."

"I'll see that bet." Michelle palmed one of Iris's breasts for a quick squeeze. "I'll bet that they're sixty-nining. She showed me her dream diary once, and that little fantasy shows up quite often in there. Winner gets to fuck Felix first?"

"We'll see." Iris batted playfully at Michelle's grasping hand. "Okay, we better stop, or we're never going to get back in there. I'll go first."

As she stepped back into the suite's hallway, Iris's heart was hammering in her chest. *I can't believe I'm doing this. I'm dragging another beautiful woman into our bed, for a real life, honest to goodness orgy. Group sex, butt play, public blow jobs, fingering Rachel in the elevator. Dear God, what other kinks do I have hiding in the back of my skull? Not that I've regretted any of this for an instant, hell no!*

As she held onto Michelle's hand, Iris reached the opening to the bedroom, and smiled at the sight before her. Felix was sitting on the foot of the bed, and Rachel was kneeling on the carpet before him. Her arms were around his waist, his hands were stroking her dark blonde hair, and her head was moving up and down in a slow rhythm, his renewed erection between her lips.

Iris paused to watch, Michelle still hidden behind her.

Felix turned his head and looked up as Iris stood there. "Did you and Michelle have a nice moment together?"

His smile was wide, and Iris's surprise was pleasantly overruled by her affection for this man. She loved seeing that playful twinkle in his eyes.

Rachel's eyes flew open, and she pulled up abruptly, Felix's length falling from her lips. "What?"

Iris laughed and tugged Michelle into the room with her as she approached the bed. "Sure did. You knew she was there?"

"Hi, roomie!" Michelle gave a nervous laugh. "Sorry about this."

"When we were all climbing into bed together," Felix continued, his length standing straight against his naked stomach, "I heard someone moving in the hallway, heard Michelle's voice whisper an *oh wow*, and then I'm pretty sure I heard her playing with herself." He smiled and trailed his fingertips along the underside of his stiff erection. "I didn't want to interrupt the moment we were having, and I thought it might be fun to have an audience."

Rachel stood. "You were here the whole time?"

"I was in the bathroom when you came in. The dance was a bust, and I didn't know you were coming here." Michelle let go of Iris's hand and glanced around nervously. "Look, I'm sorry, I should—"

"I'm so glad you're here!" Rachel enveloped Michelle in a huge hug, and to Iris's eyes, Michelle was not only surprised, but also more than a little turned on at the feeling of Rachel's naked body against hers. "Tonight has been so amazing, and knowing that my best friend was here to see it happen just makes it even better!" She stepped back, her hands on Michelle's shoulders, grinning from ear-to-ear.

"Well, I wasn't exactly planning on this, but, um." Michelle glanced towards Felix, and Iris grinned as she saw Michelle's eyes locking on the sight of him stroking himself. "Here I am."

Pulling Rachel into her arms, Iris answered the blonde's smile with an eager kiss, finishing the embrace with a giddy kiss to the tip of Rachel's nose. "Princess, I think it'd be wonderful to have Michelle join in, and I'm pretty sure I already know Felix's answer, but I wanted to make sure you were okay with it."

"Are you kidding? I kinda wanted to ask her to be here, but I figured she would've said no!" Rachel glanced at Michelle and paused. "Oh, wow."

Michelle stood in front of Felix, one hand between her legs, the other caressing her own stomach. "Hey, Felix."

"Hey, Michelle." He continued his slow pull along his cock, his eyes gazing into hers. "I'm glad you're here."

She dropped slowly to her knees before him, her hands caressing his thighs. "Of course, you are, Felix," she said with a grin. "You look good, real good, and I'm going to pick up where Rachel left off. Unless you have any objections?"

He chuckled. "I completely, totally, unquestionably object." He let go of his length and ran a hand through her dark hair. "Don't you dare go down on me. Don't you dare get me nice and hard so I can fuck you tonight. Don't even think about it."

"I wouldn't dream of it." Michelle grinned, and then lowered her mouth over him, leisurely sucking on the head of his cock as one hand caressed the root of him.

Felix's eyes rolled back, and he sighed contentedly. "One more off the bucket list," he murmured, his deep voice tinged with a note of amazed disbelief.

Iris led Rachel back to the bed as they watched, and directed her to lie back. "I figured you might be a little tender and messy from that pounding we gave you, so I brought you this." She spread Rachel's legs, and then laid the still-warm washcloth over her flushed-pink vulva.

"Oh, that does help. Thank you, Iris." Rachel fully unfolded the washcloth, and gently patted it against her sensitive folds. "I'm still going to need a few to recover. Why don't you three play while I watch?" She moved to the far edge of the bed, sitting against the headboard as she held the washcloth in place.

Iris climbed into the bed and got onto her hands and knees, facing the direction of the headboard. "Michelle, if you're done warming up my boyfriend, would you turn him around so he can see what's waiting for him?" She bent down, crossing her arms in front of her, and lifted her hips into the air as high as she could, her knees wide to give a show. She could imagine what a sight she was, her large lips swollen with need, slightly parted, dripping, and ready for anything.

Behind her, Michelle gave a happy laugh, and Felix inhaled sharply as his weight shifted on the bed.

A pity I can't see his face right now, but you can't have everything.

"Come fuck me, handsome," Iris called over her shoulder. "My pussy aches for it, and you're exactly what I want."

He grabbed her hips, and moments later, his warm rod was deep inside her again. "Mmm. Just perfect, Felix. Fuck me just like that."

"Anywhere and anytime you want, Iris. Without question." He was taking his time, filling her with long drawn-out strokes, one of his hands gently stroking the small of her back, and she loved every second of it.

"You know," she said as she rocked against him, "I don't think I've ever had anyone fuck me so many times in one day. That's how much you turn me on, mister." She grunted as he pushed even deeper than before. "If you're not doing anything next weekend, I want to barricade you in my bedroom and do nothing but rut like animals every waking moment. Think you can do that, lover?"

"Hell, yes. Consider it done." He had both hands on her waist again, and she loved the sound of his hips slapping against her cheeks with every thrust.

A new hand glided along her back. "Iris, think you could use that pretty mouth for me while Felix has his way with you?" Michelle settled onto the bed in front of her, leaning back against the headboard next to Rachel. She opened her legs, and gave Iris a closeup view of how wet she was. "Show me what you've got, goddess."

"Exactly what I was hoping for, Michelle." Iris slid her tongue from top to bottom along Michelle's opening, and she stroked

Iris's thick mane of curly hair. "Oh, am I off to a good start, then?"

"*Genjue hen hao*," she heard Michelle whisper. "That's good, Iris. Real good. Real...."

Rachel and Michelle shared what looked to be their first kiss. Their eyes were open, and they both looked as nervous as they were turned on.

"I've been wanting to kiss you for a long time," Rachel said.

"I know. I've been looking forward to it. Thank you, Rachel." Michelle broke the kiss, her back arching as Iris happily licked around her clitoris. "Hold me, roomie. Watch them fuck me. Iris, keep doing that..."

Rachel lowered her head to Michelle's breast, licking circles around a hard nipple. Michelle's breath shuddered, and Iris smiled as she lowered her face to fully concentrate on licking their new companion to a screaming climax.

After a few moments, Iris settled into a nice rhythm. Felix would thrust into her, and she'd lick Michelle's clit as her body moved forward with that thrust. She'd then rock back against her man, he'd pull out, and then repeat the same motion again. A long minute passed with no sound made but the steady drumbeat of Iris getting happily pounded from behind, and the staccato squeals Michelle made with each new touch against her wetness.

"Rachel."

Iris perked up her ears at the sound of Felix's voice. He eased off his previous tempo, and was now grinding hard into her on each push, a move that definitely hit some good spots, and Iris eagerly moaned into Michelle's wet folds to signal her approval. Felix seemed to be saying more, but Michelle chose that moment to clamp her thighs tight around Iris's head, muffling most of her hearing. That wasn't enough to cut off the increasingly louder sounds that Michelle herself was making, though.

Without warning, a jolt ran down the back of her legs, and her clitoris was suddenly blazing with raw sensual ecstasy. She screamed deliriously into Michelle's overflowing wetness, and her flailing tongue pulled a loud moan from Michelle. After another thunderbolt of pleasure ripped through her, she realized Rachel had reached underneath her, rubbing and pinching her mons and clitoris, and gods knew what else, and it was if Rachel instinctively knew exactly where to touch her for maximum effect. Iris was about to come, there was no stopping it.

Grabbing Michelle's hips, Iris slid her tongue up along one side of the hood of Michelle's sex, and then the other, back and forth, left-right, left-right like a slippery metronome, determined to bring Michelle off before her own climax hit her between the eyes and made it impossible to continue. Thankfully, it seemed to be working.

"Iris, don't stop. Iris, right there...there...yes!"

As Michelle's strong thighs quivered around Iris's ears and then finally relaxed, Rachel chose that moment to go for broke and hit clusters of pleasure nerves Iris didn't even know she had. She managed to lift her chin, gasping for breath.

"Rachel, don't stop. Felix, that's so good, keep going. Harder, both of you!"

Michelle caressed her hair, Felix's warm hands grabbed her hips, Rachel's slender hand between her legs...and the world suddenly went white.

She heard her own voice, completely out of her conscious control, and it sounded as if she was sobbing.

The white faded, and everything went black.

Iris opened her eyes, and the world had shifted. She was on her back, still on the same bed with a very comfortable pillow tucked under her head. Felix was cuddled up to her. Rachel was curled in the crook of her arm Michelle knelt between her open thighs, gently rubbing a joyously warm washcloth against her still-quivering sex.

"Oh, my God. What happened?" Tears stung her eyes.

Rachel smiled at her. "You came like a banshee, that's what. You pulled me into your arms like I was your teddy bear, and then when Felix curled up with us, you turned onto your back and wouldn't let go of either of us." Rachel craned her neck to make a show of kissing the side of Iris's breast. "Not that I'm complaining."

"You did conk out there," Felix added, "but only for a few moments. Are you feeling okay?"

"I have never had an orgasm like that in my life." Iris took a deep breath. "It felt so damn good, but I think my brain kinda overloaded." She looked back and forth at the two in her arms. "I know I get grabby and cuddly after sex. I guess, at this point, it's a reflex." She gave a small laugh, and got smiles in return. "And thank you, Michelle. That feels super nice, exactly what I needed."

"Hey, it's only fair. You gave me the tongue-lashing of my life. Best oral sex *ever*, no hyperbole. Treating you right afterwards is the least I could do." Michelle gently pressed the wet towel against her again. "God, you three are hot together, and I have never seen anyone come as hard as you did a minute ago."

She bent down, bracing herself with her hands on either side of Iris's midsection. "So, I want to say something to all of you while we're enjoying this pause in the action." Michelle's mouth turned up at one corner, and she placed a kiss between Iris's breasts. "I can tell you three are on the road to something pretty serious, and I think that's amazing." She kissed Iris again, this time on her stomach. "I'm not going to ask to be a part of that because I really want to go into this next year of school without any commitments. I've just got way too much on my plate, but... I was telling this beautiful piece of perfect sex appeal earlier that I wouldn't mind being a friend with benefits. Anytime I'm in town, if I'm still single, I'd love to get together for more playtime like tonight. Your thoughts?"

Rachel squeezed Michelle's hand. "As far as I'm concerned, four is not a crowd. Friends, and in my case, roommates, with benefits sounds awesome."

Michelle blew Rachel a kiss, and then made a show of breathing warm air across the thick pubic mound below her, making Iris squirm happily. "I don't plan on lifting your skirt too often back in the dorms, Rachel, but the occasional dalliance when we're both feeling lonely and horny could be pretty nice." She paused. "Let's not tell the rest of the Journey crew about this just yet, though."

"My thoughts exactly." Rachel smiled, and snuggled closer into Iris's side, and started happily fondling one of Iris's breasts, seemingly getting a rise out of the pink nipple. "We'll cross that bridge later."

"And you two?" Michelle stroked Felix's half-hard length, which jumped to full standing only moments later. "Can I be your happy little fucktoy? Pretty please with lube on top?" Without waiting for an answer, she closed her mouth around Iris's hood, giving very delicate little touches with the tip of her tongue, still stroking Felix all the while.

"Ooh, that's nice, but be really gentle down there. Still a little sensitive." Iris took a deep breath, and turned a heavy-lidded look to Felix on her right. "For the official record, Felix, I give you carte blanche permission to fuck this slinky little devil any-time you want, even if I'm not around."

"Ditto," Rachel chimed in. "Iris, can I just play with your breasts all night? No wonder men stare at our chests. Boobs are the best thing ever. Who needs anime? Not I. I've got Iris."

Michelle looked up from her licking with a raised eyebrow and a sarcastic snort. "Hey, let's not go crazy now. I've got a mad girl-crush for our resident sex goddess here, but give up anime? Never."

"You just haven't experienced the true power of the Iris-boobs yet," Rachel said with a dramatic delivery that was marred somewhat by the giggle at the end. "Suck this nipple for me right now," she directed, reaching over to hold up Iris's other breast. "And I will make a believer out of you."

"Hey, do I get a say in... Oh, that's good." Iris was half-laugh-ing, half-purring as the two young women each attacked one of her breasts. "Felix, were you, ah, about to say something?"

Felix sat up, holding out his hands like a movie director fram-ing a shot. "How in the world did I get this lucky?" he said with a grin. "Well, I was going to say I also have zero problem with you ladies fooling around as the mood strikes. I mean, I'd be an idiot to get in the way of something so beautiful."

"Well, let's not leave you hanging there." Iris stroked the hair of the two angels leaving delicious kisses all over her bosom. "Let's give Michelle the hard fuck we all know she's been looking forward to."

"I want you to put it in deep, Felix." Michelle looked up from the nipple she'd been licking. "I haven't had a cock in me in six months, and I want yours tonight." She licked along the curvy flesh in her hands. "And goddamn, I'm a believer in the power of the Iris-boob. Praise fucking be." She looked up. "Less talk, insert cock. Please?"

Iris and Felix exchanged a look, and nodded together.

"I won't lie," Felix said as he stood up and walked around to the foot of the bed. "I've been looking forward to this."

Michelle looked over her shoulder. "Ever since I dry-humped you in the restaurant?"

"Oh, no." Felix lined the tip of his cock against Michelle's opening. "Long before that."

Iris was watching Michelle, and was treated to a front-row seat for the wide array of expressions that flitted across the woman's face as she took Felix inside her.

"When do you mean...?" Michelle grabbed ahold of Iris, burying her face in her cleavage as Felix built up speed. "Let it all out, Felix, don't—*unh*! Don't be gentle, just fuck me hard, take me!"

"Goddamn, Michelle...so good..." Felix was definitely working up a sweat now, his eyes wide. Michelle rammed herself back onto his length as his hips built up speed like a freight train grinding away at the open track.

Something was placed into Iris's open hand. It was the vibrator from her suitcase. Rachel had just put it there, and was holding her own similar toy.

"You said you brought some toys, so I just raided your bag to find it." She sat against the headboard again, spread her thighs wide, and called out to Felix. "Look what I've got for you."

When he looked up, Rachel plunged the toy inside herself, and Felix's eyes nearly bulged out of their sockets. His thrusts into Michelle quickened, but his gaze was locked with Rachel, who eagerly pleasured herself for him to see.

"I never had a chance to tell you, Iris," Rachel said without looking away from Felix. "Felix told me tonight that one of his favorite fantasies is to watch a woman fuck herself with a dildo, up close and personal. Don't you think you should help out?"

Carefully untangling herself from being partially underneath Michelle's quivering body, Iris scooted over a little, and followed Rachel's lead. "Felix, is that what you want? Do you want to see this opening my wet pussy nice and wide while you watch?" She raised and opened her knees, and as soon as Felix's gaze moved toward her, she drove her Old Faithful home, tapping the switch on the base to send a gentle vibration throughout her insides.

"Holy hell," Michelle muttered. "Ladies, keep that up, he's fucking me so good..." She grabbed the edge of the comforter in clenched fists as Felix's speed increased.

Rachel was pinching her own nipple with her one hand, while rapidly dipping her vibrator in and out of herself with the other. "And you know what, Felix? You said your other fantasy was to have someone listening in while you fucked a girl to orgasm, so that you could hear them getting off on hearing you fuck, isn't that right? You knew Michelle was watching us, and you could hear her playing with herself, so you got *both* fantasies tonight, isn't that right?"

"Hell, yes. I was so hard inside you, Rachel. I'm so hard right now, so hard. Michelle, I'm close, I'm real close." Felix was holding onto Michelle's hips with a deathgrip, pistoning into her at high-speed, and Michelle looked to be thoroughly enjoying it.

"Me too, me too, don't stop...!" Michelle's body twitched as if she'd just been hit with a cattle prod, and surged forward. "Too much, but damn, that felt good." She looked back at Felix, who was still kneeling.

Before Michelle or Iris could move, Rachel practically leapt across the bed and inhaled Felix's entire length, frantically deep-throating him.

"Rachel!" He grabbed her hair and her shoulder, his hips bucked twice more, and with a sudden bark of exhaled breath, his entire body tensed.

"Damn, Rachel. Well done." Iris eased the toy from inside herself, and hit the off switch.

Felix was having one very long orgasm, but Rachel seemed to have no trouble swallowing every last drop.

Finally, she pulled away, licking her lips with obvious satisfaction, and Felix slumped forward into the center of the bed. "I have never, ever come that hard before. Sweet Christmas, that was a rush."

"Felix, I'm so sorry!" Michelle curled up next to him, kissing his cheeks and his lips. "I get really sensitive when I come, and I pulled out without thinking. I didn't mean to leave you high and dry like that. I am so, so sorry."

He shook his head. "Nothing to apologize for, seriously. Best night of my life, bar none."

Michelle shook her head. "Still, I'm going to make it up to you. I promise."

"You don't have to." Felix sprawled out on his back. "But I'll look forward to anything you've got in mind. Hoo boy."

Iris curled up behind Michelle, while Rachel snuggled in on the other side of Felix.

"Thank you all for this," Rachel said with a dreamy smile. "I couldn't have made this night any better if I'd planned it. You're all incredible."

"Anything for you, princess," Iris said with a happy purr. "Anything and everything."

CHAPTER FORTY-SEVEN

FELIX

Felix stood in front of the bathroom mirror, chugging ice-cold bottled water as if it was the nectar of the gods. "I still can't believe that happened. God, what a wonderful day."

As Iris stepped out of her shower and turned off the extra-large tub controls, he handed her one of Rachel's towels, and she proceeded to dry herself off. "Thanks, handsome. Yeah, I'm still feeling the glow myself. About ready for bed?"

He nodded, giving his hair one more rubdown with another towel. "Now that I feel a thousand times less sweaty? Oh, yeah."

"Don't forget, you need to do that hair-washing trick to Michelle and Rachel tomorrow morning. Although, then again," she said with a laugh and a kiss to his shoulder, "they might not let you leave this room if you do."

"Heh. *Slave of the Cosplayer Seraglio: A Felix Jackson Adventure.*" He struck a pose, holding a hairbrush as if it were a microphone, his voice sounding like a 1940's radio announcer.

"Chapter One: His mighty-thewed hands wrenched screams of pleasure from the timid maiden as he worked the herbal shampoo into her silken blue tresses." He snorted, and tossed the hairbrush back onto the sink counter.

"Oh, laugh now, but you'll be chained to this giant bathtub tomorrow, just you wait and see." She moved behind him, wrapping her arms around his waist and resting her chin on his shoulder, looking at the two of them together in the mirror. "But, yeah. What a day."

He squeezed one of her hands. "Still got two days left to the con."

She laughed. "I think tomorrow's going to be pretty quiet by comparison. If nothing else, I know you said you're going to be pretty busy with staff stuff." She left a quick peck of a kiss on his neck, and then settled back into their quiet embrace. "Do I really make you happy?"

"You really, really do. Like I told Rachel, I'd all but forgotten what that felt like. But not anymore, and I've got you to thank for that."

"And Rachel."

"Absolutely. Right now, I'm here with you, and I wanted you to know what you mean to me." She squeezed him tight at that, and his heart skipped a beat at her smile. "I'm crazy about you, Iris Weinberg. I don't think I can sum it up any better than that."

"Well, Felix Jackson, here's what I have to say to that, and if I'm saying the wrong thing, then so be it." She kissed his shoulder again, and looked right into his eyes in the mirror. "I'm falling for you, handsome. Falling hard, and I'm so glad you've been there to catch me." She turned him around, and put her arms around his shoulders. "Somewhere down the line, I think we're going to work our way up to a scary word that starts with L. I'm not ready for that word right now, and I bet neither are you. But I want you to know it's there."

She kissed his forehead, and then each cheek, and then his lips. "Felix, you make me want to be the best version of myself I possibly can, not just for you, but for me, too."

He rested his forehead against hers. "Hell, yes." He took a deep breath. "I've been coasting since college. Getting by on jobs that I don't really care about. Rousing myself to hang out with Prowl and friends on the weekends. That was the only bright spot I really had." He kissed her forehead. "You inspire me, Iris. 'Fortune favors the bold', I said to someone just last night. Let's be bold together."

"Absolutely, handsome." She gave him a playful *boop* on the nose with her index finger. "But let's be bold tomorrow. You three wore me out tonight, and that little shower I just finished is the only reason I'm not already crumpled in a heap on the floor. C'mon, let's go to bed. Our paramours are waiting."

As the foursome climbed into the giant bed, he looked around and marveled at the company he was keeping. On the far side of the bed closest to the window, Iris was clad only in a giant white t-shirt that reached nearly to her knees. Next to her, Rachel had donned a pair of simple red cotton panties and nothing else, and was already half-asleep, her eyes fluttering. Felix was on Rachel's other side, and as was his usual habit, was sleeping completely in the nude. He hated the feeling of pajamas getting bunched up around him as he tried to find a comfortable position. Michelle had curled up on his other side, taking the edge of the bed closest to the bathroom, and she was wearing nothing but a silky black number with spaghetti shoulder straps, more like a short slip than a nightgown.

Michelle hit the light switch on the nightstand. "Thank you again, everyone. What could've been the worst night ever became the best."

"Amen," mumbled Iris. "Now if you'll all excuse me, I'm going to curl up with my little blonde teddy bear princess."

"I'm her princess." Rachel's fatigue-smothered voice was barely coherent, burrowing tightly into Iris's embrace. "Felix, Michelle, snuggle up, too, please."

"Good night, everyone." Felix spooned Rachel's back, happily leaving a tender kiss on the back of her head.

Michelle wrapped herself around him from behind, and he reached back with one hand to find hers, giving it a warm squeeze.

"Sweet dreams." He closed his eyes, and sleep descended immediately.

Several hours later, Felix abruptly found himself wide awake. The room was still dark, save for a sliver of moonlight from between the curtains. His bladder prodded him with a reproachful cramp, and he slowly sat up, his eyes adjusting to the darkness.

Rachel was still lying on her side facing away from him, her face buried in her pillow, and her arms tucked in tight against her chest. Iris was flat on her back, one arm hanging off the side of the bed, her beautiful mane of curls spread out in all directions. Both were still deep asleep.

He turned towards Michelle, who was on her stomach, but her face turned towards him, and tried to work out how he might climb over or around her without waking her up. He was just starting to carefully lift up the covers so that he could try slithering straight down to the foot of the bed when Michelle stirred.

She blinked, and looked at him, her voice a soft whisper. "Did I wake you up?"

"I was about to ask you that," he responded quietly. He moved a few errant strands of her hair out of her eyes. "I just need to use the bathroom for a sec. You go on back to sleep."

She pushed herself upwards, and then moved to stand, one hand held gently against her abdomen. "I gotta go, too." She winced, and reached out to take Felix's hand. "C'mon, come with. Keep me company, but I go first."

"Seriously?" Felix couldn't help but laugh a little (if quietly), but he stood up, slowly and carefully. "You don't care if I'm in the room with you when you pee?"

Shaking her head, she helped pull him to his feet. "Felix, if I'm comfortable enough with you that I text you pictures of my naked wet vagina, and then fuck you with it a few hours later, then peeing in your presence is the least of my concerns." She started walking, pulling him along. "Besides, I wanna chat, and we won't have to whisper in there. Now come on, I really gotta go."

He shook his head in disbelief, but allowed himself to be towed along to the bathroom. As they made it inside, he turned up the room's rheostat light switch just a couple of tiny notches, adding enough light to see a little better, but not nearly so much as to blind them.

Michelle had wasted no time, hiking up her nightgown around her waist, and sat to relieve herself.

He closed the door and leaned against it, running a hand through his hair. "So, what's on your mind?" He wasn't whispering anymore, but he was still trying to keep his voice down, just in case.

"I have a question." She looked at him, a mischievous smile on her lips. "It's a two-word question, but I think those two words carry a lot of additional meaning."

"I'm an open book," he said, hold his arms out wide. "Ask me anything."

She raised an eyebrow. "Well, here goes... Bucket List?"

He grinned and looked away, a warm glow in his cheeks. "So, I did say that out loud. Heh." He nodded. "Yeah. Getting naked and intimate with you was on my big list of things I really wanted to do with my life at least once."

"Oh, it'll be more than once." She unrolled a wad of toilet paper around her hand, and reached down to dry herself. "When did I make this list of yours?"

"Exactly one year ago. When you walked onto the stage during the Cosplay Contest last year."

She stood, flushed, and then moved aside to the sink so that Felix could take a turn. "Seriously? I was cosplaying Emi Yusa from *The Devil is a Part-Timer* last year. I wouldn't call her dowdy, but she's not exactly brimming with sex appeal." She turned on the faucet and started washing her hands.

After a moment's thought, looking down at the toilet, he sat down instead of going standing up. "Less noisy this way," he said, and grimaced as his bladder unclenched and allowed nature to take its course. After a moment, he continued. "And I will respectfully disagree. That pencil-skirt made your legs—and your beautiful backside, if I'm going to be totally honest, here—look absolutely delicious. It took a lot of willpower not to stare while you were on the stage."

She rinsed soap off her hands, and ran another washcloth under warm water. She reached underneath herself with it, giving that area a quick once-over before rinsing the washcloth again. "And who else do I share this bucket list honor with?"

He thought for a moment. "Two others. One was this girl from high school named Amber who I had a huge crush on my junior year. Real sweetheart, and drop-dead gorgeous, but she never saw me as anything but a shy nerd who made the mistake of asking her to Homecoming when she already had a date." He shrugged. "She at least let me down kindly, but the rest of her crowd made it very clear I was never going to be invited to any of their parties. Even so, I had fantasies for years about meeting her again later, away from all the bullshit of high school." He paused. "The other one is Salma Hayek. Watching *Desperado* was a very formative moment for me as a young lad."

"You think I'm as hot as Salma Hayek? I'll take that compliment." She stood there watching him. "A pity you didn't say anything to me last year. I might have said yes."

"You were still clearly dating what's-his-name. I didn't want to intrude." He stood up and flushed. Thankfully, the toilet wasn't very loud.

"Randy and I weren't monogamous, but you wouldn't have known that. Still, a pity." She wrung out the washcloth in her hands. "Hold still." She reached down, and wrapped the warm cloth around his penis and testicles, gently massaging and rinsing them. His length stirred under her skilled touch.

"Oh, that's nice. To what do I owe the pleasure?"

"Two things." She paused to bend her head and playfully kiss one of his nipples, and he shivered in pleasant surprise. "First, since I've been given a free pass by your girlfriends, I thought maybe you and I could have a little more quiet fun tonight, maybe take it a little more slow and gentle this time." She dropped the washcloth into the sink, and returned to touching him with her bare hand, gently caressing his balls. "Assuming you're interested."

He reached out to caress her cheek. "You assume correctly. I mean, you're gorgeous, funny, and you've got a playful streak that not only makes me smile, but is one hell of a turn-on. Damn right, I'm interested. So, what's the second thing?"

Stroking his length, she broke into a wide smile as he visibly stiffened and grew in her hand. "Mmm, there we go. The second thing is that I still feel bad for almost giving you blue balls tonight, pulling off before you could finish. Personal foul, fifteen-yard penalty..." She dropped to her knees, and kissed the tip of his cock. "Repeat first down." Her mouth descended over him, and she reached around to squeeze the cheeks of his ass as she deep-throated him.

He took a deep breath, and let himself experience every moment of the exquisite treatment Michelle was giving him. He didn't say anything, he just stood there and enjoyed it to the fullest.

After a long moment, she stood up, her cheeks red as she flashed him an embarrassed smile. "I can't believe I said that. Repeat first down. You must think I'm a total dork."

He pulled her into his arms, and indulged in a long and sensuous kiss, ending with his lips travelling along her jawline and gently nibbling on her earlobe. "Maybe a little, but that's what I like—and you're a total dork that's going to have some nice, slow, take-our-time playtime with me. Assuming you're interested."

"You assume correctly." She kissed him again, rubbing her slip-covered body against his naked chest. "I may not want a relationship with a capital R right now, and I'm damn sure I don't want to mess up what you've got with Iris and Rachel, but I haven't been this revved up or had this much raw fun with anyone in bed, ever." She pulled the thin lingerie up and off her shoulders, then wrapped the soft fabric around his rod, giving him a soft, silky squeeze. "When I kissed you in the restaurant, when we were texting, when I could feel your eyes peeling my tight pants off my ass in the hall, and when you were fucking me like a stallion while Iris and Rachel watched—I was having the time of my life."

Tossing aside her slinky garment, she reached down with her other hand, rubbing the tip of his hardened length against her mons. "I want you inside me again, right now. I want to feel you come inside me, the way you came inside Rachel."

His fingers traced the curve of her hips, up past her waist, and then teasing the edges of her breasts. "Yes, but not in here." He reached past her, and opened the bathroom door, his voice dropping to a whisper. "Let's find something more comfortable." He turned off the bathroom light, and led her back into the suite.

She took a look around the room, and then gestured to one of the large, padded recliners.

As he settled into the seat, she moved past the bed to the window, and opened the curtains just a little bit, enough to give the room more illumination. She made her way back to him, her silhouetted hips swaying seductively as she was framed in moonlight.

"Stroke it for me," she whispered, her voice soft and eager. "Believe it or not, I've never had a chance to watch a man play with himself before tonight, and I love watching you touch yourself."

"Glad to be of service, then." He took himself in hand. He started by stroking the underside of his length with two fingers, but then wrapping his entire right hand around it as he reached full hardness. He pulled upwards, squeezing firmly when the tip of his cock reached his palm, and then relaxing his grip as his hands slid back down to the base. Over and over again, he repeated this motion at a slow and steady pace.

His eyes never left hers throughout this, and she was stroking a finger along her inner folds as she watched him, her gaze flickering back and forth between meeting his gaze and savoring the sight of him making love to himself.

Moments later, she turned around, and then eased herself down onto his lap. He held himself upright and still, and her folds descended around his erection, her back pressed back against his chest as she writhed upon him.

"I want to ride you a little," she whispered through a steady stream of gasps. "But what I really want is for me to lie back on that bed, and have you give me a good old-fashioned missionary screw, nice and slow, until you fill me with everything you've got."

"I like that plan," he said between kisses to the back of her neck and shoulders. "Nice and quiet, so we don't wake anyone."

"I wouldn't mind if they do. I love having an audience." Her hips ground into him, trying to take as much of him inside her as possible. "But since this might be our last chance to have a little one-on-one before the con's over, I want to be a little greedy and have you to myself for a few minutes." After a few more exhilaratingly wet grinds, she stood up, purring as she did so.

He had to stifle a loud moan from the way her tightness clung to him, almost refusing to let go. Her eyes heavy-lidded with lust and her knees a little unsteady, she beckoned him to follow her to the huge bed. She pushed aside part of the thick comforter and lay down on her back. Even with her legs spread open wide, she still wasn't in any danger of bumping up against the sleeping Rachel in the middle of the gigantic bed.

"Cover me with your body, Felix," she whispered. "Put it in me. Give it to me rich and slow."

He smiled in disbelief at this day's amazing fortune, and he carefully climbed in after her. His length slid into her with ease, and her legs lifted so he could enter her completely, right to the hilt. "You're a dream come true, Michelle," he whispered in her ear, and he reveled in the feeling of her breasts pressed against him.

"A wet dream, Felix. A wet dream with a wet pussy that loves your good cock." She grabbed her own legs under the knees, the better to hold herself wide open for him. "Did you dream about lifting up that pencil skirt? I wore tiny black mesh panties and garters under that. Did you dream about pulling me backstage, bending me over a table, and ripping my little thong away so you could fuck me?"

For all that he was moving very slowly inside her, Michelle's whispers were already filled with an intense, needy growl.

He nibbled along her neck, allowing himself to speed up just a tiny bit. "All that and more. I dreamed that you fucked me to sleep every night of the con, and woke me with a blowjob every morning. I dreamed that you'd let me watch while you filled yourself with a thick dildo. I dreamed that, every year, you'd come back to the con, and we'd do it all over again."

"Lick me good after you come down my throat every morning, and you've got yourself a deal. You bring Iris, I'll bring Rachel, and we're going to come so hard, people across the ocean are gonna feel it. Fuck me deep, Felix. So good, so good..."

"My God, you two are insatiable."

He looked up, noting Rachel and Iris were both awake and watching him.

Rachel's sleepy smile gleamed. "Not that I'm complaining." She was lying on her side, her nipples visibly hard in the moonlight.

Iris was spooning behind her, raised partly up so she could see over Rachel's shoulder, with one hand sliding down the front of Rachel's simple cotton underwear.

"Iris is going to make me scream her name while I watch you fuck my roommate, Felix."

Michelle let a full-throated moan echo across the suite, spurred on by her new spectators. "The three greatest words in the English language are friends with benefits. Keep drilling me like this, and I'll be an eager little fucktoy for all three of you for the rest of my life." She pulled him into a brief kiss, running her hands down the length of his arms. "Show your girlfriends what it looks like when you take me, when you come deep inside me. Come for me, Felix. Give it to me nice and easy, just like that."

"I am so glad I gave you two a free pass," Iris murmured, her palm grinding Rachel's mons. "Waking up to the sound of Michelle gasping on your cock is just heavenly." She bent down to kiss Rachel's ear, who squirmed happily. "Fill her up, Felix, because after you're done, I'm going to lick every last drop of you right out of her."

That declaration seemingly sent a new wave of lust through everyone. Rachel pulled Iris down for a long kiss, her hips shaking with need.

Michelle gasped aloud. "Do you hear that, Felix? Give Iris what she wants. Don't worry about me, it's your turn. Just come hard for me. She'll take care of me after. Use my wet pussy, fill my wet pussy."

He shivered, propping himself up on his forearms as his hips ground into Michelle's tight embrace. "You three...are the best thing to ever happen to me. I'll do right by all of you, I swear." He buried himself deep inside her again, loving the feel of her wetness gushing around him.

"We know you will, Felix." Rachel squeezed the back of his hand. "I'm going to visit every chance I get. We're going to make this work."

He looked down, and the pure bliss on Michelle's face nearly sent his approaching climax hurtling over the point of no return. She wanted him, she was turned on by him, she was gasping his name.

He turned to look at Rachel. Admiration, gratitude, and raw desire were in her eyes, and he did his best to return those feelings in kind in his own returned gaze.

They both silently mouthed the words "thank you" to each other.

He next met Iris's beautiful blue eyes, almost glowing in the moonlight, and the world narrowed and slowed until there was nothing else in this room beyond her. The depth of emotion he had for her after only one day was almost terrifying, as if it couldn't possibly be real.

It wasn't just raw physical desire, although she embodied the very word erotic in his mind, already able to send him into a dizzying lust with the smallest word or look or touch.

It wasn't just that they were two sides of the same coin, with so much in common it might defy belief.

It wasn't just that she made him happy. Although, happy seemed inadequate for describing how Iris and Rachel had started the healing on that terrible wound in his heart.

It wasn't even the renewed determination she inspired in him, the drive to become the best man he could, both for her and for himself.

This day had seemed to last forever, and nearly all of it was spent with her, and he realized in that moment, he wanted to be with her for as long as time allowed. Unbidden, he imagined Iris, Rachel, and himself, many years older, the lines on their face never dimming their smiles, curled up on a couch together, basking in warm sunlight. He had never been more at peace than at this moment.

His eyes widened, still locked with Iris, and he wondered if she was thinking the same thing. She seemed to be looking right into him, taking in and considering all he was and ever would be. Her eyes widened to match his gaze, and she nodded, biting her lower lip.

This was real, they were here together, and they would be still for a long time to come.

Michelle suddenly mewled in pleasure beneath him, and the spell was broken, time returning to normal, the heated sensations of carnal pleasure resuming with full dizzying force.

He took a moment to resume his previous rhythm, savoring the feel of Michelle's outer lips trembling around his length as her inner walls clenched. He looked back at Iris, and gave her an amused half-smile, almost in disbelief at the situation—realizing such deep emotion for one woman as he urgently fucked another right in front of her, and as she pleasured another mutual lover with her skilled hands at the same time. With one returned grin, she showed she understood, and was equally amused, and not in any way unhappy.

"Come for us, Felix," Iris called to him. "Give us everything you are."

He did. And it was good.

- □ -

Afterword:

Anime Horde is not a real convention, but rather inspired by the many anime conventions I've attended and staffed over the years. In addition, Yoroi Senshi: Knights Daitai, aka "DKD", is not a real anime, but my own creation.

I do plan to write more stories with these characters and the backdrop of Anime Horde. Angelica, in particular, along with her parents, Marcus and Abby, are part of the supporting cast of my upcoming urban fantasy romance titled, THY ETERNAL SUMMER.

I love hearing from readers, and the best way to contact me is to email me at isaac.sher@gmail.com.

CHECK OUT THESE OTHER ROWAN PROSE READS:

Isaac Sher's books are known as out of this world magical escapism. He is a master at blending sci-fi, urban fantasy, and romance for a unique read. He is a two-time brain cancer survivor, and resides with his family near Chicago.